The Book of Memory

The Book of Memory

PETINA GAPPAH

Farrar, Straus and Giroux

New York

•

Farrar, Straus and Giroux
18 West 18th Street, New York 10011

Printed in the United States of America
Originally published in 2015 by Faber and Faber Ltd., Great Britain
Published in the United States by Farrar, Straus and Giroux
First American edition, 2016

Grateful acknowledgment is made for permission to reprint the lyrics to
"Black September" by Master Chivero, used with the permission of the
Master Chivero Estate, with the kind assistance of the Zimbabwe
Music Rights Association.

Library of Congress Cataloging-in-Publication Data
Gappah, Petina, 1971–
    The book of memory / Petina Gappah. — First American edition.
        pages ; cm
    ISBN 978-0-86547-907-4 (hardcover) — ISBN 978-0-374-71488-8 (e-book)
    I. Title.

PR9390.9.G37 B66 2016
823'.92—dc23
                                                                    2015022198

Our books may be purchased in bulk for promotional, educational, or business use.
Please contact your local bookseller or the Macmillan Corporate and Premium
Sales Department at 1-800-221-7945, extension 5442, or by e-mail at
MacmillanSpecialMarkets@macmillan.com.

www.fsgbooks.com
www.twitter.com/fsgbooks • www.facebook.com/fsgbooks

1   3   5   7   9   10   8   6   4   2

This book is dedicated, with all my love,
to Lee Brackstone,
who brought me home

The cradle rocks above an abyss, and common sense tells us that our existence is but a brief crack of light between two eternities of darkness.

VLADIMIR NABOKOV, *Speak, Memory*

PART ONE

1468 MHARAPARA STREET

I

The story that you have asked me to tell you does not begin with the pitiful ugliness of Lloyd's death. It begins on a long-ago day in August when the sun seared my blistered face and I was nine years old and my father and mother sold me to a strange man.

I say my father and mother, but it was really my mother. I see them now as I saw them on the day we first met Lloyd. They are in the clothes that they wore to church on Sundays and when we went to town for window-shopping, because if you are going to hand your daughter over to a perfect stranger, you need to look your best.

My mother wears a white dress with big red poppies all over it. Around her waist is a cloth belt in the same material, and on her head a red hat with a white plastic flower on it. Her shoes and bag are white. My father is in a safari suit whose colour I can no longer remember. Or perhaps it wasn't a safari suit at all that he wore, and I have only put him in one because it is what all the men wore in those days. His hair shines with Brylcreem.

It was a happy day for me. I wore my favourite dress, a white lacy dress with a purple sash, my Christmas dress from the year before. I was in town, far from the torments of my school-playground nemesis, Nhau, who tormented me as much at home as at school because he lived on our street. I was in town with my father, who held my hand as we walked. I was happiest about this, that I had him to myself, with one sister at school and the other recently dead.

To crown my joy, a white woman in the chocolate section of the department store came up to us as we moved towards the lifts. She wore glasses with frames that elongated upwards into points on each side of her face, giving her eyes a distorted look, as though I were seeing them through the milk bottles, the gold- and silver-topped ones, that we bought at the shops. 'She looks like an angel; isn't she an angel?' she said. She gave me a dollar coin. It felt large and unfamiliar in my hand.

That brings with it another, earlier memory, of the twenty-five-cent coin that a nurse gave me when I cried hard after an injection at Gomo, the government hospital for the poor. I had bought sweets, which Nhau persuaded me to plant in the street outside his house. They would grow into a large sweet tree, he said.

From the chocolate section on the ground floor, we walked to the lift. A man in a maroon uniform with a large scar running down his face announced each floor as we reached it. 'Third floor: children's toys, children's clothes and tearoom,' he said as we left the lift.

My parents and I sat on one side of a booth. A bee hovered over my glass of Cherry Plum before toppling into the fizzy purple drink. It tried to fly out but its wings were wet and heavy and it floundered in the bubbles. And there was ice cream to go with the Cherry Plum, an elaborate sundae that Lloyd bought for me – Lloyd was on the other side of the booth – complete with a whole banana and sprinkled with hundreds and thousands.

I remember, too, the first words that Lloyd said to me. 'Speak, Mnemosyne,' he said.

I had no way of knowing then that Lloyd was teasing me, or

that Mnemosyne was another word for my name, Memory. But perhaps I am confusing this with the second day that I saw him, the day he walked me to his car and into my new life.

I could also start by telling you all about Lloyd. I could start by telling you that I did not kill him. 'Murder,' said the prosecutor who laid out the case against me at the High Court, 'is the unlawful and intentional killing of a human being who was alive at the time.'

After the police came for me on the night he died, after they arrested me and took me to the police station at Highlands, after I had spent three days without food or drink, after I had wept myself hoarse and my marrow dry – for Lloyd, I told myself, but really it was the fear – and after the dreams started coming again, I told them what they wanted to hear.

Their disbelief exploded in bursts of laughter. 'Just tell us the real truth. You were his girlfriend and he was your boyfriend. He was your sugar daddy. Just tell us the truth, that you killed him for the money.'

It is strange, the inconsequential thoughts that come at a time like that. As I looked at the constable who headed my interrogation, I noticed that his jutting-out eyes gave him the staring effect of a drunken gargoyle on a public building. 'Or maybe he made you do funny things to him in bed? This is a serious case, this one, it is no laughing matter.'

His laughter erupted thickly into the room. Two large dimples appeared in his cheeks, producing a startling transformation. The gargoyle had become a cherub.

'And it was the money, isn't it. They have too much, these whites,' said his partner, a stocky woman in a faded uniform that seemed ready to burst with every movement she made. A button had already fallen from its place on her tunic.

I could not stop looking at the pink plastic rollers in her hair. Even in my distress, the orphaned thought came to me that surely, no one made plastic rollers like those any more, the spiky ones that attach themselves to your hair together with sharp plastic pokers.

'A nice-looking young woman like you,' she said. 'You are not so bad-looking but for the, well, you know. You certainly know how to take care of yourself; I must give you that. But honestly, why else would you live with a white man like that, alone, just the two of you alone in that big house?'

She dug her right thumb into her left nostril as she spoke.

I repeated what I had already told them. 'I lived with Lloyd Hendricks because my parents sold me to him as a child.'

Even as I said it, I knew that no one would believe me, and why should they, when I could hardly believe it myself, when I had struggled to understand it all my life. From the moment I saw my mother stuff the money that Lloyd had given her into her bra, from the moment after Lloyd shut the door of his car on me, I have wondered how my parents could have brought themselves to do it.

'My parents sold me to him,' I repeated.

Officer Rollers looked at Officer Dimples and laughed.

'What is she talking?' she said. With her index finger, she flicked dried mucus from her thumb. 'We do not sell children in this country,' she said. 'What are you talking?'

There was a loud scrape as she pushed her chair back from the table to walk out of the room. Her voice came back to us from down the corridor. '*Huyai mundinzwirewo zvirimuno.*'

At her invitation, the room swarmed with officers. As they crowded around me with their mocking laughter and loud voices, I knew that there would be no convincing them. And if they did not believe the truth of this basic fact, how could I convince them of how he had actually died? What imaginative powers did they possess, these men and women in their brown-and-grey uniforms, this woman in her strained seams and pink rollers, this man who leered as he imagined funny things with white sugar daddies, what could make them see the horror of the moments that followed after I found Lloyd dead?

Lloyd rarely talked openly about how I came to live with him. When he spoke of it at all, it was always in euphemisms. He spoke of 'taking me in', of 'giving me a home', the good-hearted rich man taking in the poor black child, the cheerful Cheeryble giving room and board to an ungrateful Dickensian orphan. Except that it was really a case of the white man buying the black child, apart, of course, from the '*well, you know*', as Officer Rollers called it, the condition that makes me black but not black, white but not white. That is how it was, and I will tell you all about it.

2

I should feel afraid. I should wake in the night, soaked in sweat from fearful dreams. I should have palpitations, no appetite and endless runs.

I have felt afraid. In those early days, as I awaited the trial and bail was denied, I shared a cell with Mavis Munongwa, the only other woman who is here for murder. That was before I got my own cell.

I covered my ears as Mavis screamed out the names of the children that she had killed. I was sometimes afraid to close my eyes and go to sleep. But even then, fear did not hold me completely to itself. I was insulated by my sense that none of this was real. That none of this was true. That it was too preposterous to be real.

I still feel afraid now, sometimes, but it is mostly in my dreams that fear comes to me and I find myself drowning before I startle myself awake. Outside of those dreams, I sleep well, or as well as I can on a prison-issue bed in a cell whose dimensions fall short of those prescribed by international treaties on the sagacious and humane treatment of the prisoner. I eat well, or as well as one can eat when the food is as bad as it is here.

Mostly, I just feel bored. You do something often enough, even something like waiting for your own death, and it too becomes routine.

I am writing this in my cell because Loveness has allowed me to take the notebooks and pens back with me. It has been three weeks since you gave me the notebooks and I started writing. You were my first visitor from the outside. And you were certainly the first visitor that any of us have ever had from overseas. Even here in Chikurubi, as in the rest of Zimbabwe, we value above all else the things that come from outside ourselves. Well, maybe not Synodia, the head guard.

They talked about you after I left, Loveness and Synodia. They were perplexed as to why a white journalism woman, as Loveness called you, would come all the way from America just to talk to a murderer like me. Synodia snatched from me the card that you left behind, and read your name and address as though they were lies that I had made up just to annoy her. 'Linda Carter,' she said as she read your card with her thumb over it. 'Who is this Linda Carter?'

'It's Melinda Carter,' I said. 'She is a journalist who lives in Washington, in America.'

Synodia twisted her face into a moue of disbelief. 'Pwelinda, Pwelinda,' she said, and flung the card back at me. 'Pwashington, Pwashington. Can you eat America? I said, can you eat America? If you can, you shall eat America until you are full of America. Pwamerica, Pwamerica.'

I call these statements Synodic Utterances. I am sure they make perfect sense in her mind as she is formulating them. They just somehow lose all meaning when they are uttered.

You were the first visitor that I have had, outside of my lawyer, Vernah Sithole. My first outside visitor in the two years, three months, seven days and thirteen hours that I have been here. Until Vernah became interested in my case, the only outsider I saw was the woman from the Goodwill Fellowship.

It was Vernah's idea that I should tell my story to you. Before she sent you to interview me, she told me that I should write down every detail that I could remember, that I should record everything that could make a sympathetic case. 'It is important for the appeal,' she said. 'It is important because the death penalty is mandatory in cases of murder, and we have to find extenuating circumstances. It is the only way to commute the sentence.'

The appeals here are not looped in the endless cycle that goes on in America. And there is no governor to grant clemency at the last dramatic minute. I have just one appeal, to the Supreme Court. Vernah has appealed both the sentence and the conviction. The judges can do any of three things: they can confirm the conviction and uphold the sentence; confirm the conviction but quash the sentence; and, best of all, they could quash both the conviction and the sentence.

Look at me, with my legalese. I have become an expert in my own case. Perhaps I would not be here at all if Vernah had been my lawyer when I was arrested, or if she had represented me at my trial. I had no lawyer at all. When I confessed to killing Lloyd, I had not slept or eaten for days. That is another reason Vernah is convinced my appeal will succeed.

As I have said, writing to you was another of Vernah's suggestions. 'Write it to Melinda Carter,' she said. 'Tell her everything, even the things you think she already knows.'

You cannot imagine how strange it is to be addressing this to you. Like every person who has read the magazine you write for, I am familiar with your work. Every time I bought your magazine, I skipped the big celebrity interviews, the Iraq War and financial-scandal exposés, and made your column the first feature I read every month.

So I know that you have made a career out of exposing miscarriages of justice. Vernah has told me that you are here for a year to research a series of essays on our benighted justice system.

Verity Gutu, that veritable fount of endless and often irrelevant information, told me that I was in good hands with Vernah Sithole. She said, and these were her exact words, 'You are in good hands with that Advocate Sithole woman.'

Loveness told me about her defence of a woman in Gweru who had thrown her baby down a pit latrine. The baby had not survived; she had drowned in the faeces and urine and rank sweat. Loveness said Vernah got her off with a one-year suspended sentence. 'A pity,' the magistrate said, 'that the lawyer showed more remorse than her client.'

Until the reprieve that Vernah is fighting for comes, if it comes at all, I write this in the shadow of the gallows. If the Department of Public Prosecution and the Department of Prisons have their way, I will swing from a rope and hang until my neck lengthens to breaking point or it snaps and my bowels open and my life is extinct and I am given a pauper's funeral and an unmarked grave.

I was thinking today about the question you asked me on our second meeting: why none of the journalists here have been interested in my story. On my less cynical days, I would answer that other things matter more: who will win the election; who will govern next; which man has killed his wife with what instrument; who will win *Big Brother Africa*; football scores and cricket results; mysterious happenings involving sorcery and grave robberies, goblins and curses.

In many ways I am glad that no one has chosen to tell my story. When the papers first reported Lloyd's death, they focused on my condition, just as had always been done in the township where

I lived before Lloyd bought me. There was a brutal honesty in how the children regarded anyone different. If they saw a person with no legs, they did not point out a person living with no legs, or a person living with no sight; they shouted, *hona chirema, hona bofu*, come and see the cripple, come and see the blind man, calling attention to each deficiency.

Their attitude was implicitly rooted in the language itself. *Bofu* is in noun class five, denoting things, just like *benzi*, the word for a mad person. *Chirema*, like a *chimumumu*, is in noun class seven, also denoting things, objects, lifeless objects or incomplete, deficient persons. As *murungudunhu* or *musope*, I find myself with normal people in noun class one. But *murungudunhu* is heavy with meaning. As a *murungudunhu*, I am a black woman who is imbued not with the whiteness of *murungu*, of privilege, but of *dunhu*, of ridicule and fakery, a ghastly whiteness.

I thought at first that writing all of this down for you would be difficult, but the memories are flooding my mind, faster than I can write them down. Mobhi's feet, the soil of Mharapara Street on her soles, stick out from the bucket of her death. Copperplate thunders across the Umwinsidale downs. Lloyd and Zenzo's laughter becomes the voice of the Baptist telling me to reject Satan. The waters of the Mukuvisi close over my head as I scream in terror.

The memories have been coming since I have been here. Long before Vernah Sithole asked me to write it down for you, I have had yawning space in which to do nothing but think and reflect. There is nothing to do here in those twelve dead hours between four thirty in the afternoon, when we are locked up for the night, and four thirty in the morning, when the siren goes. Except for the Bible, there is nothing to read, and there is no one for me to talk to because I have my own cell.

We are allowed to take our Bibles back to our cells, but Synodia does not often let me take mine back with me. My very existence irritates her. She hates that I speak English, she hates that I once lived with white people, she hates that I studied outside the country, she hates that I am here for murder.

So I reflect on my life, to rework the events that brought me here, to rearrange and reimagine them in an endless cycle of what-ifs.

Jimmy Blue Butter envies my old life with Lloyd. She envies Summer Madness, the house that her imagination has transmuted into a mansion of monstrous proportions. She does not understand how someone who once lived in such a mansion can so calmly sleep on a mattress on the floor of a prison cell or eat bread with green mould on it. She does not understand how I can stand with the others repairing the condemned goods in the dirty storage room we call the Condemn, or how I can stand hour after hour in the laundry, washing and ironing the clothes of the guards who insist that we call them by the affectionate term Mbuya Guard even as they exercise their petty tyrannies over us.

I would like to tell her that poverty holds no terrors for me, because I have known it and I have conquered it. I want to tell her, but I am not sure that she would ever understand it, that even the big mansions hold their secret miseries. I would like to tell her that they hold more of them because there is more room for them.

3

_____

They still come to me sometimes, my father and my mother. They come to interrupt the rhythm of my waking moments, they come unbidden when I am in the laundry room or the Condemn, when I am singing hymns under Synodia's direction before breakfast. They come into me in the prison garden when my thoughts are on something else and I have not willed them into my mind. They come with my sisters, Joy, whom we called Joyi, and Moreblessings, called Mobhi. They come with my brother, Gift, whom we called Givhi.

Until you attempt to write the story of your life, you cannot quite understand just how hard it is to grasp at the beginning. I wish I could start this the traditional way, by telling you all about my father and mother and how they met and who their parents were and all the begats that preceded their lives, but I cannot. Until they sold me to Lloyd, and I moved away, I knew nothing about them beyond the fact that they were my mother and father.

The ritual of oral autobiography here is that we introduce and begin stories by locating our position in the family. 'I am the eldest in a family of seven.' 'I am the last-born in a family of four.' 'I am the middle child in a family of seven; two died, and only five are living.' Identity begins in that one sentence: I am the first, the middle, the fourth, the second, the last.

So perhaps my proper beginning should be there. I was the

second child in a family of three. The eldest was my sister Joyi, who was an equivocation in that she was the oldest living child but not the first-born child. That sainted place, of coming first, and thus bestowing the name by which my parents would for ever be known, belonged to my dead brother, Gift.

My mother and father were called MaiGivhi and Ba'Givhi, but instead of a living Gift, there was my sister Joyi, who was a year and a few months older than I was, then me, then Mobhi, the youngest, who was only four when she died.

When they come to me, they come as I remember them, except Givhi, who was only ever a name to me, or at most a small blurry face in the black-and-white photographs in my mother's album. He comes to me as a form without shape, wrapped in the green blanket with dark-grey stripes at the edges, the blanket that was also his shroud. When he comes to me in my dreams, he is drowning. Sometimes we are drowning together. I reach for him, but the Chimera pulls me down, down, down . . . It will not let me go and I see him no more.

Joyi is small and fast with skin like heated caramel. She comes with the voices of the children on Mharapara Street. From the spare bedroom, I can hear the songs to their favourite games. '*Tinotsvaga maunde, maunde, maunde. Tinotsvaga maunde, masi-kati ano.*' '*Tauya kuzoona Mary, Mary, Mary. Tauya kuzoona Mary, Mary, Mary woo.*'

Mobhi comes on fat toddling legs, behind her a trail of water. Up in the air she goes, she laughs, then down she comes. My father catches her and throws her up again. The world seems to shake with her laughter.

My father comes with the voices from his wireless radio set, with 'Mirandu' and 'Sina Makosa', with 'Sweet Mother' and

'Celebration', with the lugubrious music that preceded the announcements on the death notices programme, *Zvisiviso Zverufu*, and with the joyous greetings on *Kwaziso*.

He comes with Evans Mambara's voice rising to a staccato of excitement as Moses Chunga and Joel Shambo bring the crowd to their feet in the Castle Cup final at Rufaro Stadium, and with Peter Lovemore's voice that rises and rises as the invisible horses that he wills into our living room thunder from a place we had never been. 'Here comes Prince of Thieves, closely followed by Midnight Oil, and taking it away is Prince of Thieves, oh, I don't believe it, Midnight Oil has fallen behind and it is Prince of Thieves, Prince of Thieves, Prince of Thieves that wins this magnificent race on this wonderful afternoon at Borrowdale Park.'

They come with the novels that we listened to on the radio, stories with portentous titles hinting at unpropitious destinies and at the heaviness of life. *You Shall Remember Me One Day*, *I Am Now Dead, and I Hope You Will Be Successful*, *Embarrassment Is Often Worse Than Death*, *What Did I Ever Do to You?*, *If You Have Made a Plan, You Must See It Through to the Bitter End*. The radio brought to us the world of these books, a world that was hard and cruel, full of betrayal, conspiracies and unexpected danger.

And they come with the music that we listened to on the nights we did not listen to novels on the radio, with my mother's records, and the songs that we loved the best, which were the ones that were also stories. We did not always understand all the words. What did it mean that the Gatlin boys took turns at Becky? What did it mean to 'know when to fall down', and to 'know when to hall down', in 'The Gambler'? What was an almanac? Where were all these places, almost heaven, West Virginia, where was my Tennessee mountain home, where in this world was Sweet Home Alabama?

And my mother? She is all of these songs and more. She is Jeannie, who was afraid of the dark. She is Tommy, the coward of the county. She comes with the scratchy sound of a record player. She carries a birthday cake that she hurls at the wall. She is the long, thin branch from the peach tree next door. She is the voice of the Chimera that haunts my dreams. She is the stranger that glances back from my mirror when I least expect to see her. She is my beating heart, my palpitating fear.

4

In the time that I have been here, I have come to know well this formatted place, its long corridors and narrow cells. The Condemn, where we bleed our fingers on blunt needles as we try to restore to wearability the uniforms that should have been thrown out a long time ago; the laundry, where we wash and iron the guards' clothes; the ablution block, where we wash our bodies in basins meant for faces; and the canteen, where the infernal din of four hundred spoons scraping against four hundred metal plates accompanies every meal.

For reasons that will be obvious to you, we are not allowed forks and knives. But nor are we allowed to use our hands like normal people. We eat all our food with tablespoons, everything from the waterlogged porridge to the lump-filled *sadza* and the cabbage that smells of sweat. I have even learned to use a spoon to cut into the slime-brown rubber that the guards, in a simultaneous combination of euphemism and optimism, give the name of meat.

There is no happy medium to our food; it is either overcooked or undercooked, or it has too much salt or not enough, or there is not enough oil in the fried vegetables or there is so much that you almost fear that America will invade. And like the food at the Jewish wedding of the joke, our food is almost inedible, but there is never enough of it.

We march from the canteen to the grounds, from the laundry

to the Condemn, a regulated army in our green dresses and, when it is cold, red-and-white-striped jerseys with matching socks. In the winter months, the prison looks as though Dr Seuss has run riot through it with his *Cat in the Hat* inks.

Every aspect of our lives, from where and how we sleep to what we eat and how fast we eat it, from how much water to how much toothpaste we use, is chosen for us.

Our companions, our words, our very thoughts and dreams, are not ours to choose but are given to us from the sixth floor of the New Government Complex. We live on rations. Each woman has only half a roll of toilet paper, if that, twenty-five millilitres of toothpaste a week and four and a half sanitary pads a month. And it is half a pad, cut neatly down the middle, complete with a dangling wing. It is all written down somewhere, in some statutory instrument or other. Vernah Sithole can probably tell you the precise number.

If the products run out before the next allocation, we make do with what is there. So we use newspapers for tissue, or any other printed material. There was a huge commotion when Synodia conducted an inspection in Block C and found pages of the Bible mixed in with the leavings in the toilet bucket that we call *gamashura*, or the Catcher of Wonders. After she saw pages from the Proverbs and Psalms and the First Letter to the Corinthians mingled in with other wonders, she gave us a two-hour sermon in which her voice reached a pitch of such anger that she found herself unable to speak. Better than the sermon, though, she authorised more toilet rolls.

In the endless moments that I spent in the cells at Highlands police station, I did not imagine that I could ever be in a worse place. That was before Chikurubi. As it turns out, hell *is* other people, especially when those other people are your fellow women prisoners and there has been no water for a week and flies are buzzing over the *gamashura* and the only ablution possible is to run a dry towel across your body, hoping that the dirt and smell that cover you will somehow be absorbed by as inadequate an object as a prison-issue towel with a visible thread count.

I should be accustomed now to the strange rhythms of the jail, but it seems the two years that I have been here are not yet enough to make me used to the distorted sense of time. Rising at four thirty. Breakfast at six, followed by chores and lunch at eleven in the morning. This is followed by more chores.

The prisoners allowed outside go to the farm, where they hoe and weed and tend the vegetables meant for our table, but which go to the guards. I spend almost all my time with the other offenders in 'D' section. Of the four hundred-odd women in the prison, we are considered the most dangerous inmates – our sentences are the longest; we need the most watching. In the men's prison, they call the longest-serving prisoners the 'staff'. There are so few of us here that we do not qualify as staff.

'A' is for the remand prisoners who were refused bail. The main distinction between them and us is that they can wear their hair as they please, except that no weaves are allowed, lest they dim the glory of Synodia's fake-hair weaves. They spend much of their time outside. 'B' is for the petty thieves, the pickpockets, shoplifters and drunken brawlers with less than two years to serve. 'C' is for the majority of prisoners here who have more than two but less than five years to serve.

'D' is for Dangerous, for Deadly, for Death.

There are fourteen of us in D at the moment, women from all over the country: Mavis Munongwa, Nomvula Khumalo, Ellen Gumbo, Ruvimbo Mherekuvana, Benhilda Makoni, Manyara

Makonese, Sinfree Mapuntu, Evernice Gundani, Jimmy Blue Butter, Verity Gutu, Monalisa Mwashita, Beulah Shereni, Esnath Matema, and me, the only woman on death row.

Mavis Munongwa has been here longer than anyone, even the guards. She is the only other woman in here for murder, but she is not on death row. She poisoned her brother's young children, two boys and two girls. They were all under the age of twelve.

Esnath Matema was a housemaid in Mount Pleasant. She lived in the same quarters as the gardener of the house, who was also her father's brother. After they had sex, she fell pregnant. When the baby came, they strangled it and buried it in a shallow grave in the grounds of the university. Unable to live with what they had done, she confessed the truth to their employer. When their case came to trial, she was charged with incest and infanticide. Her uncle was convicted of incest and murder.

As Vernah can tell you, when a mother kills her own baby it is infanticide. If the same child were to be killed by a man, even where the man is the father of the child, it would be murder. The judge found no extenuating circumstances in her uncle's case. He is on death row.

In the night, when it is still, we sometimes hear the men from the male section singing away dead prisoners. When they raise their voices, and the air trembles with songs of sorrow, we know that a prisoner has died. Every time the songs reach our section, Esnath screams in the terror that her uncle is dead.

Nomvula is in for culpable homicide. She and her boyfriend were in a car that knocked over and killed a cyclist in Enthumbane Township in Bulawayo. She says she wasn't the driver, that it was her boyfriend who was behind the wheel. They had been driving back from inspecting the venue where they had hoped to have their wedding. She only agreed to say that she had been driving because her boyfriend had asked her to. She would get a lighter sentence than him, he said, because she was a woman. She would probably just get a fine.

She got five years.

He married someone else.

Ellen is blind in one eye. She has a gash on her cheek. Her husband did that to her. Synodia calls her 'small house', the derogatory term for a woman who is somewhere between a mistress and a spare wife. Only the wealthiest men have small houses. Ellen was the mistress of a man who was seeing other women. She seduced a homeless man to use his semen for medicine. She hardly ever speaks, and until you see her staring out of her good eye, you hardly remember that she is there.

Ruvimbo was a teacher at a school at a platinum mine near Kwekwe. She hit one of her young pupils so hard across the face that he fell and hit his head against the blackboard. He died after a concussion. She is serving six years for culpable homicide, just like Benhilda Makoni, who poisoned her married lover. Benhilda told the court that she had given her lover a powder that she had bought from an herbalist who specialised in love potions. She merely meant to turn his affections away from his wife, she said, but instead of turning to Benhilda, he went into some sort of anaphylactic shock and died. 'Now,' Benhilda says to us, her eyes shining with malice, 'his wife does not have a husband either.'

Manyara is in for stock theft. She and her brothers stole five cows belonging to a farmer near their village in Chivhu. Each cow was considered a separate count, and each count carried three years, so she and her brothers were each sentenced to fifteen years, which were reduced to seven on review.

That is something that may interest you, by the way: that the magistrates here hand out stiffer sentences for stealing cows than for raping children. You only have to look at Sinfree's case. She is from Binga, and is often the target of the guards' wrath because she is Tonga and cannot speak Shona. She is here for attempted murder. Her maths teacher raped her when she was thirteen. Her teacher paid a fine for the crime. When she was sixteen, her family forced Sinfree to marry her rapist so that she did not have the shame of the rape following her all her life. After years of ill-treatment, she burned down his first wife's hut.

Evernice Gundani was part of a protection racket in Mbare that promised market women security from harassment. The harassment came from Evernice herself, and her gang. She is serving six years for extortion.

Beulah Shereni is the youngest person in D. She should be in A category, with the other prisoners on remand, because she has not yet been sentenced. She has been on remand for more than a year. But in that time, she fought with the other women in A. After she tried to bite off the ear of a woman who had accused her of looking like a witch, Synodia decreed that she move to D, 'where she belongs'.

Jimmy has served four of her six years for attempted murder. Her real name is Rejoice Saruchera, but she is called Jimmy for reasons you would not understand. Let me see if I can explain. There is a children's game that is played to the rhyme:

Jimmy blue butter, Jimmy blue butter,
Zengeza my umbrella, my nylon,
My chachacha and my shoe!

I remember playing that game in Mufakose, or, I should say, watching the children on Mharapara Street playing that game while I imagined that I was a part of it, waving an imaginary umbrella, shaking the skirt of my dress at the *chachacha*, and sticking out my foot with a flourish at *my shoe*.

I don't really know what it means; what do children's rhymes ever mean? It is nothing more than a jumble of words and associations. The Zengeza of the rhyme is in Chitungwiza, where Jimmy lived before she came here. Jimmy looks like a cartoon lesbian would look, except that she has had sex with more men than all the women in this prison if they lived ten lifetimes. And she is not really from Zengeza, but from Chipinge.

Like our old neighbour MaiNever on Mharapara Street, Jimmy speaks in the lilting cadence of the Manyika dialect. '*Ndakaende wonini*,' she says. '*Ndakaringe wonini*.'

She is in prison for biting the penis off a man who refused to pay her after sex at a nightclub. 'Prostitute Bites Man's Privates' is a frequent enough headline in the papers to make it a commonplace occurrence, but Jimmy's attack was so ferocious that her victim fainted from blood loss. When he recovered, it was to find that Jimmy had fled to the women's toilets, where she spat out an essential part of him into Harare's sewers.

Verity Gutu and Monalisa Mwashita should not be in D at all. They are both C-class offenders, each serving four years for fraud and theft by conversion. But they had money to bribe the guards into putting them into the comfort of D, such as it is.

Verity is the most notorious woman here. I remember reading about her when I came back from England; it was hard to miss her story because she was on every front page. The newspapers loved her: a beautiful woman, always groomed to the nines, who photographed well, gave good quotes and had a documented sexual history with well-known men. Verity is possibly the only prisoner here for whom remorse is a foreign word. She confesses freely to anyone who cares to ask that yes, it's true, she defrauded the International Olympic Committee and she has nothing to be sorry about. 'What they jailed me for is nothing compared to what I did,' she says. 'Who do you think bought my house and paid for my son to go to university?'

There is an Olympic programme to fund athletes from small, poor nations in sports that are not well known in their countries. Verity signed up Zimbabwean athletes to take up fencing, curling, the modern pentathlon, handball and the steeplechase. When the country failed not only to field a single athlete in these events, but also to hold any qualifying rounds at all before the last games, the Olympic Committee in Lausanne launched an investigation, which found that Verity had used the grant money to buy houses in Borrowdale Brooke and Zimre Park, a BMW and a Range Rover, and to pay for her son's degree from a university in South Africa. The Olympics have also funded countless manicures, beauty treatments and shopping trips to Dubai.

Her case was messy and public. 'Myself, if I choose,' she says, 'I can bring the Olympic movement to its knees.'

It makes me smile to imagine the collapse of the Olympics. From the naked Greeks racing for laurels to Hitler refusing to shake Jesse Owens's hand, the whole Olympic movement could come crashing down because of Verity Gutu. She has her Protectors (the capital letter is hers); she has been the mistress of at least two high-ranking politicians, three businessmen and an assistant police commissioner. Between one and all of her former lovers, she is sure that she will be out soon. 'Myself, I will be out faster than a javelin can land.'

If Verity Gutu is the Queen of Cynics, Monalisa Mwashita is their empress. She defrauded a European embassy of more than half a million euros over two years. She was a Special Projects and Programming Officer in charge of funding projects on sustainability, governance, accountability and the rule of law, one of those jobs for whom the phrase 'job description' was invented – a job that cannot be explained by a simple word like 'lawyer' or 'journalist', 'technician' or 'accountant'.

Her job was to determine which projects should get how much of the embassy's funding. She created two fake organisations, one for the Advancement and Empowerment of the Girl Child, and another to support OVCs caught up in political violence. 'Girl Children,' she says, 'are the easiest con in the world.'

There is apparently no easier way to raise money from donors than to present a child, female and barefoot, with a plea for money to ward off all the dreadful things that could happen to it: the HIV infection, the orphaning, the household-heading, the poverty-miring and the single-mother-becoming.

Monalisa also realised that the term 'political violence' is to donors what Pavlov's bell was to his dogs. She diverted funding to the fake group she had set up to 'assist, encourage and raise awareness to further the empowerment of OVCs subject to political violence'. OVCs, if you are not up with donor lingo, are Orphans and other Vulnerable Children. More than food, shelter and all the rest of it, OVCs and Girl Children need empowerment – empowerment and awareness-raising.

It was an easy fraud for Monalisa to pull. All that the embassy required of grant recipients was that they produce quarterly reports of how the money was spent, and these she provided, complete with glowing pictures of Girl Children smiling for the cameras.

When she told me how simple the whole thing had been to set up and pull off, I was surprised that Chikurubi is not bursting with more such fraudsters. Scams go on in almost every embassy, Monalisa said, but most embassies simply fire the persons involved without prosecuting them. They do not want to report to the police for fear of drawing attention to the kinds of activities they fund. In her case, the embassy brought its case against her on the basis of the Girl Child fraud; they said nothing about the OVCs as they did not want too much attention to be given to the political side of their funding.

It seems strange that anyone would voluntarily choose to come to D with the more dangerous criminals, but I understand why Verity and Monalisa bribed their way in from C. There are more than a hundred women in C, baby dumpers sleeping next to drug smugglers and fraudsters and thieves. And there are sometimes babies sleeping with their mothers. There are frequent fights – one woman can look at another in a 'funny way', or someone will get worked up because one of the babies is crying too long and too loud and waking up the others.

And there is only one toilet bucket in the cell for all the women to share. If anyone breaks the code that says that only urination is allowed in the bucket after lock-up, the acrimony can turn ugly. This is why there is a scurry of activity outside the ablution block every day just before lockdown. Two C-category prisoners, Truthness and Locadia, went for each other in the garden last week. Truthness had accidentally tipped a bucket over Locadia's baby, and Locadia had her revenge with blows the next day.

As I am on death row, I should, in theory, live and work separately from the other Ds. I should be in my own section, with my own guards. But the prison is too small and too poor for them to make any real distinction between the others and me. So during the day, I work in the laundry, clear out the Condemn or go out into the garden or further afield, to the prison farm.

I am even allowed to play the occasional game of netball with them, and have learned, like all prisoners soon learn here, that when there is a game of netball against the guards, we should always, but always, lose the game. Jimmy told me that the first time she played, she led the prisoners to an 11–7 rout, and so angered Synodia that she brought forward lock-up by two hours.

If I can ignore the inevitability of the sentence that awaits me, there are a number of advantages to being the only one in D on death row. After lock-up is when I most feel the benefits of being on death row. I am locked up in my own cell. And, luxury of luxuries, I have my very own completely unshared toilet bucket. I have my own Catcher of Wonders.

~ ~ ~ ~ ~ ~ ~ ~ ~ ~

When I first arrived, I found the usual fear-laced fascination and superstition around my condition. I am the first woman in more than twenty years to be sentenced to death. And it is not every day that one comes across a murdering albino outside a novel by Dan Brown. But it was my skin and my crime that caused the other prisoners to shrink into themselves as they walked past me.

In those days, a woman called Marvellous gave me the hardest time. She has now been paroled after serving six years for culpable homicide. She told me that all new prisoners had to give their food to her at meal times. In the first weeks, I gave half my food to her without protest, but I soon came to see that I would starve if I did not find some way to defeat her. So I took to giving her long unbroken stares as she ate my food. 'Don't look at me with those eyes,' she snapped.

I was reminded of my mother. 'Don't look at me with those eyes of yours,' she often said, which never made sense to me, for I could only look at her with my eyes, and nobody else's, but I know now that she meant those eyes with no colour or pigment to them.

Three days after I began this, Marvellous received news that her son had died. When she asked if she could go to the funeral and Synodia laughed in her face, Marvellous wailed at the top of her voice for more than an hour and only stopped when Synodia threatened to have them add another two months to her sentence. 'No need to go to court, either,' Synodia said. 'We will just mislay your release papers.'

At the next meal, I stared again at Marvellous, and again at every meal for four continuous days. After a week, she asked to be moved away from me. Jimmy told me that she had told the guards that the looks I gave her are what killed her son, 'just like she killed that white man'. Marvellous became afraid of me, and would not look at me when she passed me. After that, I did not hesitate to use my condition to my advantage.

The chameleon that I picked up in my third month here also added to my mystique. We were out on the prison farm, weeding the maize patch, when I saw a movement among the small green shoots of the new maize. When I saw that it was a chameleon, it immediately reminded me of our old neighbour Liz Warrender, the first person I had ever seen touch a chameleon. I thought of her colourful expressions and her love for gossip. 'You should see her go after him; I promise you, she is busier than a blue-arsed fly.'

A wave of homesickness washed over me. Without thinking, I reached out to take it into my hands. The creature changed colour from green to grey to brown as it struggled with the sudden change in its environment. Then it took on the colour of my skin and the greenish colour of my uniform as it made its hesitant and slow movement up to my shoulder. In the fugue of my concentration, I did not realise immediately that the cry that rang out had anything to do with me, or the creature on my arm.

I looked up to see Benhilda staring at me with a look of revulsion on her face, the same look of shock that I must have had on my face as a child at Summer Madness the first time I saw Liz pick up a chameleon. The others turned, and instantly moved together, as though their solidarity would ward off the miasma of my evil.

'It is only a chameleon,' I said.

'Only a chameleon?' The whisper went up and down the line of women.

'How can you say it is only a chameleon?' This was Beulah. 'Are you some kind of a witch that you play with such things?'

The chameleon made a more determined effort to go round to my other arm. I picked it up in both hands, and made my way to a cluster of baby dumpers who gave little shrieks of shock as they scattered. I set the creature down and watched it as it changed colour again before disappearing into the maize.

I had forgotten that, like those creatures of the darkness, like owls and hyenas, chameleons are portents of evil, associated with witchcraft and black magic. The news spread throughout the prison and made me safe from all bullying, at least from other prisoners.

The fear did not extend to the guards. Synodia and Loveness, assisted by Mathilda and Patience, are responsible for guarding D and C sections. To them, we have no names. We are cattle rustlers and murderers, arsonists and prostitutes. They look different from each other. Loveness, the principal prison officer – she is short and round and light-skinned, with several missing teeth. Synodia, recently promoted to assistant superintendent, and thus Loveness's superior, is a little darker, a little taller, and a lot more sour-looking. Patience is simperingly pretty, all eye- and lip-liner, and Mathilda is well padded, with a slow and heavy gait.

But they also look the same, as though they are interchangeable one with the other, as though the specifics of their individualities are subsumed into the uniforms that they wear.

Through the weekly ironing that we do for them, we catch glimpses of their lives outside the prison. Loveness has a daughter and no husband, Synodia three children and a husband who works in some sort of factory; I have ironed his blue overalls. Mathilda's children, three boys, like to play with toy cars, real or made up, I don't know; their trousers are frayed on the parts that cover their knees. It is all I can do not to damage them further with the iron. Patience lives alone; she likes her clothes in lurid patterns and wears too much oil in her hair. She is not married, but we sometimes find men's underwear in her laundry.

'She will never keep the Commissioner at this rate,' said Benhilda as she waved a pair of underpants over her head. 'She must know, surely, that the only way to keep a man is to make sure that you wash these yourself.'

Unlike the others, Patience prefers to speak to us in English. She is in training to be a court interpreter. 'Irregardless of the absence of water,' she says, 'you should make sure the hoarse pipes are connected.'

'You must make sure that your plates and bowels are clean.'

'You have the wrongful number!' she screamed into her phone the other day. 'I said this is the wrongful number!'

'Can you believe it,' she confided to Loveness, 'there are women, married women, whole married women, five, six children later, who have not had a single organism?'

'You don't say,' said Loveness.

'Not even one organism, just imagine,' she said, and in the next breath she shouted at me for listening and told me to get on with my work. This is what surprises me most about Chikurubi, that we can laugh as much as we do. But there is a hysterical edge to my laughter, because every time I laugh I know that I am laughing into the darkness.

5

I did not see my family again after my parents sold me. I remember once sitting at my stool before the long wooden desk in the science lab at the Convent, melting potassium permanganate crystals in a test tube over a Bunsen burner, when the thought suddenly occurred to me that I could no longer picture Mobhi's face in my mind's eye. I closed my eyes to see her, and concentrated so tightly that I did not hear Sister Mary Gabriel shouting that my crystals were burning.

There are some things about her that I still remember. Her fat legs, her pudgy arms thrusting out to be picked up, her laugh against the sky. But over the years, her face has become a blur, like a jelly that has been out of the fridge for so long that it has lost its shape, and I cannot see her face. I remember her feet the most because they stuck out of the bucket in which she drowned.

I have no pictures that could have helped me remember. I took none with me. My mother's photo album remained with all the other things that I left behind in Mufakose. And even then, even if I had wanted to take some, there were not many pictures in that album.

These things that I am telling you about, at least in these early years, all happened in the middle of the 1980s, before the digital revolution, long before the days where every person in the world had a camera. For people like us who lived in the townships, to be photographed was a commitment that required money and serious effort.

On the rare occasions that we were photographed, we dressed in our best clothes, in our Christmas clothes that doubled as our birthday clothes, my sisters and I in the same lacy dress but in different colours. My brother, Gift, in the few pictures that remained of him after he died, wore a suit and a velvet bow tie.

Getting our picture taken meant taking the bus to Highfield Township, where there was a photography studio. Joyi and I tried to walk without shuffling our feet; we were afraid to disturb the dust of the township street, which had a stubborn propensity to stick to freshly washed and Vaselined legs. Mobhi was up on my father's shoulders.

Past Gwanzura Stadium we walked, past the Mushandira-pamwe Hotel, past the Huyaimuone Superette and Butchery, past the Chirwirangwe Cash and Carry and the chemist's, until we reached the studio.

The photographer was called Bester Kanyama. This was serious business: he did not like it when we smiled. He posed us with incongruous objects around or before us, an open umbrella in front of a velvet curtain in one case, or next to a radiogram or wireless set in another, or else holding a vase of artificial flowers fashioned from discarded thin wire and coloured women's stockings.

When he photographed Joyi, Mobhi and me separately from our parents, he sat us next to a large doll with a porcelain face that had staring eyes and a blank smile. Our pictures thus had a frozen quality; our eyes were brighter than new dollar coins, as though a light had been shone directly into them.

I always looked pale, paler than everyone else, like a ghost against the others, as though I were a live and large version of the porcelain doll on my knee; the same doll that frightened me in my first week at Summer Madness, or a doll very like it.

The only time I can remember that we did not prepare to get photographs taken was a few weeks before Mobhi died. My mother was happy, which made us all nervous. This was around the time she had joined Reverend Bergen's church and he had singled her out and made his great prophecy about her fate.

A photographer who walked from door to door taking pictures passed our house. He was not Bester Kanyama, but someone else, a man who lived in Kambuzuma Section 2 and whose studio was the street.

My mother called him into the yard. 'How much for a picture?' she asked.

The man replied, 'One dollar for one card, and three dollars for four cards, but if you want more we can negotiate.'

After a long negotiation, my mother led him to the side of the house, from where my father worked. Joyi, Mobhi and I followed. As 'Mirandu' played on the radio, the photographer took our picture. He wore a small fedora hat with a red feather in it. When he creased his brow, the hat moved, and with it the feather. We laughed out loud, all of us, my father, my mother, my sisters and me; we burst into hard, sudden laughter. In that moment he took the picture.

We did not see the developed photograph until after Mobhi died.

The photographer had said that my mother should come and pick the photographs up from his house in Section 2 after two weeks, which was how long it would take him to move around the township to finish his roll of film and persuade people to have their pictures taken. In the tumult and turmoil that followed Mobhi's death, the pictures that my mother had ordered lay unremembered with all the other photographs the photographer had taken.

After my mother failed to collect them from his house, as he had asked her to do, the photographer returned to our house. When he heard of Mobhi's death, he took off his hat and tried to give the photograph to my mother. He did not ask for money. She did not take it; she was then in a catatonic state. He left it on the starched-lace doily on top of the display cabinet. In a brief moment in which she came to herself, she tore it up and scattered the pieces on the floor.

If I try hard enough, I see that image still. My father sits on a half-finished wardrobe with Mobhi in his arms, her face cracked in two by her smile. His head is thrown back. Joyi and I are grinning, arm in arm. My mother's face is radiant with laughter. I am next to my mother, trying to ignore the unfamiliar lightness of her arm around my shoulders.

After everyone had gone to sleep that night, I looked for the pieces of the photograph and tried to stick everyone together with my saliva. It did not work. I contemplated stealing sticking tape from the desk of Mistress Nyathi, my class teacher. Until I could steal the tape, I kept the pieces in the stapled middle pages of the novel *Muchadura*, which I had just won for coming first out of all the four classes of grade threes.

I thought the picture would be safe in there. Not only was it a novel about a terrifying avenging spirit, but it also had a cover featuring a creepy unsmiling child, the torso of a ghostly woman and a disembodied eye. My father had made me cover it in brown paper. Our neighbour had the same book, and Mobhi used to burst into tears when she saw it and Joyi would not look directly at it. For all her fear of the book, Joyi took *Muchadura* with her to school one day without telling me and did not return it. Even when I beat her up until she had a nosebleed, she would not tell me what she had done with the book.

Under the bed, I found a little piece. It showed one of Mobhi's fat legs against the light fabric of my father's trousers. I held on to that piece of Mobhi as long as I could, before I lost it, and it too disappeared like the rest of the photograph.

~ ~ ~ ~ ~ ~ ~ ~ ~ ~

Vernah Sithole explained to me at our first meeting that the best I can expect to get in the absence of a completely new and fresh trial is a life sentence. 'I am fighting to get the conviction over-turned,' she said. 'But if that does not happen, the Supreme Court could commute the penalty to life. And there will be no early release,' she added, 'unless something changes after the election. There could be an amnesty that affects you too. But otherwise life really means life, you know.'

She could also have used the words of the recent editorial in the *Herald*. It was in response to a report by the Goodwill Fellowship that said prisons had become places of despair disproportionate to the severity of the crimes that brought people there.

With its usual charm and perspicacity, the *Herald* got to the heart of the matter: 'Let no one be in any doubt that in this country we really know how to deal with criminals. We put them in prison, then we throw away the key, and leave them to rot there with all the other filth and dregs of society. And if they do not like it, well, they should not commit crimes.'

Synodia could have written these words. At her approach the

milk of human kindness curdles. To every complaint, that there are too few blankets, that there is too little food, or that there is no water to flush the toilets, or not enough sanitary pads, she says the same thing. 'It was not me who made you a criminal. If you don't like living in this place, you should not be a criminal.'

So life means a life like poor Mavis Munongwa's, a life with no parole. There is no hope of escape either, no floating to freedom on sacks of coconuts like Papillon, or, like Andy Dufresne, digging my way out with a rock hammer and crawling through a river of shit to come out clean on the other side.

6

When I close my eyes and will it to, Mufakose Township comes to me complete in every detail. I still know all the streets that I passed on the way to school; we always took the same route with my father. We passed Chiguyakuya, Mbizi, Kafudzamombe and Mutarimbo. We went past Handira and Mbada and Dapi, and turned into Zongororo, which means millipede, and I imagined that the houses on that road were the legs of a millipede. From Zongororo, we passed the church, turned into Muonde, left into Munondo, then left again into the school gate.

I discovered when I left Mufakose that it is possible to live in Harare in total unawareness that there are areas to the west and to the south containing the detritus of human existence, that it is possible to be unaware of the teeming townships with the houses that look exactly the same, redbrick houses with a square inch of space around them, houses in which humans, plants and dogs managed to flourish. Families lived together all packed one on top of the other, like sardines in a tin: mother, father, another mother, sometimes; aunts, uncles and cousins.

You will discover as you walk around the city that it was planned to keep the direct heat of the sun away from the faces of white people. In the mornings, they left the northern suburbs to go into town to work, and the sun was behind them, and in the evenings, when they went back home, the sun was behind them still. The streets of the northern suburbs are lined with avenues of jacarandas and flamboyants that give cooling shade. But in the townships, the sun is always in the faces of the people. And there are no tree-lined avenues, no cool grass beneath the feet, only the hard heat of the dusty streets.

When I found myself living with Lloyd at Summer Madness, I surprised myself by missing the sounds that I had heard from inside the room that I shared with my sisters in Mufakose. This was the room that my mother called the *speya*. In the township, the parents' bedroom was just the bedroom, and the second bedroom, for there were only ever two bedrooms, was always the *speya*. This indicated rooms so plentiful that one was spare, but as the *speya* was always where the children slept, it also suggested that our rooms were not our own, and we were mere interlopers, temporary guests who could be evicted at any time.

In Umwinsidale, with Lloyd, on the other side of Harare, I was as far from Mufakose as it was possible to be. Umwinsidale was still tranquillity. There were no sounds that did not belong to nature. Lloyd's house, Summer Madness, sat on its own small hill, and when I looked out into the night, I saw nothing but the darkness of the valley, and the far-away lights of the neighbours shimmering like fireflies in a distant forest.

In Mufakose, the night was torn with sounds of couplings, snoring, howling dogs, the running feet of thieves chancing it in the darkness, and children mimicking *zvinyau* dances under the huge tower light that lit up the township street.

In the daytime, the township pulsated to the symphonic movement of the everyday. From the *speya*, I heard the children of Mharapara Street play their favourite games. I knew all the rules to all the games. I knew it was bad form *kuita chiziso* when playing *rakaraka* or *dunhu*. I knew just how to challenge a rival to a fight by forming a small mound of earth then destroying it while looking around dramatically and saying, '*Ndaputsa zamu raamai vako*. See, see, I have smashed your mother's breast', so that the rival had no choice but to fight in defence of the smashed breast.

I knew all the words to all the games, and sang along to them. '*Pansapo paribe, askende rimwana, pansapo paribe, askende rimwana auPretty auke aukende sikende s'ke skende sikende auke auke wawa.*'

From the *speya*, I heard the woman who walked up Mopani Road from Mufakose to Kambuzuma crying out the vegetables that she sold. I heard MadzibabaConorio, with his shaven head and bushy beard, shouting, '*Mabhodhoro*', as the pots that he collected for mending clanged and jangled against the bottles at his side.

I heard the beggars, the blind men and women led by their children, pleading from one end of Mharapara to the other, '*Tooooooooooookumbirawo rubatsiro vanhu vaJehovah*', and their grateful claps and acclamations when anyone extended them a kindness. '*Mwari venyu vakukumborerei, vakukomborerei, vakukomborerei. Mugare kure kwemoto vakukomborerei vakukomborerei vakukomborerei.*'

I heard SekuruAlexio, whose eyes dripped with yellow pus and who spoke in a Malawian accent as he tempted the children into buying *mbwirembwire*. If a child bought more than one pocketful, he exclaimed at what he saw as the child's riches and said, in delight, '*Uri mwana wambozha!*'

We were poor without knowing it. There was nothing ennobling or romantic or life-affirming about our poverty. It just was. And you could say that we did not know just how poor we were because everyone else around us was the same. We accepted the simple order of our lives in the ignorance that other, richer lives were possible.

We were intimate with the ways of our neighbours and they with ours. Little happened that did not invite the scrutiny and commentary of the township. We knew when our neighbours were having chicken, and they knew when we were having *matemba*. We knew that, at one end of Mharapara, Nhau's mother habitually burned the meat as well as we knew that there would be no meat smells from the kitchen of the Malawian family at the other end, who seemed to live on Lacto sour milk.

What we did not see and smell ourselves, we got from our most gossipy neighbour, MaiWhizi. No one entered any yard on Mharapara without her knowledge. She had countless relatives with endless virtues. She ended up being related to most people on the street because she had an uncle or a nephew or a *muramu* who had just that minute arrived from *kumusha*, he was looking for a job, he would get a good job, it was just a matter of time before he got a very good job, an excellent job, and all he wanted was a good wife to cook for him.

Vero, who lived next door but one to MaiPrincess, married MaiWhizi's husband's youngest brother. She had set her eyes on Rispah, MaiNever's aunt's daughter, for her own aunt's eldest son, but Rispah fell pregnant. MaiWhizi knew about Rispah's shame before anyone, down to the names, heights and ages of all the inhabitants of the house in Mugaragunguwo Street to which Rispah had fled to escape the wrath and shame of MaiNever, Ba'Never and her parents.

For all that she knew more about Mharapara than any of us, MaiWhizi was more capable of astonishment than anybody else.

She compared everything shocking or startling, anything surprising or unexpected, to a bioscope. 'Ah,' she exclaimed, and put her hands together in a quick clap in front of her face before quickly releasing them, '*Zvariri bhais'kopu!*' She spent hours polishing her veranda red with Sunbeam polish or wiping her windows. When MaiWhizi's curtains twitched, you knew that something was happening.

Although they later became fast friends, MaiNever once threatened to beat up MaiWhizi because she told MaiPrincess that MaiNever's husband had been seen at a shebeen in Mbare. 'Ba'Never *vakasvikopikire chipostori zvariini?*' MaiNever shouted in Manyika. '*Magemenzi andinobvire wonini, andinobvire wacha zuva ngezuva.*'

MaiPrincess was also called MaiMaTwins because she had given birth to two sets of twins. She had six children under the age of twelve. She was the most pregnant woman that anyone had ever seen. She seemed always to have just given birth, be about to give birth or be feeding a child at her breast. Her first two children, the twin girls Princess and Pretty, were followed by their brother, Progress, then by a girl, Promise, and twin boys, Providence and Privilege. For all I know, she had more children after I left Mufakose. Perhaps she had a Prudence, a Praise or a Promotion. Perhaps she had a Prevarication or a Predestination.

MaiWhizi, MaiNever and MaiMaTwins talked to each other over their buckets of laundry. In the year that I left, they were obsessed with Peggy, the township ghost with red lips, a shining Afro and an alluring bottom. Peggy had been seen in Highfield and at Chitubu in Glen Norah, they said, and was now working her way up Kambuzuma Road to Mufakose.

'She lured a man at Mushandirapamwe Hotel, *hanzi* they danced all night.'

'When they got to his house she said he was not to light a candle.'

'The next morning, he woke up in the graveyard, right on top of her grave.'

'And he saw Peggy, but now she was a statue, *pafungei ipapo*, just a statue kneeling on the grave, just kneeling there, stiff as anything, *kunge mukadzi wa*Lot *chaiye*. Just like Lot's wife.'

When they were not gossiping over the laundry, the township women tore the air with the names of their children.

'Nhau! Princess! Never!'

'Promise! Providence! Progress! *Imi! Chiuyai mugeze!*'

'Whizi! *Nhai iwe* Wisdom! *Urimatsisu?*'

'Run to MaiNever and give her this pot.'

'Run to MaiPrincess and ask her for sugar.'

'Run to MaiWhizi and tell her she is late.'

'Run to MaiGivhi and give her this powder.'

'Run to the tuck-shop *utenge* half-bread.'

'Run to the tuck-shop and buy seven candles.'

'Run outside and don't bother me.'

'Run away and don't ask too many questions.'

'Run along before I slap you.'

Run here, run there, run forward, run backwards. The children of the township were constantly moving dynamos, with fast legs but with heads often elsewhere, attending to the tasks at hand with half the mind on play. The ensuing recriminations would ring out across the street.

'You have spilt the sugar!'

'You silly child, you have squashed the tomatoes!'

'*Mazizheve anenge ababa!* You have forgotten the bread!'

'What do you mean, you dropped the money?'

Then the sound of a slap, or a walloping with the favoured instrument of the house concerned – a belt, a sjambok or the long, thin branch from a peach tree. Then would come wails and lamentations, *ndagura, ndagura kani nhai* Mhai, before the admonition to go out and play.

But the tears soon dried, and the pain was forgotten in chasing the Snowman ice cream man, in shouting, '*Paribe musevenzo, paribe musevenzo*', while dancing after SekuruAlexio, and in the dizzying round of play and games, *rakaraka* and *nhodo*, *dunhu* and *pada*, games that I did not play in the township where we lived.

~ ~ ~ ~ ~ ~ ~ ~ ~ ~

The strongest memory that I have of the *speya* is the smell of Mobhi's urine on the green-and-brown blankets hanging on the washing line outside our houses. I say our houses because those same urine-soaked blankets followed us to hang on other washing lines, as we moved from Mbare to Highfield before settling in Mufakose, from where I was sold, their green and brown stripes fading from the sun and washing. We were one short after Gift was buried.

I must have been three or four when Gift died. I read somewhere that long-term memory is linked to the left prefrontal lobe in the brain, which only develops after the age of three. I also read, perhaps in the same article, that memory is closely linked with the acquisition of language, that without verbal ability to articulate experience, there can be no memory, and this is why our earliest recollections date from the time we learn to speak.

So it may have been even earlier than that when my brother died. Or perhaps it is another child's funeral that I remember, nothing to do with my brother at all. I never knew exactly how old Gift was when he died because no one talked about him, though his name was with us daily in the MaiGivhi and Baba Givhi that my parents called each other – apart from those moments when anger broke through the decorum of naming conventions and they called each other by their first names. It was a shock to us to hear them call each other Moira and Benson; it was almost like seeing them naked.

Our house, all our houses, had rickety doors and thin, thin windows that shook as the doors were opened and closed, and shook even harder when my mother banged them. There was a small garden around our house; there we had a banana plant. Our neighbours had half-attempted orchards with mango trees and, occasionally, naartjies. The gardens were only just big enough to grow small vegetable patches; however long people lived in the towns, agriculture, like an atavistic instinct, was still in their blood and drove them to plant crops and till the land even on these tiny plots.

MaiPrincess and her family, who lived next door, had a large avocado tree and wanted to keep each avocado to themselves, but we did not always give back the fruit that fell and rolled under the tarpaulin covering my father's wood and tools. We mashed up MaiPrincess's avocadoes and spread them on bread.

I slept next to Mobhi, who slept next to Joyi, and I often woke up with the smell of her urine on my nightdress. My mother, enraged, would beat us, and command me to wake her in the night. But the toilet was outside and the night held terrors for me.

In the night, our main door squeaked, dogs barked, insects flew and the witches who ate children mounted an invisible presence and saw through the eyes of the barking dogs. In the night walked Peggy, with her big bottom and big Afro. Then there was the small matter of the haunted house six houses down from MaiNever's.

It was an empty house, with all the windows smashed in. It drew the gaze of everyone in the township. At least during the day it held its fascination. In the night, it was a place of terror. People had lived there once. But every time new lodgers moved into that house, they woke in the night to find themselves, and all that they owned, out in the street.

People said that there was an angry *ngozi* spirit in that house. *Ngozi*, if you did not already know, is the spirit of vengeance that follows a violent death. All the people on our side of Crowborough believed that someone had been killed there, and that, until that spirit was appeased, all those who lived in the house would live with the horror of that terrible slaying and wake to find themselves outside the house.

The haunted house was on the Dindingwe end of Mharapara, nowhere near where we lived, but it was close enough that I preferred not to go out at night. A million times better to hang up our urine-soaked blankets, a million times better to wash daily the old nightdress in which I slept. And when Mobhi drowned, her feet sticking up from out of the zinc bucket in our bathroom, I remember the relief of dry blankets.

In the township, we lived in forced intimacy. We knew which neighbours borrowed which things: shoes for a school trip, sugar, mealie meal, salt, eggs.

We revered Teacher Maenzanise, who had something that few others had – a car. When Constance fell from the avocado tree at Princess's house, her mother, MaiNever, carried her broken body all the way down Mharapara, across Shuramurove and into Mhembwe Street, where Teacher Maenzanise lived. All that MaiNever needed to say was 'Connie *wabvirodonha*', and Teacher Maenzanise put down his *Parade* and his cigarette and drove them to Gomo Hospital.

There was no thought of an ambulance. For one thing, there was no phone to call it with. Teacher Maenzanise provided an unofficial ambulance service for everyone on our side of Crowborough Way. MaiPrincess's daughter Promise had been born in that car, Ba'Nhau's old Sekuru had died in it, and both had been on the way to the hospital.

In the year before I was sold, Teacher Maenzanise's reputation was in danger of being dented because an angry woman came to school and took off her clothes in front of him. Drawn by the commotion, a crowd of children and teachers came to his classroom and heard her threaten to take off her clothes. This was meant to show that she had lost all her dignity; it was to show that the world might as well see her naked because of what he had done to her. '*Ndokubvisira hembe*, I will strip off my dress right here,' she shouted.

I did not see this myself, but my sister Joyi did because she was in Teacher Maenzanise's class. She and her classmates had seen the woman, but could not describe what she looked like naked because Teacher Maenzanise had taken his jacket and covered her up and fought her out of the door. She had held on to the doorjamb and Teacher Maenzanise had had to force her out. The last thing that Joyi and the class had seen were her naked legs kicking her light-blue plastic Sandak shoes to the ground.

The township gossips said it must have been her fault if she was pregnant, didn't she know he was married, she was a slut who deserved everything she got.

'Who would say no to being married to a teacher?' said MaiWhizi.

'Especially a teacher with a car,' MaiNever said.

'Imagine marrying a woman like that, *ukaroora zvakadaro unenge wazviparira ngozi*,' was MaiWhizi's conclusion.

MaiWhizi would come over and comment on the hairstyle my mother was working on. She was also obsessed with other women's complexions.

'*Ende vasikana* Rispah *mazotsvuka*,' she would say. '*Murikuzoreiko mazuvano*, what lightening cream are you using?' Like the bi-coloured rock python in the *Just So Stories*, her face was two different colours. The cheeks were black – from using Ambi lightening cream, everyone said – and the rest of her face was the colour that she should have been, the colour she kept changing.

But this was all in my mind. I longed to play on Mharapara with the others but I could not join in. I could not join in because, if I went out and stayed in the sun for any length of time, my skin cracked and blistered. I spent my days indoors with the sound of the township coming through my mother's shining windows, or I sat and observed them from our Sunbeam-red veranda. And when I did venture out, it was to be greeted as *murungudunhu*, so that I thought that must be part of my name.

7

The nights that I spent at Highlands police station and those early nights at Chikurubi in the cell that I shared with Mavis Munongwa brought back the old dreams that had shuddered me awake, the dreams that had not disturbed my sleep since my first two years with Lloyd.

In my dreams, I see a *njuzu* that is shaped like the Chimera. It moves beneath a dress of poppies that are brighter than the blood gushing from its mouth. It speaks in a voice thick with blood and water. 'You are dirty, you are unclean,' it says.

It pulls me down, down into its throat. I jolt myself awake just at the point that its throat closes over me and my face is submerged and my lungs fill with water. Sometimes the *njuzu*'s voice sounds like my mother's, other times like Lloyd's. In the water with me is Lloyd's swollen face, his eyes open, his neck constricted by the creature's tail. As it pulls me into itself, I hear the clanging crashing of a thousand keys. A scream that begins as mine merges into Lloyd's sister Alexandra's before becoming the shriek of the Chimera.

I don't know if you can smell in your dreams, Melinda, but in mine the creature comes wrapped in the suffocating smell of camphor, as though it has washed in it, as though its very marrow is made of it. And as it was then, I can never go back to sleep after my sudden waking. I lie listening to the sleep sounds of the prison, the stertorous breathing of Mavis Munongwa in the next cell, the high whine of a million mosquitoes, the creaks and sudden sounds of the prison talking to itself. I listen to the beating of my heart, until four thirty in the morning comes and with it the strident siren that heralds a new day.

~ ~ ~ ~ ~ ~ ~ ~ ~ ~

Vernah told me before our second meeting that you are learning Shona. I didn't know that you are planning to stay as long as that. Whatever you do, you should not allow yourself to be discouraged by the many people – white people, I mean – who you are certain to meet who will tell you how difficult the local languages are, how they twist the tongue and confuse the mind.

Lloyd and his friend Liz Warrender, who I will tell you about, were both fluent speakers. Liz had picked up hers at the farm in Melsetter where she grew up, while Lloyd's was the result of years of assiduous and conscientious study. It was partly this facility and ease with the local language that got them labelled eccentrics. Lloyd could not only speak Shona fluently, which helped me in that difficult first year with him, but he could also write it better than most Shona speakers that I know.

The main passion of his academic life was to translate Homer and Aristotle into Shona. He took pains at it, insisting that the only pure translation was one that came from the original Greek texts. For Lloyd, using the English texts would not only have been a lamentable shortcut, it would also have destroyed the integrity of the project, and taken away all its fun. They are still there, I imagine, Lloyd's books and manuscripts, on the shelves of his study in Summer Madness. *'Mambo Idhipasi'*. *'Idhipasi wekuAntioch'*.

'*Rwendo rwaOdhisiyasi*'. If they are not still at Summer Madness, I imagine Alexandra threw them out.

Lloyd's written Shona was much better than mine. My spoken Shona is still fluent, but my writing is frozen at the age of eight, which is when I last wrote it in school. This is one of the consequences of a superior education, you see. In this independent, hundred-per-cent-empowered and fully and totally indigenous blacker-than-black country, a superior education is one that the whites would value, and as the whites do not value local languages, the best-educated among us have sacrificed our languages at the altar of what the whites deem supreme. So it was in colonial times, and so it remains, more than thirty years later.

So I never learned how to write with lyricism or beauty in my own language. I never learned the proverbs and metaphors that give colour to the language. But there is a proverb that I still remember from Mistress Nyathi's class in grade three, which goes '*matakadya kare haanyaradzi mwana*, memories of bygone feasts will not feed a hungry child'.

My memories are not of bygone feasts, unless you count the birthday parties that my mother had for us. The day that my mother and father sold me to Lloyd is the day that our different lots, his and mine, collided to form the thread that brought me here to this cell in Chikurubi Prison. Until that day, I had been going in one direction, my sphere limited to house number 1468 Mharapara Street in Mufakose, to my two parents, my dead brother and two sisters, to my school, to my small joys and sorrows.

Fighting Nhau's daily torments and the hissing of the children. Struggling to conquer the twelve times table. Longing sharply for food that we did not have, ready-made, store-bought food like candy cakes and Colcom pork pies and cream doughnuts. Fearing always the heat of the sun, and the smell of Mercurochrome and the purple stains of gentian violet that were dabbed on my blistering skin by the rough, callused hands of the nurses at Gomo Hospital.

Trying to be invisible. I spent much of my life trying to be invisible. But I was never truly invisible. Even in London, or Sydney, where I should have blended in with everyone, the world's gaze came with a double take. On the surface, my skin looked like everybody else's, but seen closer, my features are very obviously not Caucasian. I could feel the puzzlement on the face as the mind tried to work out what was different.

The most hysterical reaction came from a pregnant inmate called Melody, who looked at me with her one eye round with fear before screaming so loudly that the guards had to take her away. Jimmy said that she was afraid that I would infect the baby she carried. Years ago, this might have hurt me, but it doesn't now. It no longer hurts with the acid pain I felt as a child. It is a long time since I wanted to crawl out of my own skin.

I once found, in an old book at one of the antiquarian bookstores on Charing Cross Road in London, a facsimile of a handbill exhorting the public to witness THE AMAZING WHITE NEGRO, YOURS TO SEE FOR 2S ONLY in Piccadilly. By then I had left home, but I had not completely let go of a childhood game that I had once played alone, in which I moved myself across time and space and imagined the alternative lives I could have had, had I been, for instance, born in Pompeii or in Egypt or in Atlantis or the Wild West.

It struck me as I looked at that handbill that any alternative life that I might have had in a freak show in Piccadilly in the seventeenth century would not have been particularly different from my childhood in Mufakose. The only difference was that, in the twentieth century in Mufakose, I was a freak who made money for no one.

In a township, everything odd, particularly oddities of appearance, is remarked on. But in my case, even the people who looked odd, like Sekuru Jonas, who limped on his left leg and lived across the street and made manyatera sandals at Siyaso, spat whenever he saw me.

MaiTafadzwa, who could only afford to feed her family on Lacto sour milk and *matemba*, muttered something under her breath and spat. The Phiri family two houses down from MaiNever's place, generally mocked because they were Malawian and the father had a sing-song voice and joined the *zvinyau* dancers on the banks of the Marimba River, looked at me with eyes of pity.

And when my family made rare visits with me outside the township, the children of other townships did that thing that children do, they shouted to remind me I was a *murungudunhu*, and not content with that, danced around me and announced my presence to everyone.

What made my situation worse – at least, as I saw it – was that I was not the only albino person in the township. The other was Lameck, who had a squashed face and red, blotchy skin that broke over his arms and face.

His hair was almost orange. Mine was just as strange, not black like everyone else's but closer to white, the same colour as my skin. Lameck stood in the same place every day; he sold tomatoes and maputi at the market that sprouted at the corner of Mharapara and Kafudzamombe Avenue. He had placed himself so that the people who lived at our end of Mharapara did not need to go all the way to the shops at kwaMhishi. For all the convenience that his store provided, he was not exactly inundated with customers.

When he was not selling tomatoes, Lameck squinted at a James Hadley Chase novel, his fingers as white as the almost-naked women on the covers. He wore one of those transparent tennis visors on his forehead – they were the rage in the township then, along with those tiny Adidas shorts that barely skimmed the bum. His visor was red, and its shadow cast a bright light on the pages of his novel.

Every time that I passed him, I saw the flies that settled on his mouth. I did not wonder that people were so afraid of me – I, too, was afraid of Lameck. It was terrible to me that he sought me out, that he offered me this solidarity; it was terrible that people should look at us and conclude that we were the same; terrible that when we passed him with my father on our way to school it was always to me, and only to me, that he sent his greetings. '*Hesi*, Memo,' he called, each time, his cracked face smiling.

I gave him no affirmation at all. His attempts to get me to enter some sort of melanin-free club failed. On those only-too-frequent occasions when I had to go to his stall to buy tomatoes, I looked down as he chatted endlessly about the novels he was perpetually peering at.

Lameck always contrived to give me things I had not asked for, masau when they were in season, or mazhanje. I ate them quickly, with no guilt. I did not want to say anything that might suggest kinship. I see now, of course, that he was just as much a misfit as I was. I do not imagine that his parents named him after the original Lameck – Lameck, the father of Noah. Sister Mary Gabriel told me that Noah was an albino; that God had chosen to save an albino above all the people he flooded in his wrath.

*And my son Methuselah took a wife for his son Lameck, and she
became pregnant by him and bore him a son. And his body was
white as snow and red as the blooming of a rose, and the hair
of his head and his long locks were white as wool, and his eyes
beautiful. And when he opened his eyes, he lighted up the whole
house like the sun, and the whole house was very bright.*

That day, when I went home to Lloyd, he said to me, 'It is your
choice, Mnemosyne. You can spend your life feeling sorry for
yourself, or you can simply choose not to. You can invite people's
pity or you can refuse to be an object.'

Lameck in Mufakose had no Lloyd or Sister Mary Gabriel to
tell him of the wondrous origins of his name, or to spend money
at the dermatologist's and buy creams and lotions with sun filters,
as Lloyd did for me after he bought me, ointments that healed
and mended my skin.

I wanted to believe that I did not look to others as Lameck
looked to me. He looked incomplete, as though he had been fashioned at *mahumbwe* play by a careless child, and then been fought
over before being abandoned to be stamped on as the children
hurried in to their suppers.

Like Lameck's, my skin often blistered, but it was never as bad
as his. My father made me wear a large grey school hat, and he
made me wear it everywhere. Consequently I did not have the
protuberant pustules that Lameck had all over his face.

On Mharapara Street, I had a torrid time of it, but at school,
where children from other streets in Mufakose joined the children of my street, the tormenting reached unbearable levels.

Nhau and his gang ran up to me to form a cordon beyond
which they hissed at me and shouted or laughed. I was at least

lucky in one respect – they never touched me. In grade two, when we had first moved to Mufakose, a boy had slapped me in the face. If my skin had been like the others', the slap would not have left a visible mark, but because of the absence of colour in my skin, his hand had left its outline on my face.

From this incident had come the children's fear, and the saying that *ukamurova anotsvuka ropa* – if you hit her, they said, her blood rises to the surface. So no one touched me.

Once inside, I could get my revenge on the children who hissed and called out to me when I walked outside. In here, I could humiliate them by showing them that a *murungudunhu* like me had better brains than them.

Had it not been for my condition, I would have been every teacher's dream. I sat quietly in class, in the front of the room, where my father insisted to my teachers that I sat. I was not one of those children who eagerly put their hands in the air and yelled, 'Mistress, mistress, mistress', but when called upon to answer a question, I always knew the answer. I was quiet and watchful, and my report every term spoke of a one hundred per cent pass rate in every subject.

I longed to be like all the others. I tried to get as dark as the other children. I longed to belong. I felt a sharp and burning envy of everyone I saw. I sought out obsessively the children with flaws. I would have given anything to be Nhau, who had a slash across his face. Lavinia walked with a limp. The grade four class had cast her as a cripple in their end-of-year play, and she had added a gritty sense of realism as she walked on the stage, exaggerating her limp as she moaned, '*Ini zvangu mushodogo, hee mushodogo.*' Whizi was cross-eyed; it was never clear if he was looking at you or not. Never, who was tall as a man but still played in the street with the children, and who talked out of the corner of his mouth, was given the nickname Drunken.

I would have taken Whizi's eyes, and Lavinia's limp, and added to it Nhau's scar and Drunken's speech, only to have some colour in my skin.

I prayed every second I could for God to darken my skin. After Reverend Bergen said, 'Ask anything of me, says the Lord', I redoubled my prayers. I made all sorts of bargains, made promises about being good, about coming top in class. I promised not to slap Mobhi, and I even vowed not to hate my mother. But my skin remained what it had always been.

Religion having failed me, I turned to science. When my father was not looking, I sat in the sun and wished for my skin to darken. It only made my skin red and sore and blistered. I noted obsessively the different shades of the skins on my family.

My father was dark brown.

My mother had a smooth, light caramel complexion that was almost the same colour as her feet. Joyi looked like her, but it seemed to me that, in me, my mother's skin had lightened to the point of disappearance. The lightness of skin that made my mother and my sister beautiful had been bleached to the point of distortion in me. I was just three, possibly four, shades away from beauty.

I tried my mother's Pond's Foundation Cream, and her face powder, the same caramel as her skin. Its brown colour lay invitingly in its blue compact plastic case, and I smeared and smeared it all over my face until I realised that I would need more than one compact to cover my hands and arms. I hid the evidence of my attempt, and washed the cream away from my face.

Over and over again, I ran my fingers over the faces of the women in my father's *Parade* magazine. Joyi liked *Parade* because of Max Eagle, the private detective with gravity-defying karate kicks, but more absorbing to me were Caroline Murinda and Sarah Mlilo, the two Miss Luxes who advertised Lux Beauty Soap. I stared for hours at Caroline Murinda's cream dress, and the yellow belt that matched her yellow hat. I was dazzled by Sarah Mlilo's neat Afro hair and by her slim fingers making a chord on her shining guitar. But most of all, I was drawn to the radiant beauty of their brown skin. 'She cares for her beautiful complexion with Lux Beauty Soap' said the captions below their smiling faces.

I believed that my skin could be as beautiful as theirs if only my mother bought Lux instead of Choice or Geisha soap. I even thought of stealing from my mother's purse so that I could buy the soap that would cure all my problems. Or perhaps it was not Lux, but Cleartone that I needed. If I could not be like the others I would be invisible. To befriend someone like me would defeat that desire to disappear, to melt and only observe, and so I ignored Lameck, because to acknowledge him was to see that in myself which I would rather not have been.

8

There is a Psalm Sister Mary Gabriel loved that also forms the basis for a supplication in the Book of Common Prayer. 'Let me know, oh Lord, my life's ending,' it goes, 'and the measure of my days. Let me know how frail and fleeting my life is. You have made my life a mere handbreadth. Each man's life is as a breath to you.'

She wanted us, she said, to know that our days in this life were numbered, that we were mere blinks in the life of the universe, and that our lives should have a purpose. 'A life without a purpose, girls,' she often said, 'is like a needle without a point.'

Sister Mary Gabriel was not blessed with either felicity of expression or originality of thought. 'And what,' she often asked, 'is God's telephone number?'

'Jeremiah thirty-three verse three,' we chanted in unison.

'That's right, girls,' she would say, her face beaming. '"Call to me and I will answer you."'

Poor, sweet Sister Mary Gabriel, with her nine types of angels, her cherubim and seraphim, her thrones and dominions. Her Christianity did not have the formal stamp of Rome's approval – it was based entirely on the non-approved gospels, with a dash of Milton thrown in for good measure. She told us stories from the Apocrypha, from the Gospel of Nicodemus and the Book of Judith, stories about the boy Jesus moulding pigeons and blowing life into them so that they flew high in the sky like the first birds on the fifth day.

Instead of doing what she was most temperamentally suited for – founding a religion in some backwater, like my mother's Reverend Reiner Bergen, or standing at street corners thundering the more stirring passages of Amos and Hosea – it was poor Sister Mary Gabriel's lot to be a sister at the Convent, with its deadening self-effacement livened only by teaching girls with reedy voices to strum-strum-strum on cheap guitars in accompaniment to songs of saccharine banality. D change to A, A change to G, G change to D. One-two-three, one-two-three. Bind us together Lord; bind us together with cords that cannot be bro-o-ken.

I have a Good News Bible here. It is the only book that Synodia will allow us to read. It is a simple one, this version, with none of the grace and majesty of the King James that Sister Mary Gabriel taught me to love.

I only mention this Psalm because I wondered often, when I was a child, how I would die, from which you can rightly conclude that I was a particularly morbid child. I was simultaneously fascinated and terrified by the idea of the guillotine, with that glinting steel that was sharp enough to slice off a royal head while the knitting needles clacked.

Safe in the knowledge that I was not a French royal, I imagined other deaths. Being poisoned by a tarantula, for example, and dying in a paroxysm of ecstasy; do you remember an Inn, Miranda, do you remember an Inn, and the tedding and the spreading of the straw for a bedding.

When I began to ride Copperplate across Umwinsidale with Liz Warrender, I was terrified that I would fall and break my neck. But the exhilaration of guiding my horse over the downs and of riding across the Nyanga hills soon came to conquer my fear of falling.

It was drowning that terrified me the most, because with water I associated the *njuzu* that people said lived in the Marimba River. I am not quite sure how to explain *njuzu* to you; there is no direct equivalent in your mythology. It is convenient to translate it as a mermaid or a water sprite, but it is more sinister than either. Mermaids sit sedately on rocks; they flick their tails and comb their hair. They sing and seduce. Water sprites cavort in, well, spritely fashion. *Njuzu* are violent, they are wild beyond taming. They rise up in the air and become one with the clouds. They become hurricanes and storms. They transform into snakes and crocodiles. *Njuzu* capture the unwary and pull them down, down beneath the waters. They are especially fond of children.

Under the water, they train you in the art of magic. And if any member of your family weeps for you, *njuzu* will kill you at once. But if no one weeps, if your family allows you to go unmourned, you emerge after years and years with gifts of healing and prophecy.

I had no distinct image of *njuzu* in my mind. It was all fear and speculation. It was only when I was sold and sent to Umwinsidale that I gave it form. *Njuzu* became, to my imagining, the frightful creature that I saw in one of Lloyd's books, Bellerephon's Chimera, the fearful beast of immortal make, snorting terrible flames of bright fire.

In my dreams, it pulled me to itself; it dragged me down into the water. Umwinsidale gave my fear its form, but it also cast it out. The fear of drowning stayed with me. Not even Lloyd's doomed attempts to teach me to swim in the chlorine-blue safety of the pool at Summer Madness helped me.

There is an old English superstition that holds that if you escape death by drowning, you will be hanged. You could say I escaped drowning twice. I try not to but it is hard not to imagine the coarse, woven noose around my neck, my feet scrabbling in the air. I imagine people talking of me as the albino woman who was hanged. I find that idea repugnant, almost as abhorrent as the thought of my feet dropping into that empty space.

'They will not hang a woman,' Vernah Sithole said to me.

'They hanged Nehanda,' I said. 'And Dorothy Strydom. Loveness told me about her.'

'Nehanda was in 1898,' was her rejoinder. 'And the Strydom woman was pardoned. The same could happen to you; anything can happen after the election.'

But there may be yet another reason to hope. Last week's *Financial Gazette* carried the headline 'Country Lacks Hangman'. It would appear that, in addition to all the other shortages – no doctors, no nurses, no teachers, no books, no democracy, no sense – we are enduring a chronic shortage of people willing to tie nooses, slip them around the necks of their fellow men, string them up and drop them to their deaths.

'The country's severe economic crisis is having an effect on the delivery of justice,' a Ministry of Justice official was quoted as saying. I laughed hard, great whooping laughs that made me choke. My eyes watered and the *Financial Gazette* became a film of pink in front of me.

There are currently fifty men and one woman 'eagerly anticipating', as the journalist put it, 'the hangman's noose'.

The same journalist wrote another story in the same paper about a crowd of women at the airport who were also 'eagerly anticipating' the President's return from Asia. The country anticipates the President's return as eagerly as we anticipate our death. From such unintended statements often comes the truth.

'The fifty men and one woman on death row,' the story continued, 'might wait for ever. The last hangman resigned his post ten years ago.'

There was a large paragraph about my case, with Lloyd's name misspelled. As the only woman on death row, I could not escape attention, but it was still strange to read about myself.

A few metres away, on the men's side of this complex, are men who have been waiting for more than ten years for the hangman, living each day without knowing whether the vacancy has been filled at last. Loveness told me that there are five men who have been waiting for fifteen years to die. They have woken up every day, those men, expecting each day to be their last.

And at the end of the day comes the horrible reprieve, and they have gone to bed again and woken thinking: maybe this is it. Have they seen the paper, has anyone told them that they are waiting day after day because there is no hangman? Have any of *their* guards told them why they wait?

It was Loveness who brought me the newspaper with the news about the hangman. In the last two months, she has been bringing me a variety of papers. It is just one of the many odd things that Loveness has been doing lately.

She let me keep these notebooks and pens that you brought me, even after Synodia protested. It was strange to me that Synodia did not put her foot down; all that she did was flick the fake hair of her hairstyle of the month and look at me in that way that suggests that, if I am not invisible to her, I should be.

Loveness has become considerate – chatty, even. In fact, she will not stop talking when she is around me. It is bad enough to have to spend all one's time here without a prison guard going on and on about her interminably dull existence, which seems to centre on her church and her daughter. If I did not know better, I would think she wanted something from me. Loveness is not nearly as odious as Synodia or as dismissive as Patience, but in the last month or so she is positively the soul of benevolence.

'This is for you; something special today,' she said as she gave me the paper.

It was all I could do not to snatch it from her. It was the first complete newspaper I had seen in the two years that I have been here. This is what I have missed most in here, the simple, unremarkable wonder of having the printed word within my line of vision, on stop signs, adverts, newspapers, billboards, packaging on products.

The paper you discard without reading it, the books, the books, the glorious books. The crackle of an old manuscript, the dead smell of a hundred-year-old letter. Until I came to Chikurubi, I had never gone more than three hours without reading. Whenever Loveness brings me the newspapers, I drink them in quick, thirsty gulps. When I first got here, I thought I would go mad. I hallucinated pages rising like mirages before me, the letters dancing away when I reached out to touch them. I felt restless and unrooted. My thoughts chased each other. I understood finally what a desert-island book was.

I kept my mind sane through a constant repetition of the things I remember. 'The House will once again, Mrs Dombey, be not only in name but in fact Dombey and Son. Hence! home, you idle creatures get you home: is this a holiday? It little profits that an idle king, by this still hearth, among these barren crags, match'd with an aged wife, I mete and dole unequal laws unto a savage race. I have spread my dreams under your feet; tread softly because you tread on my dreams. I was took up, took up, took up, to that extent that I reg'larly grow'd up took up.'

There were books here once, Jimmy said. There was a small library of circulating books. But since Synodia's religious conversion, the Bible is the only book that she will allow. Before that, the guards used to wade through the books that the Goodwill Fellowship sent, to weed out tales of homicide, suicide, crime, politics.

Monalisa once suggested that some of the more qualified prisoners could teach the less educated, as there was so little to do after lock-up.

'We can have a small library,' she suggested.

'Pwlibrary, pwlibrary,' said Synodia. 'Who said you are here to get an education? If you are so educated, why are you here? You come here with your English and you think you are special. Let me tell you something. Here I will give you all the education that you will ever need. Here you will feed on education *kusvika wazvimbirwa* and your stomach bursts from education. Pweducation, pweducation.'

Every time the Goodwill Fellowship donates books to the prison, covering all sorts of subjects, science and history, novels and poetry, the guards sell them. So when Loveness gave me the paper, after all these months, it was all I could do not to snatch it from her. I devoured every page of it. I read the perplexing story of a baby called Kingsize who changed sex overnight. 'When we put him on his bed to sleep that night, he was a boy,' his mother said. 'But when he woke the next morning, we found that he had turned into a girl.'

I read a long opinion piece on what was wrong with the new

constitution; I read every letter to the editor on why the country is now ready for the coming elections. I even read the sections that I would normally not have glanced at, like the property and motoring reports. I drank in the technical specifications of the latest Range Rover.

I read the special supplement about a new shopping complex near Warren Park that is operated by a Chinese company. 'This image shows the magnificent balancing rocks made out of hardened plastic that are exact replicas of the rocks cleared away in the construction of the building,' an admiring caption said. I studied the congratulatory faces of the Chinese manager, the smiling passivity of the workers in yellow hard hats and blue overalls, and the bonhomie of the fat-bellied minister who had cut the ribbon around a fake rock.

Loveness's act of generosity is both incomprehensible and alarming. The guards are not supposed to bring us whole newspapers. When we get them at all, the newspapers are always at least a month old – the opposite, in fact, of news. And they are, well, *incomplete* does not begin to describe it.

The first time that I saw a newspaper here, I thought there must have been some mistake. Parts of it had been cut out so efficiently that when I held up the whole thing, I could almost see through to the blonde hair extensions falling with wild abandon on Synodia's mammalian graces. Synodia took great pleasure in telling me that the guards cut out all the court news and any reports of crime, so that – her words – 'You lot will not get any ideas if you ever get out.'

The guards also cut out the politics sections because they do not want us to get agitated. I must concede that this is a fair point. The inaccuracy of your average local newspaper is enough to

[67]

raise anyone's blood pressure. They cut out the business news, presumably for the same reason. What's left are the sports and entertainment sections, the adverts and the classifieds, but even they are not guaranteed to remain, particularly if Synodia is on newspaper-cutting duty.

She applies the scissors with such zeal that we often end up with just the adverts and the classifieds and empty margins with gaping rectangles. The empty spaces hide the news we are not allowed to know, the collapse of the fragile agreement that has held the government together, the coming new constitution to be followed by more elections. And everyday news, such as how many pupils passed their O levels, and by how much the prices have gone up.

But if you read carefully, the classifieds are revealing in their own way. When I saw that the price of baked beans had gone from three million dollars to one dollar fifty, it meant one of two possibilities: the unlikely one, that our vertiginously collapsing dollar had found a way to shoot upwards; or the more likely, and correct, one, that the currency had been changed.

The guards sometimes leave in the occasional headline. 'President Returns from M', said a section with a huge rectangular space below it. I suspect that most of the cut-out space was devoted to the President's image. Returns from *Mwhere*, I wondered? Given the President's predilection for travel, it was probably somewhere *Mforeign*. Malaysia, Maldives, Mauritania, Malta, Madagascar, Mozambique, Malawi.

'It would be easier,' I once pointed out to Synodia, 'to just cut out the bits that we *can* read and hand them to us in a pile.'

For that bit of wit, Synodia confiscated my Bible for two weeks. She must imagine that it is the ultimate anguish to be without the Good Book. But to make assurance doubly sure, as it were, to make sure that my physical person was punished in addition to the spiritual deprivation she had devised for me, she assigned me to sanitary duty, a polite way of saying that I spent two weeks collecting foul-smelling and bloody pads with my bare hands before piling them into the large metal drum that serves as an incinerator.

Haven't there been studies that show that, when groups of women live in close confinement, their cycles become synchronised? This is how it feels here, like there are two to three hundred women who are on at the same time.

Once a week, in the evenings, the prisoners on sanitary duty collect the sanitary towels in one bin and lug them to the incinerator behind the Condemn. As we had no gloves, we improvised with old plastic bags, stuffing the repulsive things into the incinerator, where they crackled and burned and sent up a stench that covered our clothes and hair and which we could not wash out because there was no water.

When there is water, it is normal for the women to wash out the blood from the pads before disposing of them. 'If you don't,' Jimmy advised me when I first arrived, 'someone is sure to use your blood for something.' *Something* being, of course, the witchcraft rituals that everybody here accuses everybody else of. So you wash off the excess blood before throwing it in the bin. That week, there was no water to be had. No water to wash in, no water to flush the toilets. It was not as distressing as it could have been because it has happened far too many times to cause comment.

Jimmy prefers to be the last to get the paper because she likes to pore over the classifieds without worrying about the next person in the line. She laps up the mansions that cost billions and trillions of dollars, occasionally emitting a sibilant sigh of admiration when she finds one that seems particularly impressive. '*Inzwaka*,' she will say to whoever is near her. 'Mansion available in Ballantyne Park, ten bedrooms, six bathrooms, four en suite. Kidney-shaped glitter-stone pool. Floodlit tennis court. Massive entertainment area. Lock-up garage for six cars. Landscaped garden. Self-standing three-bedroomed cottage. Imported tiles and fixtures from Dubai. Right in the heart of the golden triangle. Must-view.'

She was almost beside herself when she found out that I once lived in a 'mansion'. '*Hesi mhani*, Memo,' she said, and spent the next hour asking about it. Jimmy uses the diminutive of my name.

Jimmy Blue Butter does not know that I lived in Mufakose once. No one here knows that part of my past. I have told her very little about myself, but things have nonetheless managed to reach her and the others. I trace it all to Evernice, who seems to know everything about everyone. Within days of any new prisoner's arrival, Evernice will have found out everything she can about her.

Having been convicted of killing a white man gives me an almost talismanic effect. Even after the killings on the farms, there seems almost something surreal about the violent death of a white man; it does not seem real in the way that everyday deaths of black people are real. It is so out of the ordinary as to be fantastical, like something out of history: Nehanda ordering the death of Pollard.

To Jimmy, it does not seem to matter that I have been convicted of killing a man. All that she sees as essential in me is that I lived in a huge mansion in one of the northern suburbs. I once told her, exaggerating slightly, that each of our bedrooms had built-in closets and en suite bathrooms. '*Hesi mhani*, Memo,' she sighed. 'Jealous down!'

It was nothing at all like this. It is always hard to remember the impression that things made on you when you were a child. It is easy to recast what you now know to how you first saw them, and to see them again with an adult's understanding. The first time I saw Summer Madness, I saw only a big house with pillars and columns and a veranda that seemed to go all around it.

What I see now is a house of heart-stopping gracefulness. It was one of the few private houses designed by James Cope-Christie, the neoclassical architect who put his graceful stamp on the city's first buildings. Its simple purity, its almost unbearable loveliness, shines against the monstrous promontories that surround it now. It is the type of house that people with new money, diamond money, money from steel deals in China and Saudi Arabia and oil deals in Angola, will destroy to replace with a mansion of ten bedrooms, a kidney-shaped glitter-stone pool, a lock-up garage for six cars, and imported tiles and fixtures from Dubai.

The house is mine now; at least, I know that Lloyd left it to me in his will. That fact spoke against me at the trial. I have watched enough legal dramas to know that a convicted person cannot profit from the fruits of his own crime. I must remember to ask Vernah Sithole, the next time that I see her, what will happen to the house, whether it will be confiscated by the state, or whether Alexandra, as Lloyd's next of kin, will inherit it now.

I try not to think about being released. Even if the thing I dare not think about happens, and I am set free, I cannot see myself ever living there again. I do not see myself ever going back to Umwinsidale. Jimmy calls it Umwinsdale, dropping the 'i' and consequently making a strange swallowing sound.

She knows the area well. For two terms when she was in grade four, she lived with her uncle, and went to St Joseph's

School in Chishawasha. She has never forgotten the long walk down Umwinsidale Drive, past the stables at Mahobohobo, crossing Enterprise Road and into Chishawasha, an inverted Umwinsidale with its thatched rural huts and sinewy, hard Mashona cows.

She keeps asking for more and more detail about the house. I have added more and more rooms, and a sauna and a Jacuzzi in addition to the swimming pool and tennis court that need no exaggeration. As we cleared out the Condemn, I heard her tell Verity that I was so rich that, when I wanted to get really hot and sweaty, I would go into a small room built just for that purpose, and that our house had rooms that existed only to lead into other rooms. 'Lots of halls, entryways and corridors. Jealous down,' she said. 'Memo really lived the life. *Kwete imi vana* Verity *munoite wonini.*'

Verity protested that she had never hoed a field in her life. Jimmy said, well, just those two feet alone walking in a field is enough to do some hoeing. 'You can get all the pedicures in the world, Verity,' she added, 'but you cannot do anything about your hoe-shaped feet.'

This is how things usually are with these, my unlikely best friends, Jimmy and Verity, the prostitute and the con artist. I moved away to get out of the sound of their argument.

9

The biggest surprise about prison is the laughter. There is laughter to go with sudden quarrels; there is malice and gossip along with acts of generosity. It is not unusual to find two women who were accusing each other of witchcraft the previous week clapping hands to each other as though nothing had ever happened between them.

It is not possible to sustain one emotion for too long. It is too taxing on the mind to always be angry, or always sorrowful. Pain in particular is too big a burden when you are in a confined space. I do not mean to sound like I am writing a self-help manual, but your mind truly is the only thing you can control when you are in prison. Your emotions are the only thing you can call your own.

Much of our time here goes to helping women with court cases, women on remand facing trial, women facing appeals on sentence, helping them to weave convoluted tales of innocence. It is at these trial preparation sessions that you find the most laughter.

Vernah Sithole has told me about the strategy sessions she has with her colleagues at the Advocates' Chambers. It would amuse and impress her, I am sure, to know about the strategy sessions we hold in here, where the prisoners gather in groups to discuss strategy and rehearse procedure. Unlike the lawyers, what we discuss is not the law, as such, but how to play the system, how to beat it.

Jimmy, who has seen more police cells and courts than anyone else, and Verity, who knows everything there is to know even when she doesn't, are the most active. Evernice also takes active part. Enough of her comrades have been rounded up in the last year to make her familiar with court proceedings.

Last week, as we took a break from working in the garden, we went over Beulah's case. She has been on remand for more than a year. The charge she faces is assault with grievous bodily harm. If she is convicted, she faces a long sentence, at least five years, for hitting another woman with a bottle and wounding her.

'You must point out that you have been on remind for a very long time now,' said Verity.

'Remand,' corrected Monalisa. 'It is remand, not remind.'

'And you must remember,' said Jimmy, 'that a magistrate is your worship, not your lord. Your lord is a judge.'

'No, no,' said Verity, 'what are you talking? She must say my worship and my lordship.'

'My worship *sei futi*. Do you think you are in church?'

'But anyway,' Evernice interrupted, 'you don't need all that, because you can just speak in Shona and the translator will find the right words for you.'

'Those translators are the dangerous ones, *manje*,' said Verity. 'Why do you think that Patience wants to be a translator? They are the people with the power. They are the very people who will really fix you for ever, like if you say something that is too difficult for them to translate, *hodo*, they will just say whatever comes to their heads, and the next thing you know, *ketshke*.'

She made the sound of a key in a lock. '*Ketshke*,' she said again.

'So I should speak in English, should I?' Beulah asked. 'I have four O levels plus a D in English. I can speak in English if that will help.'

'Yes, use English,' said Verity. 'The magistrates will be impressed because they do not expect someone who goes around thumping people in the street to speak in English.'

'Don't speak in English,' said Jimmy, 'because everyone will think *kuti uri wonini*, that you are just too high-class and they will want to fix you.'

They all turned to me. I had famously used English, and only English, at my trial. In my first week in prison, I had overheard Jimmy tell Evernice that even when I cried, I cried in English. 'And she even laughs in English,' she had added, with what sounded like admiration. '*Kwete imi vana* Evernice *munongoseke dzvandu.*'

'Just speak in Shona,' continued Jimmy, 'but speak simply, and just stick to explaining what actually happened. Explain right now. We are in court. Verity is the prosecutor, and I am the magistrate.'

'And I am the interpreter,' said Evernice.

Jimmy protested. 'Interpreter *wekwadini* when we are saying she should speak in Shona.'

'*Horaiti*, I will just sit here with these other people in court.'

Evernice moved to join the five baby dumpers on the grass who were giggling as they watched.

'I am the court reporter,' said one of the baby dumpers. She rose from the grass to join Jimmy and Verity.

'And I am the policewoman in Court Five, the one who always looks like she is smelling rotting onions,' said Manyara. She twisted her mouth to the right. The watching women gave great gulps of laughter.

'The court shall come to order,' said Jimmy. She made as though to gavel a table. 'Mr Prosecutor, please proceed.'

'I would like to ask the accused where she was on the day in question,' said Verity.

Beulah blinked and licked her lips.

'*Hona bwai bwai yacho*,' said Evernice. 'There is your D in English. You see why you need an interpreter.'

'Actually, it's translator,' said Verity.

Jimmy said, 'Okay, fine, translator, interpreter, it is all the same thing. Evernice, you can be the interpreter.'

Verity said, 'Translator.'

Jimmy said, 'Fine, fine, whatever. Please, Mr Prosecutor.'

'I said where were you on the day in question?' Verity asked.

'Where were you on the questioned day which is the day that we are questioning you about today?' Evernice translated.

Beulah blinked, licked her lips again, drew breath, and said, 'I was just coming from the shops, *ndazvitengera zvangu yekera yangu*, *ndazvitengera* drink *yangu*, it was the first time that I had seen Cherry Plum in ages, from the time I was a girl I have always liked it even though it makes your tongue purple, so I bought some and I was so happy, and I bought it with my own money, and I was drinking it and laughing with my friend Shupi who lives in Jerusalem when this woman called Rosewinter who lives in Canaan walked past us, and I know her because she tried to take my boyfriend, he used to live close by Shupi in Jerusalem, in fact that is how we met until his landlord kicked him out for not paying rent on time, but I can't really say that he was my proper boyfriend as such because he was married even though his wife lived at their village.

'So as she passed us she was talking and I heard her say to her friend, *ndiye uya anoroya*, and I said what did you say, and she said, *ehe*, I said you are a witch who eats people, what are you going to do about it, you witch?

'And I said, what, what do you mean I am a witch, and I said to myself, no, I cannot allow this, how can I allow this Rosewinter person, *mumwewo mukadzi zvake akabarwa seni*, to call me a witch while I just stand here drinking Cherry Plum like nothing is happening, and she said again, you are a witch, and then I took my bottle even though it still had some drink in it and I took it and I hit her with it and she screamed, *maiwe*, the witch is killing me, and that made me even angrier so I hit her again and the bottle broke on her head; you have never seen anything like it because the bottle broke and there was this blood now mixed with the Cherry Plum and I turned to Shupi for help but she and the other woman's friend were busy fighting, but when the police came, they both of them managed to run away even though Shupi left her new wig behind, it was a boy-cut style, which was a pity because *kanga kakamufita zvisingaiti ka*wig *kacho*, and this woman was now shouting, my head, my head, my head, *kani* my head, like I had killed her.

'And then they took us to the police camp and they arrested me even though I explained to the police that I was minding my own business drinking my Cherry Plum which I had just bought for myself with my own money when this woman spoke to her friend and said, *ndiye uya anoroya*, and I said what did you say . . .'

The women were now in fits of laughter. Abandoning her role as court reporter, the baby dumper was rolling on the grass, while her friends clapped their hands to each other in delight.

'Okay, okay,' said Jimmy. 'Just stop there. You need a simple story. Leave out the stuff about this *wonini*, this Cherry Plum; no one cares about Cherry Plum or what colour it makes your tongue. And this Canaan, Canaan business . . .'

'Did I say Canaan?' Beulah said. 'I actually meant Egypt, yah, he moved to Egypt before he went to Canaan.'

'Egypt, Canaan, Jerusalem, it would not matter if it was Gethsemane. Just cut all that out and get to the point. Just say what actually happened. She called you a witch and you became angry.'

'And you were angry because of your dead grandmother who was once called a witch,' said Evernice.

'*Ehunde*,' said Jimmy. 'That is a good one.'

'But both my grandmothers are alive,' Beulah said.

'Yes, but what about your grandmothers' grandmothers?' Evernice asked. 'Are they not your grandmothers too?'

'But they were never called witches,' Beulah said.

'And how do you know that?' said Evernice. 'Were you alive in the time of your grandmothers' grandmothers? Do you know everything that happened to them? Were you there? What are you, a witch?'

'Don't call me a witch,' Beulah said as she flared up.

In a low voice, making sure that Beulah did not hear me, I said to Verity that it was just as well that there was no bottle of Cherry Plum handy. Verity swallowed her laughter and gave me a punch on the arm.

'*Iza*, Beulah, *iza*,' said Jimmy. 'Evernice has a good point. Just say she called you a witch, it made you angry and sad because that is what they had called your grandmother who has now died, and you were overcome with anger.'

'Say you need a course in anger government,' said Verity.

'Anger government *kuita sei*,' said Jimmy. 'Just say you are sorry, and that you have remorse.'

'That's right, remorse,' said Verity. 'You are full of remorse and you ask to be sentenced to the time that you have saved.'

'Time served,' said Jimmy.

'Time saved,' said Verity.

'What do you mean, time saved?' said Monalisa. 'Jimmy is right. It is time served.'

'The point is that she will not go to jail because she has saved the time,' reasoned Verity.

Before anyone could answer, Beulah said, 'I am sorry, of course I am, and I will let the court know that I am sorry, and that I promise not to be that angry again, but I swear by my father who is buried in Zimuto even though he died in Seke Unit J, I swear that if I see her again and she calls me a witch or so much as looks at me like she is even *thinking* that I am a witch, *ndinopika nevakafa*, I swear by the dead that I am going to thump her, bottle or no bottle.'

As the siren sounded for lock-up, we took our laughter with us all the way to our cells.

~ ~ ~ ~ ~ ~ ~ ~ ~ ~

I spend twelve hours of every day in my own cell. There are women here who would go mad in such solitude. The guards frequently punish us by isolating us. Verity claims that the activist who was kidnapped from her home two years ago is actually here in Chikurubi, hidden away in solitary confinement in an underground room with a special guard that we have never seen.

The idea of being alone horrifies the others. They prefer to move in groups, to work in clusters, to always have a companion. It is different for me. Solitude is not the hardest thing about prison life for me. From the time that I was a child, I have been able to retreat into myself, and to find within myself the resources that have made it possible to bear my own company. Even when everyone came back from their various occupations, my mother from plaiting hair when she was well, my father from his work,

[79]

and Joyi and Mobhi from their play, I found it possible in that houseful of people to be entirely alone.

I spent so much of my time on my own that I learned early to follow the thread of my own thoughts, and to watch, and be still while others talked. I learned early to distinguish between those who spoke the truth and those who lied. My habit of watching people enraged my mother. She often lashed out at me, not because I had said something she did not like, but because I had said nothing at all.

I was not always alone at Chikurubi. When I first arrived, just after I was convicted but before I was sentenced, I shared a cell with Mavis Munongwa. Mavis has been in a kind of solitary confinement for most of her life here because there are no other women with sentences as long as hers.

She has been here since the last year of Rhodesia, longer than any other prisoner or guard. For thirty years or more, she has roamed the halls of the prison, moving between the Condemn and the canteen, between her cell and the prison farm.

She has no knowledge at all of Zimbabwe, no idea of what life has been like in the last thirty years, no concept of the immense contradictions that make up this country – national unity achieved through the massacres in the south, discrimination against the white people whose Olympic victories form an integral part of the nation's self-declared successes, the multiplicity of laws that guarantee women equality and a culture that ensures that they remain subservient.

When she talks, she talks of Salisbury, of Que Que, of Charter and Melsetter. Like the mink-and-manure set in which I once lived, the fact of independence does not translate into any reality for her. But the people that I lived amongst in Umwinsidale lived in a cocoon of privilege that was untouched by the political changes around them, while Mavis is more like that Japanese soldier who continued to fight the Second World War decades after Japan's surrender. She simply does not know that anything has changed, and when she is confused has the vacant emptiness of a marble god.

Every name that she gets wrong is more abuse from the guards. 'I have had enough of your boomshit,' says Patience. 'Acting like a deaf-moot. Do you think we still live in Rhodesia?'

On the first night in our shared cell, in long urgent whispers interrupted by fits of raspy weeping, she told me why she was here. In her life before this one, Mavis had been married in Gutu. Her husband fell sick and died suddenly. She and her brothers consulted a diviner to find out what had killed him. The diviner had told them that her sister-in-law, Mavis's brother's wife, and her friends in sorcery, had killed Mavis's husband. 'In the night, in the graveyard,' the diviner told Mavis, 'they feast on his flesh and drink his blood. They have made his penis into the whistle that they use to summon each other.'

Mavis bought rat poison and put it in the drinking water inside her sister-in-law's cooking hut. But it was not Mavis's sister-in-law, or even her sorcery friends, or her husband, who drank that water and died. Instead, it was their four children. It was Mavis's two nieces and two nephews, aged eleven, nine, seven and three, who drank the water and died in pain on the floor of their mother's hut.

In those nights that I shared with her, I would have given anything to be back at the police cell at Highlands. When her spirits were high, she filled the cell with manic laughter, chanting the alphabet name song over and over again. 'Anna, Boniface, Cecilia, Dickson, Edina, Fungai, Gibson, Henry, Ida, Jakobo, Keresenzia, Lameck, Manuere, Noeri, Otilia, Patson,

Que Que, Ruth, Stephen, Timothy, Urita, Vikita, Watson, Xhosa, Yachona, Zambia.'

And when her spirits were low, she groaned out the names of the children she had killed. 'James and Lydia, Cecelia, Boniface.'

If I managed to get any sleep at all, I would wake up to find her whispering to me, telling me of the children's distended stomachs, their bleeding mouths, their horrible deaths. 'They vomited out their own intestines,' she whispered. 'I saw everything that was inside them. They put the bodies in my hut and refused to bury them until I told them what I did to them. They locked me in with them. They would not let me out.'

After the third night of her weeping, I could no longer take it and I shook her to keep her quiet. It made no difference. Again and again she called out, 'You have eaten my husband. I have eaten your children. James and Lydia, Cecelia and Boniface. James and Lydia, Cecelia, Boniface,' she sobbed. She put her hands to her cotton-white hair and rocked herself as she wept with no tears.

So when they put me on my own, I was relieved to escape. Mavis rarely goes out. The guards don't like that she frightens the other prisoners. She sometimes acts as though she sees the dead children before her. She smiles at the empty air, holding out food and saying, 'Eat, eat.' When that happens, the guards put her back in her cell, from where she shouts for James and Lydia, Cecelia, Boniface.

Verity is convinced that all that time alone has made Mavis mad. Jimmy argues that it is no mere madness, but the spirits of the dead children that have come back as *ngozi* to haunt her. When they can find them, which is not often, the guards sometimes give her sedatives to go along with the casual, easily given diagnosis of madness. But no one has called a psychiatrist to make any kind of official diagnosis.

'Who is going to pay for a psychiatrist – is it you?' Loveness said, the first time I asked if Mavis had been seen by anyone. 'And even if we find that she is quite, you know, quite mental, where will she go? There are no women in the mental ward.'

Mavis may well be better off here than on the mental ward. If they can barely afford food for us, what means do they use, without drugs, to calm the prisoners? And what of the torment that the strongest there visit upon the weak? She is better off here, poor Mavis, where every wrong name is a rap on the knuckles, where Synodia imitates her to her face and the rest ignore her when they do not mock her.

Mavis did not hang because the judges found extenuating circumstances in her case. Vernah Sithole told me that Mavis Munongwa's was the case that set the legal precedent that a strong belief in witchcraft, like excessive alcohol or catching your wife in an adulterous coupling, could be considered extenuating circumstances in mitigating sentence, and could even go as far as amounting to provocation, which, more than mitigation, is an actual defence.

As you travel around the country, you will find that a lot of people believe in the power of witchcraft and dark magic. Jimmy is full of stories from her village in Chipinge about wives who put spells on their husbands so that when they go with other women, their genitals disappear. 'The men become as smooth as anything down there, Memo,' she told me. '*Kuite* smooth *kunge wonini, kunge chidhori cheplastic chekuChina chakagadzirwe nge*plastic, just like a plastic doll.'

I told Jimmy about the baby in Loveness's paper, Baby Kingsize, who had changed from boy to girl overnight. She clutched my arm and nodded. There were many such examples in Chipinge, she said, but they did not all make the papers. Perhaps this is a comparative advantage, sex-change operations without hormones and surgery, all eased through the wonder of African technology.

Jimmy did not understand what I was talking about. I explained about sex changes, but it took time to convince her that it was possible to take hormones and undergo surgery to change your sex. She only accepted it because of the authority that enveloped me, from having lived with white people. Monalisa, too, had some of this authority, but she had only worked with them. I had lived with them; I knew them inside out, thought Jimmy, so that meant if I said such things were possible then they must be possible, even though it seemed to her like a form of unnecessarily complicated witchcraft.

But it is not only Jimmy with her little education who believes in witchcraft. Even Verity Gutu, smooth, urbane, Zurich–Harare-hopping with a stop in Dubai, believes in the power of a *n'anga* from Malawi called SekuruMuchawa, who specialises in restoring stolen property. If anything goes missing, she believes, like when her car was stolen, SekuruMuchawa flicks a whisk, asks, *ndiani aba mota*, *ndiani aba mota*, and rattles some bones, and just like that he restores your lost property, or, at the very least, he tells you who stole it.

I do not believe in any of those things, at least not any more. I had those beliefs once, too, but I was a child then. I believed in the haunted house on Mharapara. I also believed in the God of Sister Gilberta and Sister Mary Gabriel, the God of incense and Mass and the Benediction and the Trinity.

It has been the work of many years, but I no longer believe in anything. That these beliefs can shape a human life is horrible to me. It frightens me how much something like this can change a life. One minute there are four children, James and Lydia, Cecelia and Boniface, and the next they are just gone.

I no longer believe, but sometimes I find myself envying those who do, just as I envy Synodia's certain assurance that there is hellfire waiting for all of us prisoners. How much easier must it be to navigate a Manichean world in which black and white are so starkly marked.

But for the most part, I am glad that my life has not been touched to this extent, that I left superstition behind with the dust of Mufakose. I am glad that my life has been untouched by this, as it is untouched by that other belief, that there is a heaven and a hell in which, in the words of one of Synodia's songs, we sinners shall gather and stand at the throne of the Lord, weeping for the kingdom we have lost, after the people of the Lord have gone away.

10

If I am to tell you the truth, Melinda, I had not expected that I would enjoy this. I am enjoying these words, crafting sentences, seeing paragraphs form. I am well into the first notebook already, but I already feel like I could write all day, and every day.

Vernah sent a message last week to say that my appeal has been set down for the end of July, which is when the judicial year begins. That means that I have five months to complete this. But it is all confusion at the moment because, before the opening of the courts, there is the election.

Vernah is convinced that things will really change this time and that the opposition will not only win, but will actually be allowed to take power. But that's what we thought in the last election, too, and in the one before that one. I am not pinning all my hopes on anything that might happen after the election. Even if there is an amnesty, Vernah has explained that it does not apply to death row prisoners.

I am writing this for you and for Vernah, for the appeal, as she told me to, but I am also writing it for myself. Around the time that Lloyd and I met Zenzo, I was in a Stephen King phase, gulping down stories about rabid dogs, pyrotechnic children, telekinetic aliens and demonic cars. My favourite then was a book about a writer who was forced to write a novel by the deranged fan who held him prisoner as her own modern-day

Scheherazade. But in the end, he wrote to keep himself alive.

That is the sense that these notebooks have given me. It is the best part of my day when I can go back to my cell and write. Scheherazade told stories to keep her head where it rightfully belonged. I am writing to keep myself alive. But I am also laying out the threads that have pulled my life together, to see just where this one connects with that one or crosses with the other, to see how they form the tapestry from which I will stand back to get a better view.

But, as it turns out, writing this is not as simple as I had imagined. I had thought that when I sat down to write, it would be to tell a linear story with a proper beginning, an ending and a middle.

I did not realise the extent to which my current reality and random memories would intrude into this narrative. I do not flatter myself that I am writing in the tradition of the prison diary. There is an imprisoned writer who wrote a whole diary on tissue paper. I can't recall whether it was Wole Soyinka, Ngugi wa Thiong'o or Albie Sachs, or all three.

This would have been in the sixties, or seventies, perhaps; before the invention of three-ply tissue paper. The tissue must have been particularly tough to withstand all that ink. I wonder how many rolls he used. How did he get it out? And who transcribed it afterwards, unrolling roll after roll?

Loveness allowed me to write in my cell without me asking. She continues to make these unexpected overtures to me. She talks constantly of her life outside these gates. I have generally met her overtures with silence, but that has not stopped her talking.

Her conversation is so dull that she makes the option of gazing at the grey concrete walls of my cell seem wildly attractive. When I stare at the wall, my mind is free to wander where it pleases.

With Loveness, my mind cannot stray. She can spend more than thirty minutes just talking about groceries; telling me that it is better to buy bread from this supermarket than from that one, because the bread from that supermarket does not last as long. Toothpaste is more expensive in the supermarket with expensive bread, but washing powder is more expensive in both so it is best to buy from yet a third.

More than anything, she talks about her daughter. She has talked enough about her that some of the details have seeped through and stuck. I know that her daughter is called Yeukai, and she is in primary school. I would know this even if she hadn't told me because I iron her school uniforms every week. I know that she has some sort of illness that Loveness is vague about.

'Yeukai is having problems at school, such problems.'

'There are no teachers at all.'

'They have been on strike for three weeks, and the only time they teach is when you pay for extra lessons.'

'You need six million a month these days, just to survive.'

'I am going to South Africa month-end to buy clothes, weaves and hair extensions to sell on. This time I will buy lots of blonde weaves. It is not just loose women who wear weaves now, even the very yellow ones. Even proper women, like Synodia, women who go to church and who have husbands, like to wear them now.'

I pricked up a little at this: so it is Loveness who sells Synodia the raw material for her extraordinary coiffures. She has hair-styles like none that I have ever seen. All her hairstyles are named after celebrities. 'This one is a Naomi Campbell,' Synodia said once, as Patience, Mathilda and Loveness crowded around her.

Evernice, ever ready to curry favour, crowed about how good she looked. '*Ende makafitwa*,' she cried.

All I can say is that the short-fringed blue-black bob may have been de rigueur as Naomi strode down the catwalks of Milan and Paris, but on top of a round-faced, short-necked woman straining in her prison uniform, it looked more like a very small mushroom atop an unusually bulbous stalk.

'And this one is a Rihanna,' she said a month later.

I can assure you that there is nothing more menacing than a prison guard glaring at you out of one eye while the other is hidden, Veronica Lake–style, by a mane of flaming red plastic hair with gold highlights. The ghostly presence from *The Grudge*, all sodden hair and wild white eyes, had nothing on Synodia in the Rihanna.

But back to Loveness. In the week after she gave me the newspapers, she also brought me a tub of camphor cream. 'I picked this out for you,' she said as she handed over the green-and-white tub. 'I thought better camphor than, what, than Vaseline.'

The feeling of dread that began at the pit of my stomach spread up and up my body until I was vomiting my lunch all over the floor of my cell. As Loveness exclaimed over me, I tried and failed to ignore the pungent smell that came from the open tub. Again I heaved, but there was nothing left to expel. She soon connected my reaction with her gift. From the time I was a child, I could not bear the smell of camphor, but I had never had a reaction as violent as throwing up. Wonder of wonders, she not only brought me a cup of water and a bucket for me to clean up the vomit, but she also came to my cell with a large bottle of unscented aqueous cream the next day.

Her apparent friendliness to me is all the more remarkable as she vacillates between indifference and callousness towards the others.

~~~~~~~~~

Have you ever heard of the Little Ease, Melinda? It was a cell designed in the Dark Ages so that the inhabitant could not sit nor stand nor lie in it. The last man to be imprisoned in the Little Ease lived a long time in it, and an even longer time out of it. Chikurubi is like that. You learn to live with it. Some days are obviously harder than others, but you learn to live with it.

As you read this, I do not want you to get an overly romanticised or sentimental understanding of how things are. I worry that I may be giving you a wrong impression of Chikurubi. Take my friendship, such as it is, with Jimmy and with Verity Gutu. It didn't emerge from heroic exploits, as it would have done were my life a film. I did not save either from bullying or beatings, nor did they save me. It all began about six months ago – or, at least, I can trace it to the day that Synodia targeted Sinfree. Until that day, every woman at the prison had kept her distance from me.

The chameleon incident meant that the others left me alone, but it also meant that, until the day of the incident between Sinfree and Synodia, no one talked to me if they could help it.

Like all bullies, Synodia goes for the weakest person in any situation. No one radiated weakness more than Sinfree, the new girl who arrived six months ago. She was a fragile, thin thing, flung into a world that expected obeisance to rules that she did not know. There is no induction or orientation of any kind. Synodia, Loveness and company prefer you to learn by what you might call the Montessori Method of Prison Instruction: you learn by doing, picking things up as you go along. The more mistakes you make, the more they hit you and the faster you learn.

So you soon learn that a prisoner is allowed to talk to the

guards only when she kneels before them. A prisoner may not look directly at a guard. A prisoner's hands, those dangerous implements, are to be in front of her at all times that she appears before a guard. No prisoner is called by her real name.

Sinfree knew none of this when she arrived. Three days after she got here, she sat crying at breakfast. The women around her kept their eyes focused on their plates.

'Arson!' Synodia called.

Sinfree wept on.

'*Iwe*, Arson!'

Someone must have nudged her to indicate that her name had been called.

She came and stood before Synodia.

'*Pfugama*,' Synodia said.

Sinfree spoke in Ndebele and said, 'I do not understand.' She turned to Loveness and to Patience, the other guards there. 'Please,' she repeated, this time in English. 'I do not understand what you say.'

'Who said you can speak English?' Synodia said. 'Who said you can speak English in here? Do you hear anyone else speaking in English? You think you are special, don't you, with your English? Pwinglish, pwinglish.'

By this time, my blood was boiling. I did the very thing that I have spent my life flinching from: I drew attention to myself. 'Can't you see that she does not understand you, that she does not speak Shona? Why shouldn't she speak in English to you?' I turned to the girl. 'She says you should kneel – that is what *pfugama* means. She is asking you to kneel.'

In the silence that followed, Synodia walked slowly and deliberately to where I sat. She gave me a long look. Then she walked back to where Sinfree still stood. She raised her hand and slapped the girl.

Her hand left visible welts on Sinfree's face.

Jimmy, Verity and I all made the same, almost involuntary movement. From our separate tables, we stood up as though propelled by the same force.

Synodia gave Sinfree another slap before pushing her to her knees. 'Did you not hear what the murderer there said?' she said to Sinfree, still speaking in Shona. '*Hanzi pfugama*. You want English, well – we will give you all the English you want. Here is some English. And some more English.'

Each 'English' was a slap that spun the girl's head. After Sinfree collapsed, Synodia turned to the three of us.

We continued standing.

'And so, you three are the new guards then, are you?' she said. 'Let me show you how we train new guards.'

She came up behind me, and held me by the neck of my dress. She pulled me out of my place. She pulled at my hair and gave me a slap, then another. She pushed me to my knees. 'This is how we train new guards. This is how we do it. Like this. Like this. Like this.'

Her spittle landed on me as she spoke. The smell of her rage enveloped me. Perhaps it was just the smell of cheap hairspray, but I found it more suffocating than the slaps. She then went for Jimmy, and for Verity.

The next morning, Synodia made Sinfree stand at breakfast and watch us eat. I was in enough trouble and I figured: what could be worse than the Condemn? I got up to her and gave her my bread. Synodia's voice shrieking my name was like a whip through the air but on I went. I pressed a slice of bread into her hands. In her shock, Sinfree stopped crying, though I don't know whether the shock was from my defiance of Synodia or from being touched, probably for the first time in her life, by an albino. Then Jimmy got up, too, and gave Sinfree her bread.

The others began to shout and whoop and bang their metal plates on the tables. Mavis Munongwa slapped her hands on the table and laughed. Benhilda Makoni said, 'Beat them, Mbuya Guard. *Nyatsorovai*.'

The siren sounded ten minutes later.

We were locked down for the rest of the day, with no meals.

Jimmy, Verity, Sinfree and I were sent to clean the Condemn, the filthiest part of the prison. In a prison film, Verity and Jimmy and I would form a little band of sisterhood and Synodia's cruelty would crumble under the strength of our sorority to a soaring John Williams score. It did not happen like that. Until she decided that she had had enough – of Synodia, of Chikurubi, and of the world at large – Sinfree was more scared of me than ever and Synodia more triumphant. But this is what I mean, that I am making a bad job of it, that I am still stuck here in the prison, when I should be telling you about how it all began; about my father and my mother, our house at 1468 on Mharapara, and how I left it one August day and never went back again.

11

I have said that my mother comes to me in a cloud of fear. Perhaps a better word for the feeling that my mother gave me is uncertainty. In that uncertainty lay fear. I never knew when she would laugh or cry or shout at us; I never knew when she would tell me to go outside and stop looking at her with 'those eyes'.

When she put on her records, it was a sign for us to get out of the house as fast as we could. When that happened, we went to the back of the house, where, his wireless set drowned out by the music of the records, we watched our father at work, making beds and tables and chairs and wardrobes, cupboards and shelves.

With the leftover bits of wood, he carved little dolls with vacant faces on which we painted eyes and smiles. He made delicately fashioned replicas of cars out of thin wire. Everything I knew about cars, their different shapes and their names, came from those models. He made a Rolls-Royce car – a Silver Ghost, he called it – and Citroëns that looked like crouching frogs, Beetles and Mini Coopers, Massey Ferguson and John Deere tractors.

Those little cars are everywhere now – you can buy them anywhere, along with little soapstone sculptures and baskets made entirely out of bottle tops; you can buy them wherever there is a street and a corner to stand at, but in those days, my father was one of the few who made them.

As we watched him work, the sound of my mother's music

floated out of the house and into the garden. My mother's taste ran to the maudlin. She liked the more mournful music of Jim Reeves and Dolly Parton and Porter Wagoner and Kenny Rogers, particularly the songs that were also stories. She listened to songs about Jeannie, a small child who was afraid of the dark and on whose grave there was always a light; about Little Rosa, a child crushed to her early death by a motor car; about Sue, who was actually a boy but had been given a girl's name to toughen him up; and about Tommy, who was called a coward because he had promised his father to walk away from trouble if he could.

Her favourite record was about a soldier who was arrested on a long march during the North African campaign and brought before the provost marshal. Even now, in Chikurubi, the words of that song come to me with as sharp a clarity as if I were listening to it from the back of our house. The soldier responded to the charges against him by stating that each card in the deck he carried stood for some theological principle or tenet, and concluded that his cards served him not only as a prayer book and almanac, but also as a Bible. Even as a child, I thought it must surely be easier for the soldier to carry a very small Bible than to remember what each card represented.

Three days ago in the garden, I heard Jimmy Blue Butter sing 'Coward of the County' as she worked, and I was again at home with Kenny Rogers on the radio as my mother sobbed and we waited for her mood to pass and the music to cease so that we could get back inside the house.

I do not want to give you the impression that my mother was like this all the time. But I believe that we were afraid to laugh because our laughter so very often had to be switched off if she decided she did not want to hear it.

She was most joyous on our birthdays; she went to great trouble to make vetkoeks for breakfast, which we ate instead of bread. She whisked the batter together before dropping it in little dollops in the hot oil. I liked to watch the balls become round and golden.

After we ate the vetkoeks, we all sang 'Happy Birthday', and she put on records and we danced. On those days, she retired Jeannie and Little Rosa and Tommy and the boy named Sue, and instead played 'Bhutsu Mutandarikwa' or other happy songs. But even these occasions were not without their fraught moments, as she sometimes got mixed up on the dates.

She thought one day that it was Joyi's birthday when it wasn't. She made us come inside to put on our Christmas dresses, which were also our birthday dresses. For everyday clothes, my mother went to Express Stores, but once a year, in December, we took the Zupco bus to Fourth Street and walked to First Street to gaze at the lights on the giant Christmas tree, and do window-shopping at Barbours, Greatermans and Miltons, before going to buy our annual Christmas-Birthday clothes at the Topics red-hanger sale.

Our dresses were always the same, but in different colours. The year that my mother mistook Joyi's birthday, mine was orange, which made me happy because it was a colour I loved above all others; Joyi's was blue and Mobhi's pink. She told us to change into these dresses. We could not start the party without our special clothes.

We were too afraid to tell her that it was no one's birthday, or that it was not Christmas. Instead we went along with her excitement. She went by herself to the shops and brought back a rectangular cake with pink frosting all over it. While she was getting the cake, Joyi and I changed into our clothes and helped Mobhi into hers.

When my mother came back with candy cakes, she turned on the radiogram to play 'Bhutsu Mutandarikwa'.

The song played three times and each time it played, she made us dance. Then the music stopped with a harsh scratch as she snatched the needle from the radiogram. We stopped dancing and stood in silence, looking at her.

'Stop looking at me with those eyes,' she said. 'What are you doing in here anyway, what kind of children are you, always indoors when you should be out playing with other children? And who said you can wear those clothes?'

I could see that Joyi was about to blurt that it was my mother herself who had called us in not moments ago and insisted that we change. I stopped her in time and tried to herd everyone out.

But we were too slow for my mother. She took up the record from the radiogram and threw it at me. It spun towards me, just glancing my ear, before smashing against the wall. The cake followed. We were too slow. Mobhi slipped in the cake, came down hard on her bottom and sat in the middle of the mess wailing that her dress was dirty. I walked back quickly to pick her up and ran out with her struggling in my arms.

When my father found us in the sun outside, he held the wall to steady himself before going back into the house.

The next time that my father went to the shops, he bought us a new 'Bhutsu Mutandarikwa'. At the next real party, which was Mobhi's party, my mother made us wear our Christmas-Birthday clothes. We danced to the song again and again just as we had done before, like nothing had happened.

I no longer recall where my father was on the day of the false birthday party. He rarely left the house. He did not go out to work like other fathers. He paid a boy to bring him what he needed in a scotch-cart. As he expected his customers to come to him, he did not sell much, but still managed enough that we did not have to eat Lacto or *matemba* every day.

When he left the house, he usually took us with him. He took us to the Agricultural Show every year, where we headed straight to the horses. My father was mad about racing. Away from the show, racing was part of our lives – even my mother was silenced by Peter Lovemore's voice. The radio was a part of my father's every moment.

Our father worked from the back of our house, where wood was stacked. He kept his things under a dark-green tarpaulin to protect them from the dust and the sun and the rain. Before we moved to Mufakose, he had worked in a factory. Then he had ridden his bicycle to work in the Western industries before he stopped working there and began to work from home.

My mother was angry when our neighbour said the factory that made furniture for Mashonaland Furnishers was looking for workers and he refused to go and stand in line for a job.

The other children routinely mocked us because our father walked us to school every day. Only on the first day, and some-times not even then, did parents walk the grade ones, the very youngest children, to school. While other children moved to school together in little bunches of blue-and-maroon or green uniforms, we walked with our father.

He carried Mobhi on his shoulders, her fat little legs wriggling as she laughed through the smoke and called out the names of any people that she recognised. Joyi and I tried to melt into the road as we passed staring children.

After he left us at school, my father walked back home with Mobhi and spent the rest of the day behind the house doing his carpentry work while she played around him. My mother, prone to headaches and other complaints, usually kept to her room.

When we did not go to school, he often took us to the shops in a group to buy us centacools or maputi. Joyi and I moved around and about them. Nhau, who had appointed himself my tormentor, would come after us, rolling a bicycle rim. With my father beside me, Nhau could only content himself with dancing out his torment and making faces. My father was my bulwark, my protection against my mother, and my protector against the torments of Nhau.

Now that I think about those days, I wonder what happened to Nhau. He was my main torturer, and if he became the man he promised to be as a child, he may well be next door, at the men's section of Chikurubi, perhaps one of the infamous car thieves for which Mufakose has become notorious. On the streets of Mufakose are Harare's thieves shaped, forged and burnished. Or perhaps he is a deacon in one of those ever-sprouting churches, a pillar of his community and a father of four. Or perhaps nothing that extreme but rather something in between, a perfectly ordinary man.

I have already said that my father was unlike any of the other fathers of the children that we knew because he did not go to work. He was also unlike other fathers because he did not drink. Lameck's father always staggered home from the Rufaro Marketing beer garden near the shops. On the nights that it was too hot to sit inside, I sat on the veranda and watched him stagger home, held up between Lameck and his brother Nathan, singing, '*Vakaita musangano mapositori ekwaMarange, pamusana pekuda kuziva akatipenda nependi nhema, yaive mugaba, mugaba reurombo.*' On payday, he lost most of his money at the beer hall, either spent or stolen, until the manager at his factory agreed to give his wages directly to Lameck's mother. Sometimes he was so gone that they borrowed a wheelbarrow from my father so that they could wheel him home. He would fall out and Lameck would try to coax him back in.

Rispah's mother chased Rispah's father up and down our road when she found that he had spent all his pay on horses at the Mashonaland Turf Club. Nhau's father had a woman come to their house and threaten to remove all her clothes in public if he did not admit that he was the father of her child.

My father was not like this; he was not a drunk, or a gambler or a womaniser of any kind. His love for the horses was a passive activity; it did not see him gamble his money away at the Mashonaland Turf Club. In our family it was our mother, and not our father, who chastised us. At school, the children were afraid of their fathers. They spoke of the instruments that their parents used to beat them.

Lameck's father was a policeman and used his truncheon.

Patience's father liked to use the sjambok.

Nhau's father made him and his brothers prepare their instruments of punishment: they picked a thin branch from a peach tree and stripped it of leaves, the better to leave a stinging, burning pain on exposed skin.

When she needed to thrash us, our mother used an old woven leather belt that once belonged to my father. She hit us with the buckle of it. Oftentimes, when the punishment was not premeditated, she took up whatever instrument came within her reach.

I know that this will seem like the most shocking abuse to you, but to us it was our everyday reality. We were no different from other families. We even found a certain heroism in the amount of punishment we could take. We admired Nhau for his ability to withstand the most severe lashing without the slightest whimper, and gathered round to marvel at his welts. It was not uncommon to hear children boasting about the scars they had picked up or about the pain they had endured, exaggerating it for effect.

We all pretended that we had not heard each other crying out, '*Ndagura, ndagura*', crying out in penitence to stop the lashing.

I do not mean to suggest that all levels of violence were accepted. Clarissa is here because she beat a pupil to death. She has lost an eye because the father of the child she killed attacked her outside court. It was not uncommon to find another parent, an adult, come to the rescue of a beaten child, clapping hands in respect to the enraged parent, pleading for an end to the punishment as a child had had enough.

Anything, I felt, could be borne with a sherbet or centacool in my hand and my father beside me – the same father who handed me over to Lloyd at the Post Office on Inez Terrace and walked away without a single backward look.

12

My mother spent most of her time indoors because she suffered from a headache that seemed to have no cure. On the days she was well, she plaited women's hair from our house. These were the days when only women with money had perms. The women in the township, with little money to spare, distinguished each other from neighbours by plaiting their hair in ever-more-elaborate fashions. They regarded hair as so much virgin territory to be conquered and twisted or stretched with a hot comb until it was compliant.

She was skilled in this conquest, my mother; she knew how to slather hair with Vaseline before stretching it without burning the scalp. She could plait hair into any fashion, weaving a tapestry of zigzags and other patterns across the head.

My skin made it impossible for my mother to stretch or plait my hair. My scalp was too sensitive, and grew hot in the sun.

My mother did Joyi and Mobhi's hair every Friday. She sat on a three-legged stool outside our house, and they sat on the floor before her. She scratched their scalps to remove dandruff. She then divided the hair into as many sections as the pattern demanded. Then she wound the thread around each section, connecting it to the next. She specialised in plaiting with a needle to create long, thin rows that were evenly spaced and left the scalp gleamingly exposed.

Joyi's face wore a pinched expression after each hair session; she stuck out her head as though it was now too heavy to rest on her shoulders, or like it carried an invisible load. It was worse for Mobhi, who cried herself to sleep on hair-plaiting nights. It was only after two days that their faces relaxed as the style settled in.

On special occasions, my mother stretched their hair with a stretching comb. It was only when I watched Liz Warrender groom the Compton-Jones's horses that I discovered that these stretching combs were actually intended to be curry combs for groom horses.

The moments where I was alone with my mother are so few that each one stands out. The only time I left the house with any regularity, apart from going to school and church, was in connection with what my mother called my illness. It was mostly my father who came with me to the hospital. When I was particularly ill and the flies settled on my breaking skin, and I saw the world only through a well of water, my father wrapped me in a blanket and I walked in the suffocating heat to the bus stop to take a bus to Gomo Hospital.

When they were not in school, my father insisted that Joyi and Mobhi come too. They resented this because they would much rather have been playing on Mharapara than sitting in the waiting room full of sickness and a hushed silence that did not encourage giggles and fidgeting. The only consolation for Joyi was that it gave her material to use in her games with the other children. 'Let's play Memo Goes to Hospital,' I heard her shout once, immediately followed by the loud squabbling voices of the other children insisting that they wanted to be the doctor or the nurse – no one wanted to be me.

At the hospital, the doctors lifted my eyelids, and the nurses put gentian violet on my blisters, leaving me with purple-stained skin. They told my father to keep me out of the sun. Mostly we saw the nurses, scowling beings in white who treated my illness as though it were an inconvenience. The white caps on their heads seemed to float, halo-like, in the air above them. They looked soft and clean and made me feel dirty and unwashed.

But their hands when they touched me were rough and strong as they put stinging ointment on my broken skin. They seemed to think that they could scold away my illness if they shouted loud and long enough. 'Why do you sit in the sun when you know you are so sick?'

I grew to fear the hospital, and when my father said we should go, I threw myself on the floor and grabbed a leg of the sofa and fought him when he tried to pick me up so that he often just gave up, and nature, when it chose, did the healing.

My mother rarely came to the hospital with us. Instead, she talked of consulting diviners. She was convinced that a potion or spell could be found that would make my problems disappear. Mine was not an illness, but a curse sent to her by her ancestors to punish her. This was the cause of some of the most frequent disagreements between my mother and father.

Oftentimes, my father just let my mother talk, her words a river washing over him without regard. She talked in declarative terms of the people from the east who were the only people in the country with forces powerful enough to counter the might of lightning and direct it to smite their enemies, and about the powerful *runyoka* spells cast by husbands to ensure that their wives were bound.

I recall an evening, perhaps a year before I was sold, when my father stopped my mother as she talked and said, 'You know as well as I do why these things are happening. Why do you want to cause yourself more pain?'

She had been angry, and suddenly she changed mood and said, 'Why don't you just leave me? I know that is what you want to do. Just leave. That will end everything.'

My father said, 'I will leave you only with my death.'

They were both very quiet after that, and my mother did not talk about diviners again that night.

Even though my father refused to sanction trips to healers, I recall at least three occasions when my mother and I left the house without my father's knowledge. Each time, we visited a traditional healer, and each time, my mother swore me to silence. In dusty little rooms in the townships of Harare, my mother waited for ancestral spirits to visit little round men and women who acted as mediums. But I was still unwell, my skin still broke and bruised, and I remained unhealed.

The last time we visited such a place, we found the house empty, except for a small boy of my age who was all mango; there seemed to be more mango on his person than had made it into his stomach. He interested me because he saw out of one eye. The other was big and bulging and covered with his eyelid.

I watched him out of the corner of my eye. I longed to know what had happened to that eye but feared to ask because to ask would be to expect a response and I had learned that children did not always like to talk to me.

So I looked with longing at the mango; I watched him pull it out of his mouth with a plop. He said, without prompting, 'You have come to consult the Great-Ancestor.'

'We have come to consult the Great-Ancestor,' my mother confirmed.

'Mhamha,' the child yelled, 'there are people to see the Great-Ancestor.'

The shout was directed to the veranda of the neighbouring house, where a woman looked up from a group who had gathered to plait her neighbour's hair. She had her own hair in a perm; the waves in it were damp with excess hair oil. Her breasts jutted from underneath a tee-shirt that bore the words NOT MY TYPE in shining gold letters.

'You have come to see the Great-Ancestor,' she said. 'Wait here and we will call you in when he is approaching.'

'Well,' my mother said to me, 'she is not what I expected but at least she is from Manicaland.'

The child reappeared. Cleaned of mango, he wore a small skirt of feathers and beads around his waist and carried a pair of traditional rattles in his hands. The Great-Ancestor had arrived, he said, and he would see us now. Inside the house, the medium had hidden her hair under a crown of feathers. She wore a cloth of red and black that fell from her shoulders like a cloak.

She let out a belch that must have fallen into my mother's ears with added reassurance. Here at last was something familiar, a spirit that presaged its entry, as such spirits did, with grunts and groans. The spirits never announced themselves in anything that might resemble a normal human voice.

The woman took snuff, began to shake, and then she was still. In the midst of clapping and the child's rattle-shaking, a deep voice issued from her mouth and said, 'You are here because you are greatly troubled.' The voice stopped; the woman seemed to go into a deep sleep. We waited and waited but nothing further happened. Only when my mother prodded her did the woman come back to herself.

After her return to earth, she and my mother had a slanging match, because my mother said she could not be expected to pay for nothing, while the woman said what was she to do, she could not control the comings and goings of the Great-Ancestor.

While our mothers shouted at each other, the little boy looked at me with a frank and unhesitating stare. His navel, I saw, stuck out in a little lump like on one of MaiPrincess's twins.

'Here,' he said, and offered me a mango. He put down his hat of feathers, and sat next to me in his feathered skirt. I took the mango, and we sat on the *stoep* of their veranda, a small space between us, eating our mangos side by side as we listened to the voices of our mothers.

I will not pay, said mine. Oh, but you will pay, said his, otherwise you will find yourself facing worse things than your daughter's skin. They went on like this for some time, but in the end my mother slammed down the money, stormed out and yanked my arm so that I dropped my mango.

I said, 'Mhamha, my mango.'

'How many times have I told you not to eat at people's houses?' she said, and gave me a slap. I held back my tears and did not look back at the boy. Instead, I held on to the remaining taste of mango until we reached home.

That night, when my father found out where we had been, he hit my mother full in the face with his fist. This was the only time that I recall my father ever hitting my mother. Until that day, he had been, like my sisters and me, the recipient of my mother's blows.

It was always she who attacked him, hitting him in his face while he attempted to restrain her and cover his face at the same time. He would hold his arms to his face as she went for his chest and his arms. He held her fists sometimes, and it was then that he called her name, and pleaded with her and said, 'Moira, Moira, *ndapota'*, and it was terrible to hear them, more terrible than it was to hear the sounds they made in their room when my mother cried out in the night.

That night I heard a sound from the back of our house. It was my father, crying deep gasping sobs, like he was out of breath after running a hard race, a race that he had won but had somehow still managed to lose.

13

If there is one thing that I can say I like about prison, it is that there are no baths. I have always hated water. I could not bear even to wash my face in it. I get through that morning ritual only by holding my breath and washing very quickly. It is an irrational fear, but I cannot bear to be near any body of water. This is why the hardest thing I did that night was not to dress Lloyd's naked body, or remove the belt from his neck, but to drag his body to the swimming pool at Summer Madness.

I still dream of drowning. Perhaps it is because I almost did when the Baptist held my head under the waters of the Mukuvisi, and again when one of the girls at the Convent pushed me into the swimming pool.

That was on the fourth day of my first week in school. As I stood and shivered by the side of the pool, one of the girls came laughing at me and pushed me in. I have never known such terror. When our games mistress, Miss Flack, came in to get me, I struck out at her. Lloyd tried to teach me to swim at home, but I spent most of our lessons shivering with terror, and eventually he gave it up.

And then there was the day the Baptist almost drowned me. My mother was restless in her church attendance. She had been to different churches over the years, dragging us with her, almost as though she had to try them all out before she finally settled on one.

For a short period, we joined the Salvation Army. I loved it there because of the marching and the uniforms and the whistles. After that, my mother became one of the white-robed Apostolics, and sat with other white-garmented people under the shade of msasa trees. Here the women sat separately from the men, and always there were more women because most of the men had at least two wives.

Feeling my skin burning, I watched the sun glint off the shaven heads of men with long beards who said angry prayers that made their spittle fly out over their held-out staffs and land on my face. The group she joined worshipped near the Mukuvisi River. It did not matter whether it was wet or dry – we sat outside and worshipped in our long white garments that never seemed to get dirty, no matter how rough our surroundings.

Three Sundays after we joined this church, our whole family was baptised in the Mukuvisi, which on that day was no ordinary river in Salisbury but stood in for the River Jordan. The baptism was a wet and violent process. The whole person was submerged not once, not twice, but three times.

My mother was baptised first, then my father, then Joyi. When it came to my turn, the Baptist asked whether I accepted Jesus and rejected Satan. All I could think of was that vast, terrible river, and the water that was muddy and brown. There was something in that murderous water, a *njuzu*; I just knew it, something that stole children. It would come for me, it was coming for me; I could feel it pulling me down, down.

'Do you accept Jesus? Do you reject Satan?' the Baptist said.

There was only one way that I could think of to save myself from the terror of all that water. In deadly fear, I clung to the Baptist. 'No, no!' I shouted. 'I do not accept Jesus.'

My mouth filled with water and I could say no more. The choice was a simple one for me. Rejecting Satan meant putting my face in that river. Accepting Jesus meant the flow of that water over me.

'Accept Jesus!' the Baptist was now shouting. 'Reject Satan!'

I screamed and swallowed water as I fought against him. I was now full of terror and all my strength was directed at making him stop.

He ducked me once more and when I came up, it was to scream louder than I had ever screamed before. The man ducked me again and I swallowed huge mouthfuls of the Jordan.

When he lifted my head out, I spluttered and screamed, 'No, no, I do not accept Jesus!'

'Legion!' shouted the Baptist. 'Satan, I command you. Release this child. I command you, Legion, in the name of Jesus, release this child.'

When he ducked me the third time, he held my head under the water. I struggled, then let go. I went limp and thought: it is coming, the thing is coming for me. It was then that I felt strong hands, familiar hands grabbing hold of me.

It was my father. He held me to him as I trembled. He and the Baptist then got into a shouting match. My father said he had frightened me, but the man said I had a strong spirit, an evil spirit that was in me.

'Did you not hear her?' he said, turning to the small band of congregants. 'Did you hear her refusing to reject Satan? Look at what she is. This child is an instrument of Satan.'

I clung to my father all the way home. We did not go back to that church again. For days afterwards, I dreamt of being pulled down, down into the river to be received by a creature with long arms that gripped me and would never let me go.

My mother then discovered MaiChaza's church, where the primary means of salvation was through elaborate rites of public confession, the confessions becoming more and more detailed and the sins confessed more outrageous: one woman confessed to performing as a witch from the age of three, while a man claimed to have killed his father with an axe at the age of seven. Three women confessed that they had eaten their children.

Then my mother met Sister Lucia and Brother Patrick. They belonged to a happy-clappy-tambourine church, the Church of the Felicitous Tidings of the New Gospel.

In the fields of the Apostolics, the songs were lugubrious and soporific. But in the community hall at Highfield, which served as the Church of the Felicitous Tidings for one and a half hours on Sundays, before giving way to the next church whose turn it was, the songs were catchy, happy, uplifting and infectious.

I began to look forward to going to church. I loved the music. I longed to be like Sister Lucia, beating along in time with her jangling tambourine, her red and white ribbons flying from it. My eyes closed in rapture as I sang about a wonderful treasure God gave without measure; we are travelling together, my Bible and I. One day, I vowed, I would have my own tambourine.

The God of the Church of the Felicitous Tidings seemed like someone who actually cared. For the first time in as long as I could remember, I prayed for something other than dark skin; I prayed for a tambourine of my own. I imagined that I would adorn it in my favourite colours, in purple and orange ribbons. I fantasised about playing it with the expert flicks that Sister Lucia gave.

When the frenzy took them, the women in the church dropped their tambourines, and raised their voices to speak in a babble that they called 'tongues', a large wall of nonsense that seemed to rise from the congregation and make its way to heaven. After only two weeks at this church, my mother, too, started to speak in tongues. Her tongues had to manifest in a special way. She took to fainting and falling about on the floor.

For all the falling she and the other women did, and it was only ever the women, she never exposed her underwear, and even though she shook violently, the Holy Spirit very chastely confined his visits above the waist, and never once caught her in spiritual disarray.

Her tonguespeak and falling fits established my mother as a stalwart of the Church of the Felicitous Tidings of the New Gospel. It was at this church that the momentous event in my mother's life happened. It was here that she received the prophecy that led directly to my sale.

14

The world outside comes to us through the snatches of conversations that we overhear from the guards, and through the news from visitors. The big news at the moment is the coming election. Loveness told me that all the guards have been attending meetings at which they have been instructed how to vote. But to hear them, you would not know that an election is coming. The guards are much more exercised about hairstyles and clothes, and the everyday things that happen to them, than they are about the election.

I overheard Patience and Mathilda talk about a funeral that Patience had attended at the weekend. 'They tussled at the graveside, can you imagine. They fought until he fell in and smashed his head on the coffin, and just like that he was deceased. I have never seen such boomshit. We were all in mayhem.'

I sometimes wish it were Patience, and not Loveness, who had taken such a shine to me. Her stories are so outlandish that I think the newspapers must use her as their regular source. 'There was mayhem at a grave in Warren Hills when mourners fought at the graveside.' 'There was pandemonium in Warren Hills when mourners fought one another and one cracked his head on the coffin.'

From what I have described of the prison, it is probably hard for you to believe that things were much worse here once. There was a cholera epidemic the year before I arrived. Ten women died. It could have been more but the women are not packed as tightly as the prisoners in the men's section. Still, we are so much on top of each other here that I sometimes forget that there are just over a thousand women in prisons in all of the country. There are some open prisons, and some in Shurugwi. The men are just over twenty thousand, with almost two-thirds of them crammed into Chikurubi.

Every time there is a death from their section, we hear the voices of the men rising in the night to sing away the dead. Loveness says in the cholera days they did nothing but sing, in the day, in the night, all through the months until finally the cholera died out.

I wonder if the first prisons in the country were called penitentiaries, as they were called in England, which gave us prisons along with the rest of our penal system. This is one of those things that Lloyd would have known. The Victorians founded Rhodesia, bringing with them their rigid view of religion, in which there was no difference between a crime and sin; either one meant damnation. They would have seen jails as places of penitence, where sinners and criminals, being so close together, would make their peace with their maker.

In America you call them correctional facilities, as though the buildings are factories and the inmates within so many faulty bottle caps needing to be mended. 'Jere', 'tirongo', 'college' are the slang terms for prison. Nothing suggesting rehabilitation, just being shut away, exile.

Synodia would have been at home in the world of the penitentiary. She has found a new form of tyranny. She now belongs to a church of the type that my mother attended just before she sold me. It is a Pentecostal church called, of all things, the Church of God, headed by a man who calls himself Evangelist Ishmael.

You probably know more about him than I do, but from what the papers say, he draws huge crowds to his services, where he performs cures. The lame walk. The blind are healed. The overweight experience instant weight loss. The short gain centimetres. I read in the paper last week that he has paid for doctors to perform eye surgery on people with cataracts. Considering that he claims to have the power to heal without medical intervention, I would have thought that it was cheaper to place healing hands than do the surgery, but what do I know.

It is not enough that Synodia's own salvation is secure: she wants to save us all, too. But first, she wants us to know the full extent of our own damnation. She insists that we attend a morning service on every day that she is on duty. Being saved is enough to give her absolute authority not only to interpret the Bible, but also to tell us how we are all to be judged. Who will protest that the prison is state territory, that she should keep her private views to herself?

The separation between Church and State is as foreign to Synodia as her own natural hair. She makes us stand and sing every morning before breakfast. Then she gives a little sermon, and all the while flies are hovering over our bread and the tea grows cold. The sweat shines off her face as she makes authoritative pronouncements about the fate that awaits each of us. She taps the side of her head with an open palm and her fingers splayed upwards as she talks – I suspect that it is not the passion that moves her, but her scalp that itches under her weave. 'You are whores and murderers; you are thieves and criminals. You have forfeited the Mercy of the Lord, and you will never know the grace of God.'

We have learned the expected responses.

'That's right,' we respond.

'That's right!' screams Evernice, louder than anyone.

'Are you listening to me? Are you with me? You will burn in hell, all of you.'

'Amen,' we agree.

'Only through the blood of Jesus will you know salvation.'

'Hallelujah.'

'You must open your hearts to the Lord. You must fill your blood with his power, so that even the mosquitoes that bite feel that power. They will suck the power in your blood.'

'Power in the blood!' echoes Evernice.

'*Kamasatalaha, kamasatalaha, kamasatalaha.*' This is Benhilda Makoni's contribution. She has begun to speak in what she calls tongues. She froths at the mouth and shakes her body.

We then launch into one of Synodia's favourite songs: 'Every day with Jesus / is sweeter than the day before. / Every day with Jesus / I love him more and more.' Synodia interrupts each of her sermons with a song. It surprises me that we manage to sing at all, let alone rouse any enthusiasm. And yet you find ululations and dances and thumping on makeshift drums.

All through yesterday, 'Every Day with Jesus' followed my movements wherever I went. If it was not Benhilda singing it in the ablution block, it was the baby dumpers singing it in the garden or Jimmy and Verity humming it as they swept out the cell.

~ ~ ~ ~ ~ ~ ~ ~ ~ ~

The song has also struck a chord of memory: I believe that was one of the songs that we sang when Reverend Bergen came to preach at the tambourine church that my mother made us go to after my father found out about the healer.

My mother's Christianity did not preclude atavistic beliefs in the ancestors whose job it was to guard and protect her against misfortune, against barrenness, illness, financial woes and misery. It is a curious thing, this straddling of the modern and the ancient world. One foot is in the Christian camp of the certainty of prayers answered, tambourines and organs, Latin chants and wafers that are actually human flesh. The other is in the traditional-religion camp, propelled by fears of witchcraft and *tokoloshes* and *divisi*. In this world, ancestors are a powerful force, for we have them on both sides, as did our fathers and mothers before us, and theirs before them, creating an ancestral web that cocoons us in its care and protection.

My mother believed in the spirits and the mediums through which they spoke. She believed in healers and diviners. And simultaneously, she believed in Reverend Bergen. All of this could exist in her mind at the same time. His deeds had preceded him. In Mozambique he had raised a man from the dead. When she heard that he was coming, my mother could barely contain herself.

That Sunday we got up early to prepare. My mother had laid out our Sunday clothes, our Christmas dresses, and our long white socks and shiny shoes. After we had dressed and eaten, we walked all the way to Kambuzuma, but still we were not the earliest.

There was a large crowd of people, nothing like you see now with Prophet Makandiwa and people like that. This was the Pentecostal movement at its nascent stage. Still it was a large enough congregation that it spilled out of the marquee that had been set up for the occasion. My mother fought our way into the marquee.

My father said, 'MaiGivhi, there are too many people. Why don't we sit outside?'

My mother said, 'But think of Memory.'

This was the first time that she had taken note of me, and as we fought our way inside, and a man stepped on my feet, I held off the pain as I thought that she was doing this for me.

We fought our way to seats that had a direct view of the pulpit. When I saw the Reverend, I was seized with a feeling that was part attraction and part repulsion. I thought, at first: but he is albino, he is just like Lameck and me.

I looked closer and saw that he was just a white man, with pale eyes, and blond hair that lay flat across his head. Reverend Bergen spoke through a translator. It made the services longer than usual. Babies started to cry. I was pleased that Mobhi was not with us; she had been left at MaiPrincess's house. Reverend Bergen talked of God's love, and God's mercy, and the promises of God's kingdom. He held out his hands over us and blessed us.

'Every day with Jesus,' we sang, 'is sweeter than the day before. Every day with Jesus I love him more and more.'

Then he looked out at the congregation and picked out people. 'I can see into your heart,' Reverend Bergen said to a man in a green jacket. 'What you desire will bring you no lasting joy.'

The man nodded and sat down. Reverend Bergen fixed his colourless eyes on my mother. 'Stand up,' he said.

My mother looked around; we looked around, unsure to whom he talked.

'I am talking to the woman in the blue hat with the white flower,' Reverend Bergen said, and looked at my mother in her blue hat. She had bought it just the previous week from Amato Stores. 'I am talking to the woman in the blue hat,' Reverend Bergen said again.

My mother stood up, in the way that the man in the green jacket had stood up.

'I see your suffering,' he said. 'God sees your suffering. He has all the answers. If you trust in him, he will deliver you. He says to you, in one month, I will end your greatest trouble. Believe in me and I will deliver you.'

He moved on to others, giving each his fatidic pronouncements.

In the line afterwards, my mother could not keep her eyes off Reverend Bergen. He sat at a long table filled with Bibles and copies of a book that he had written called *The Spirit Descends*. It was more expensive than the Bibles. He signed a book for my mother, and also a Bible, as if he had also written it.

When we went home, she took down the Bible and stroked the page with his autograph. The night before they handed me to Lloyd, I sneaked into the sitting room and took down the Bible from where my mother kept it on the radiogram. I ripped out the page with Reverend Bergen's sprawling autograph on it and put it in my underpants, and only removed it when I lay down to sleep in my new bedroom in Summer Madness, Lloyd's house in Umwinsidale.

I don't know whether my mother ever left that church. She was still there when Mobhi died, and the church people came to our house. And she was there still when, in fulfilment of God's promise that he would relieve my mother of her suffering, they sold me to Lloyd. The vague words spoken by Reverend Bergen gave my mother pride. Her suffering had been given official sanction and confirmation; it had been acknowledged not just by God, but also by God speaking through the undoubted authority of a white man.

Reverend Bergen himself had come – all the way from Germany, he had come; from all that way he had seen how much

I suffer, she said. In her telling of the story, the good Reverend had come for no other purpose than to see and tell to the world the nature of my mother's suffering.

When Lloyd approached my parents a short few months after this, when another white man presented himself to her, she had no hesitation in believing him the messenger sent to deliver her from me.

15

They happened a lifetime ago, these things that I am telling you about. It is hard for the truth to emerge shining clearly from a twenty-year fog of distant memory. There is a lot to sift through. I am not sure if there was one event that prompted my parents to act as they did, whether my parents sold me to Lloyd because of the church service that Reverend Bergen had led, or whether it was because of the visit to the traditional healer. Or perhaps it was because of both.

It was certainly after that service at Reverend Bergen's church that my sister Mobhi died. It was during term time that we saw him because it was the Sunday of the week in which Nhau had attacked me because I had beaten him again in a mental arithmetic test.

Mobhi died the afternoon that I saw Nhau steal the peaches from MaiNever's house. It must have been during the August school holiday because we had spent the whole day playing outside, and it was a day when we would normally have been in school. During the week that Mobhi died, my mother suffered frequent attacks from her headaches, and spent most of her time lying down on her bed. For that reason, we mainly played outside.

I sat in the shade with my father, watching him make a little wire aeroplane, and when it was finished, moving it up and down on the same spot. Mobhi slept on a blanket near where my father worked, and when she got up, she wandered off to play with Promise from next door. Joyi was, as always, playing in the street.

Not even the death of Sheila, the little girl from up the street who had been crushed by a car the Christmas before, stopped the children from playing outside. The street was the only place there was, and that August was no different. I could hear Joyi's voice joined to those of the other children playing endless rounds of *dunhu*, *rakaraka* and *chisveru*. When I asked my father if I could play with the others, he said it was too hot, and I should sit in the shade at the side of the house and help him with his cars.

Around two in the afternoon, Joyi came back home, complaining that she was hungry. My father said, 'Don't disturb your mother – she is sleeping.'

When Joyi said again that she was hungry, my father said, 'Fine, we will get something from the shops.' She cheered up at once.

My father called out to Mobhi to come, but she cried that she wanted to stay next door. I knew why she wanted to stay: MaiPrincess's daughter Promise had a new doll with curly yellow hair and blue, long-lashed eyes that opened and closed while it said 'Mama'. That holiday, Mobhi had spent as much time as she could with Promise, watching her play with her doll, never allowed to touch it, only clapping, cheering and giving little jumps when the doll said 'Mama' and Promise hugged it to herself.

While my father was trying to persuade Mobhi, I managed to sneak into the house without waking my mother. I fetched my hat from our room. When my father saw me put my hat on, he said, 'Memo, you stay here with Mobhi, and make sure she does not disturb your mother. I will bring you back some food.'

My father said to me that Mobhi could stay next door, as long as she did not go back into the house to disturb our mother. I stood near the fence and watched Mobhi and Promise play. They made the doll open and close her eyes again and again. I was angry and resentful. I wanted to go to the shops, and had a good mind to follow my father and Joyi. After a few minutes, tired of watching a game I did not have a part in, I wandered away from the fence and went to sit on our veranda, where I could watch the people passing in the street.

It was then that I saw Nhau. He was walking strangely, like he had something in his pants and shorts. Then I saw what it was: he had hidden peaches in his clothes. I realised that he could only be coming from MaiNever's house. She had a mulberry bush and a peach tree; Lameck sold the peaches for her. Nhau could only have got them from there.

As I watched him walk away from the house, three peaches fell out without his noticing. There was no one to see him disappear up the street. The peaches lay there, unnoticed, inviting. No one would see me if I took them.

I left the veranda and went over to pick them up. I rubbed one on my dress. Just as I was about to bite into it, MaiNever came and saw me with the three peaches in my hands. 'You are the thief who has been taking our peaches!' she shouted.

I protested that it was not I, that all I had done was to see them fall and pick them up. 'Fall from where?' she asked. 'Don't tell lies, how can peaches fall from the tree behind my house, how can they just fall onto the street?'

'They are not your peaches,' I said.

'As if I would not know my own peaches,' she said.

I knew that I was in fifty thousand kinds of trouble, but I could not bring myself to name Nhau. He was the most popular

of the children, the most playful, the most daring, and the acknowledged leader of the Mharapara Street children.

Perhaps, even now, the other children were congratulating him
as they ate the fruit of his exploits. I could not name him. If I did, the
other children would never talk to me again. So I did not say what
had happened. I could only protest that I had stolen no peaches,
that I had only seen the peaches fall, and that I was no thief.

As with anything in the township, our contretemps attracted
attention. Soon, there was a small gathering of onlookers, with
each person giving their opinion about how guilty I looked and
was. I could hear the whispers, '*Aba mapichisi, aba mapichisi.*' In
the middle of all of this, my father came back.

MaiNever dragged me to my father and said, 'Your daughter
is a thief.'

My father only asked me, 'Where is Mobhi?'

I looked down. I could not answer.

My father then ran into the house. MaiNever still held my
arm, and yelled about her peaches as she followed my father to
MaiPrincess's house.

'Where is Mobhi?' he asked.

'She said she was hungry and went back to your house,'
MaiPrincess said.

MaiNever still held me by one hand and in the other she held
the incriminating peaches. I saw Nhau in the crowd of people,
smirking among the children. I could almost feel the peaches in
his stomach. I imagined him sharing them with the other children, while letting me take the blame. My eyes welled up with
angry tears.

I could hear my father calling out for Mobhi. My rage against
Nhau gave me strength. I managed to break free from MaiNever's

grip, and ran to hide in the outside bathroom behind the house. She ran behind me, still shouting. I opened the door and was about to shut myself in when I stopped. MaiNever also stopped behind me.

In the silence that followed, she let out a piercing scream.

My father ran out of the house.

From a very long distance, I heard MaiWhizi shout, '*Chii chiiko, zvadiniko veduwe?*' Other neighbours followed to where I stood in stiff silence as MaiNever continued to scream.

My father moved me out of the way and there was Mobhi, or at least, there were Mobhi's legs, because all I could see of her were the legs sticking out of the large zinc bucket that was used to store the water for flushing if there was none in the tank.

I looked for a long time at her feet.

They were brown with dirt even though she was in the water. Then there was noise and confusion behind me, as my father took her out of the water and tried to breathe life into her while he called her name.

MaiNever and MaiWhizi had their arms around each other as they wailed in counterpoint. My mother came out of the house. When she saw Mobhi, she hit my father on his back with her fists. My father struggled to get her to stop.

He pushed too hard. She screamed, fell against the wall near the door and cut her head. Joyi began to cry from the sight of the blood.

My mother got up. She fought against my father's restraining arms. She slipped in the water and hit her head against the door-jamb. Her head bleeding, she ran weeping to the house next door. She picked up the front of her dress and covered her face, and everyone could see that she wore her black petticoat with the hole where the iron had singed it.

MaiPrincess came and then all the other neighbours came. The women joined my mother in keening and the lament spread from house to house in the street until everyone in Mharapara and as far as kwaMhishi knew of Mobhi's death.

In all of the confusion, I remember one thought: this meant that people would soon forget about the peaches. I was right. No one mentioned the peaches again, not even MaiNever. My father took us to MaiWhizi's house. She took me in her arms, and hugged me to her. I could smell the sweat of her armpits and from her skin the cloying and overpowering smell of camphor lotion.

~ ~ ~ ~ ~ ~ ~ ~ ~

Mobhi's wake lasted four days and three nights. During that time, our neighbours and the people from the Church of the Felicitous Tidings of the New Gospel filled up our house, cooked outside and sang. My mother and MaiSheila sat and wept together, rocking back and forth as they held each other. Joyi and I did not sleep at home.

We remained at MaiWhizi's until the day we buried Mobhi. On the day of the funeral, I went with my parents and the others on a bus to the cemetery in Highfield. Only a year before, we had walked these same streets, in our Christmas clothes, going to get our picture taken by Bester Kanyama, Mobhi in her pink lace dress seeing everything from my father's shoulders.

My mother should not have been at the graveside. There is a tradition according to which the person most touched by a death is not to see the burial. My mother was supposed to come only to see the grave after the burial, and not to witness the burying itself.

My mother refused to stay in the house, so my father gave in to her. I kept my eyes focused, not on the little coffin that was covered in dirt, but on MaiWhizi, who was dancing at the grave in time to the beating of the drums. When Mobhi's coffin was lowered into the ground, my mother tried to jump after it. My father hid my face against himself, but I could still see my mother struggling to jump in before she went suddenly limp. Even when the men from the funeral place threw gravel over Mobhi, she simply stared, and continued in the same position until the entire grave had been filled up.

It was only when Mobhi died that I realised that we had no relatives. I overheard MaiWhizi ask MaiPrincess, 'And just where are all their relatives? What is this new fashion of being buried only by neighbours and church people? There are no aunts here, no uncles, no grandparents?'

'It is as though they had just sprang from the earth,' said MaiPrincess.

'They have never received any visitors, not once as long as they have lived here,' said MaiWhizi. 'I have never seen a single aunt or uncle, sister or brother.'

'Not even an in-law, and you know how you can never get rid of those.'

'And they go nowhere in planting season.'

'Maybe they just have nowhere to go.'

They were right. Our neighbours had endless uncles and aunts, cousins and grandparents forever coming to stay. In six months alone, for instance, all of MaiWhizi's relatives would have visited.

In the holidays, instead of going to a rural home like the other children, we stayed at home, like the Manyasarandi and Bhurandaya families from Malawi or Mozambique, who everyone said were born *rukesheni*, belonging to the townships and with no proper home, and who had to be buried in the cemetery in town.

No relatives ever came to us from the village, or from any-where else. We seemed complete in ourselves, with no one ever coming, no aunts, uncles or nephews. At the time, I did not notice it, but I have wondered since then why we were so unconnected to anyone else but ourselves.

It made sense to me that we were from Malawi, which I knew was another country that was far away. In the invincible confidence of my new knowledge, I marched up to the two women and said, 'They are in Malawi; everyone is in Malawi.'

My father came up to me and I turned to him eagerly and said, 'Baba, tell them. Tell them about Malawi. They are asking where our relatives are, but they are in Malawi, aren't they, Baba, aren't they? They are in Malawi.'

My father said only, 'Memo, go inside.'

As I walked away, MaiWhizi laughed, a high, nervous sort of laugh, and said, 'Ah, children. When they overhear something, they don't always understand it.'

My mother did not leave the house after Mobhi died. She lay on her bed in her room and came out only when my father helped her to the bathroom. A few days later, I began to have strange dreams. I began to dream of the creature that hugged me to itself and almost choked me with the smell of camphor cream.

Now that I have written that sentence, it strikes me as strange that I should have begun to dream about a creature that I had never seen, because it was only at Lloyd's house, and not before, that I first saw the Chimera, but so it seems to me now.

It was then that my dreams started. In them the creature trailed water; it had dirty feet and surrounding it was the cloying smell of camphor. In another dream, the creature came and picked me up; its dirt had spread from its feet to its body, and I was covered in it. I opened my mouth to scream and my mother appeared to fight for me. She looked terrible in her nightgown; her hair stood up in spikes as though it had been stretched. For a moment I thought that she was the Chimera. Then she fought the creature and took me from it. 'You are dirty, Memo,' she said. 'Come, you need a bath.'

She picked me up, but the creature struggled with my mother and took me back from her and in my father's voice, it said, 'Not again. Not this again. She is clean, she is clean, Moira, let's go to sleep.' Then I thought that the Chimera would swallow me but all that happened is that I fell into a deep sleep interrupted by sounds of weeping, long harsh sobs that made it seem as though the whole night, the whole house, and the whole world beyond it was also weeping.

16

In the days after Mobhi died, I sometimes woke up in the night to hear my mother struggle. My father sank into himself. He spent most of the time cooking for us, feeding us and watching us play with each other. He sometimes stopped work and would sit for minutes staring into the middle distance. We had to call out to him more than once to make him hear us. He became much more affectionate in physical ways than he had been before. He had always been an easy man to touch, but now he seemed always to be lifting us up or holding us to himself.

He ate very little. I was a reasonably good cook by then; all girls who are raised in the townships and villages can cook something by age seven. Of course, it helps that most of the food I cooked was boiled, nothing too complicated. I decided to boil him an egg, and to make him some fried bread. I fried the bread, and put it together with the peeled boiled eggs on a plate. I made him tea, with powdered milk. The tea had floating lumps. I carefully walked to where he was. He was staring out of the window. 'Baba,' I said. 'Look, I made you some food.'

He looked at me as though he did not remember who he was. Then he looked down at the food that I had made. He put his arms around me and wept hard as he held me. When he let me go, he said, 'It is just what I needed.' But when I came back later to collect the dishes, I found that he had not touched the food at all, but had fallen asleep. I thought I would give my mother the food, but she too was asleep, the rope still around her hands.

The morning after one of my dreams, I had gone into my mother's bedroom with a plate of bread and jam. The room was in darkness. My mother lay in her nightdress on top of the bed. Her hands were tied behind her.

My father sat with his head in his hands, on the floor, in a dark shadow cast by the bed. 'This is so that she does not harm herself,' he said when I entered the room.

It was still the holidays when Mobhi died, so Joyi and I did not have the distraction of school. In our room, there was no Mobhi to sleep between Joyi and me, no Mobhi to wet the bed.

About two weeks after Mobhi died, my father said he was going to town. He left us in the house of MaiNever. We were not to disturb my mother, he said. This was easily done: MaiNever had a television, and we sat dazzled before it, watching cartoons. MaiNever gave us rice and chicken, which we ate while trying to keep our eyes on the TV.

Then she put before us a bowl of peaches, and seeing them, I looked up into her face. She had tears in her eyes. Joyi took the peaches, but I said *ndaguta*, and fixed my eyes on Voltron forming arms and legs. I did not eat those peaches. I have not eaten a peach since.

~ ~ ~ ~ ~ ~ ~ ~ ~

After we got back to school the term after Mobhi's death, I got into a fight with Nhau during break.

Nhau had told Joyi that, if witches didn't eat her flesh first, Mobhi would soon turn into worms. Joyi cried. When she told me what Nhau had said, I went after him with no further thought than that I would make him pay. I was still angered that he had taken the peaches for which I had received the blame, and so I lunged for him. Around us the children started to shout, *fight, fight, fight*. Nhau hit me a hard blow to my chest that left me winded.

I rushed at him as though to push him, but he stepped aside. I fell down hard. When I got up, I ran straight at him and knocked him down. He was afraid to hit me, afraid of seeing the blood under my skin. I felt a savage satisfaction as I hit and hit, and stopped only when Mistress Nyathi lifted my hands from his bruised face.

Mistress Nyathi asked what had happened, and I would not say, and neither would Nhau. She punished me by making me sit outside for the rest of the day. I refused to go to school the next day, and my father said he was going to ask me to stay at home that day anyway, because he wanted to take me to town with him. I was to dress up in my Christmas dress, he said, my favourite dress: white, with a purple sash.

This was simply too wonderful to be real. The idea of going to town with my father soon eclipsed the pain of seeing Nhau again. My mother insisted on coming with us. She was better, she said; she wanted to do some window-shopping. This was the first time that my mother had been out of the house. She looked very thin; she wore a blue costume with a pink blouse that had a bow tie at the neck. We walked Joyi to school, then took the Zupco to town. My father sat in the middle, while I looked out of the window.

I have vivid memories of that wonderful morning. It was as though my father could refuse me nothing. We walked up and down First Street, looking at the windows. I had two ice creams. I had candyfloss that my father bought from a Coloured man on First Street. I was still hungry when my father said, 'Now we need something to eat.' I kept stealing glances at my mother, but she was too taken with everything around her. She looked happy, and she laughed with my father. We went inside Barbours department store, something we had never done before. It seemed like some sort of treasure chest of glittering bottles and sweet-smelling women. A white woman in strange-looking glasses who stood behind the chocolate counter gave me a dollar. I looked like an angel, she said, just like an angel.

On the third floor, we stopped at the toyshop. I asked my father to buy me a doll – a real doll, like Princess's but much nicer. He looked at his watch and said he was hungry and why didn't we eat something now. We went to the tearoom behind the toyshop. I felt as if every eye was on us because the place was filled with lots of white people.

We sat in a booth, my parents and I all on one side. As we ate our chips and chicken, Lloyd came to our table. He called my father Benson, and talked to him with a familiarity that suggested they had met before. My father introduced my mother to Lloyd. She nodded and said nothing.

I was struck by the wonder of a white person talking to my parents so familiarly. I had never talked to a white person before: I had only heard Reverend Bergen speak to us, but never talked to him. It filled me with wonder that my father could be talking with this man; at eye level they were the same height. I was so lost in the wonder of it that I did not immediately realise that the man had stopped talking and was looking expectantly at me. 'What is your name?' he said.

My mother nudged me. 'Why don't you answer?' she said. 'Why do you act as though you do not understand such a simple sentence? Is this what you come number one for?'

[134]

I did not reply. I felt that the white man was my amulet against a sudden smack, and indeed, my mother did not touch me at all despite her irritation. My father spoke for me and said, 'She is called Memory.'

Then Lloyd said, 'Speak, Mnemosyne.'

That is the thing about memory. Sometimes you come to understand the things you cannot possibly have known; they make sense and you rewrite the memory to make it coherent. I did not understand then what he said, and looked at the ground. He and my parents talked; I only understood fragments of their conversation but they seemed to be talking about my illness and me and what grade I was in at school. I continued to eat my chips as they talked. Then the waiter brought the bill, the man paid for our food and we got up to leave.

'I will pick her up at twelve tomorrow,' the man said. 'I am glad that your wife approves, because I could not have done it otherwise.'

He took something from his pocket. It was a large wad of green bills, twenty-dollar bills; they were the highest-denomination notes in those halcyon days, before our million- and billion-dollar bills. He handed the money to my father, but it was my mother who reached out to take it. She took the money without counting it and stuffed it into her bra.

We went back home. That night, my father said to me that I was to pack my clothes, and say goodbye to Joyi because I was leaving Mufakose the next day. 'You are going to live with that man we saw today,' my father said. 'He is a doctor and you will live with him. You are going to go to his house, and you will live there with him and his wife, and it will be better for you, and you will go to a good school and you will stay there just for a little while, for just a short time until you are better.'

He said all this very fast, almost as though he wanted to believe it himself. Even believing, as I did, that anything could happen at all, that anything was possible, it seemed the most fantastical of things that a white man that I had never heard of, and whom I had only seen once for a very short time, could take me in for no reason other than to heal me, send me to school, and then return me to Mufakose.

It was when my mother made vetkoeks the following morning and let me eat all of them that I realised, as I vomited all over my new dress and still my mother said nothing, that my father had been serious. I was leaving my home and my remaining sister. I was leaving my mother and my father and everything that I knew.

PART TWO

SUMMER MADNESS

I

_____

The dreams that startled me awake in my first years with Lloyd have come back to me in Chikurubi. And when I am not dreaming of the creature that comes to me at night and speaks in my mother's voice, I find myself walking through the rooms and corridors of Highlands police station, past broken furniture and windows coated with what seems like centuries of grime, past peeling walls, the laughing faces of the officers, past the ceiling leaking blood.

I see chairs with cracked leather through which the discoloured stuffing shows. I smell the fetid smell of too many unwashed bodies in the airless space. Above all, I hear the mocking laughter of Officer Dimples and Officer Rollers in the interview room. I hear their echoing questions.

'Where in this country do such things happen?'

'Where do people sell their children to complete strangers?'

'If such a thing really happened as you say it did, such an outrageous thing, why were your parents not tried?'

'Why did no one report it?'

'Why didn't you report it?'

'Why were they not arrested?'

'Why was there no prosecution, no trial, no public shaming?'

Perhaps Vernah Sithole, surrounded by law reports and books that set out precise punishments to be meted out for the kind of crime that my parents committed, is reading these notebooks and asking herself the same questions. Perhaps, reading this, she will regret that she agreed to represent a fantasist. And even you, probably conditioned to believe in the worst that can come out of darkest Africa, are asking yourself whether this really happened.

Those questions from the police officers at Highlands, the questions that you and Vernah are probably asking yourselves now, are questions that I have asked myself countless times over the years.

It all seems so utterly improbable.

And yet it happened.

I used to think sometimes that all those books about abandoned Victorian waifs that I feverishly devoured as a child had somehow confused me; that I had mistaken my life for that of Elizabeth-Jane Henchard, sold along with her mother, or Oliver Twist, sold to be a mourner at children's funerals. But I did not imagine the wad of notes that passed between Lloyd and my parents in the tearoom at Barbours. I did not imagine my mother stuffing those same notes into her blouse. I did not imagine my father then handing me over to Lloyd at the Post Office without so much as a backward glance.

Most objectively of all, incontrovertibly factual: I have not imagined my own reality. I spent the first nine years of my life with my parents and my sisters, Joy and Moreblessings, and with the memory of our dead brother, Gift, at 1468 Mharapara Street in Mufakose. I then spent the next nine years with Lloyd, and Poppy and Namatai, at Summer Madness in Umwinsidale. I have not imagined Poppy, with her paper-thin skin and Ella Fitzgerald records. Or Lloyd. Or Liz Warrender and Sandy Knight-Bruce. I have not imagined Zenzo.

For as long as I lived with Lloyd, we did not talk about the circumstances that had brought us together. Whenever I felt the subject looming between us, I did everything I could to deflect it. Lloyd did the same. On the rare occasions that he spoke of how I came to be living with him, he spoke only of 'taking me in', of 'giving me a home'. He did not speak of buying me, of purchasing me as you might an appliance or piece of clothing.

'I took you in, Mnemosyne,' he said to me once, 'because giving you a home was the right thing to do. It was the only thing to do. You will understand it all when the time is right.'

I thought that if I said it out loud, that if I said, even to myself, that my mother and father had sold me to a stranger, it would make it more real than it already was.

You see, I thought at first that I was going to be returned home. It was all my mother's idea, I thought, because she had taken the money. She would see this as the truth of Reverend Bergen's prophecy. My father would make her see sense, I thought, and he would come for me. They would go home, and they would see my empty place on the bed in the *speya*, they would see my clothes in the wardrobe and say, 'We miss Memo.'

Or perhaps Lloyd would return me himself.

When I thought of this particular possibility, my mind seemed to freeze. I could not see how this could ever happen. I tried to imagine it, Lloyd getting into the battered Land Rover that had brought me to Umwinsidale, driving down Enterprise Road into town, past Rugare and Kambuzuma and into Mufakose, crawling up the street while Nhau and Promise and Mharapara's children ran in the dust that he left in his wake.

MaiWhizi would watch, open-mouthed, from her veranda. '*Zvariri bhais'kopu*,' she would say, and rush to tell the news to neighbours as far as Zongororo Street. I simply could not see it.

On the day that I left home, Lloyd met my parents and me at the Post Office. I did not look directly at him, but glanced from the side so that I saw him only in glimpses that I then assembled in my mind.

I sat rigid without moving. I did not look at the city streaming past the windows. I had no curiosity about where we were going. I sat stiff with my hands under my knees. I kept my eyes fixed on the little doll that hung from his driver mirror and swung to and fro as he drove. I focused on its pink hair and half-naked body and grinning face.

He saw me look at it, and unhooked it. 'It is a troll,' he said. 'It was a birthday present from my sister. You can have it.' He placed it in my lap. 'You can keep it,' he added.

I did not pick it up, but let it sit on my lap where it moved with the car. When we stopped at the traffic lights, it fell to the floor. I bent to pick it up and clutched it. I was still clutching it as we walked up to the Wimpy at the Union Arcade, next to Brentoni's.

I looked for that Wimpy when I came back, but like other places that I knew, it has been erased from the face of the city. There is another Wimpy now, further along the same road, but on the other side of First Street.

If people stared at our odd pairing, I did not notice it. I kept my eyes focused on the little troll doll. Lloyd ordered a plate of chips and a strawberry milkshake. I looked at the doll and wondered how something as ugly as that could be so comforting.

When he talked, he mixed Shona and English. His *zva* sounds came out like *zha* and it made him sound like a small child, like Mobhi. That made me less afraid of him. I watched his mouth move as he ate my untouched chips. He took out a packet of cigarettes. It was this that finally broke me down. They were

Everest – the coolest taste in smoking, said the packet; they were the same cigarettes that my father smoked as he whistled to the radio. As the smoke swirled around our table, I finally gave in to the tears I had been holding back.

The smoke floated around us in that Wimpy, he watched me cry, and I could not stop it. I held the troll doll to my face and soaked its pink hair with my tears. He ordered an ice cream sundae that sat and melted until the little coloured grains that were sprinkled on it, which I later learned were called hundreds and thousands, disappeared into little coloured blobs in the milky mess.

When Lloyd registered me at the Dominican Convent, I knew that my sale was final. He needed my birth certificate, you see. He needed it to register me.

I had last seen my birth certificate at our house in Mufakose when my father registered my brother and sister and me at our new primary school in Mufakose. My father had then returned the certificates to the Manila envelope inside the briefcase that he kept locked on top of the wardrobe in my parents' bedroom. The birth certificates were usually in protective plastic folders together with Gift's, and later Mobhi's, death certificates.

So when I saw my birth certificate on Lloyd's desk together with an application form for the Convent, on which he had put his unreadable scrawl in the space above the words 'Signature of Parent or Guardian', I knew that only my mother or father could have given it to Lloyd.

It was the final confirmation that my sale was irrevocable. It was then that I knew there was nothing at all that I could do about it; and there was no one that I could tell. Who could I have turned to? I was nine years old. I was alone. The people who could have helped me were the people who had sold me in the first place. I did not know how to get back home; I did not even know in which direction home was.

The pain was made bearable only by the thought that, if my mother and father could get rid of me so easily, I did not want to be with them. If they could do without me, I resolved, then I could just as well do without them.

This was a vow that was better made than kept.

In that first year, it seemed to me that I saw them everywhere I looked. My heart grew still when I saw any tall, straight man with a short, neat Afro. Six months after I left home, Lloyd dropped me off at the Queen Victoria Memorial Library on Rotten Row; I saw a man that I knew was my father. So certain was I that it was him that I ran after him across the street. The traffic lights changed before I noticed them and all around me car horns beeped, and I came to myself.

An irate driver who had almost run me over got out of his car and blocked my path. More horns beeped around us as he made a grab for me, but I managed to slip away. I ran all the way back to the library without stopping, and I lost sight of my father, or the man that I had imagined to be my father.

The phantom sightings continued over the years. One Sunday, two years after my sale, at the racecourse at Borrowdale with Lloyd and Liz Warrender, I heard a woman shout '*Iwe*, Moreblessings!' Even as I knew that it could not be our Moreblessings because our Mobhi was dead, and even as I saw that this Moreblessings was not a girl but a woman in a bright pink shirt and a yellow banana clip in her hair, my hope still rose in my throat until it stung my eyes.

That day, and on every day that I went to the racecourse, I imagined my father sitting at his wireless set in our house on

Mharapara Street in Mufakose, listening to the invisible thunder of the horses that I saw before me.

Throughout the years, I would catch what I thought were glimpses of one or another of my family, but as the years ran into each other, the memories faded.

Years later, when I had begun to think of Lloyd and Poppy as my family and Summer Madness as my home, at St Dominic's Secondary School in Chishawasha, the valley opposite Umwinsidale, I saw a schoolgirl, small, slight and caramel-skinned, who might have been my sister Joy.

St Dominic's was the rural version of our school. It was not so much a sister school; more like a cousin, a poor rural one for that matter, where the girls were not considered sophisticated enough for the blazers, boaters, French, swimming or tennis that was considered so necessary for us.

We had gone there for a debate; something about colonialism bringing more harm than good. After the motion was carried, we got into our bus to leave. As our bus negotiated its way along the narrow path that led to the school gate, we stopped to make room for their school bus.

As their bus passed us, I saw among the faces in the bus a girl who could have been my sister, a girl who could have been the child that my sister Joy had been when I last saw her. As though sensing that I was staring at her, she turned in my direction. Our eyes met. In that moment, our bus drove away, and I was left to persuade myself that I had imagined the resemblance.

I never saw them again. Even after I was old enough to have my own money and I could navigate the city on my own, even after I turned sixteen and Lloyd gave me my beloved orange Beetle, I did not look for them. By this time, I had reasoned to myself once and for all that if they did not want me, I did not want them either. Most of all, I did not look for them because I was afraid that seeing them would only confirm my loss.

I wondered often why Lloyd had taken me in. You see how insidious his influence is, how I am using his language. I believe he came close to explaining, after all the ugliness with Zenzo, but I did not open the letter he put under my door. I did not want to hear his self-justification.

In the years that followed, my feelings for Lloyd went through a complex spectrum that took in fear, affection, anger and revulsion, gratitude and, ultimately, pity. If you had met Lloyd, you would have been struck that such a mild and gentle man could cause feelings of such depth and intensity.

Lloyd's unstinting generosity complicated matters, particularly after the business with Zenzo. There was no question that his house was very clearly, and openly, my home. He gave me an expensive and necessary education that was good enough to get me into an elite university. Under expert medical care my skin bloomed until both Simon and Zenzo could say, with some sincerity, that I was beautiful. I discovered books that became as necessary to my being as breathing.

Living with him in that house, I fell in love with history. Through him, living in his world, I got a sense of a world that was bigger than myself. Could there have been love?

If I had not seen that passing of notes between my parents, I would have believed . . . I don't know what I would have believed. And if there had been no Zenzo. Maybe there could have been love between us, not the prurient love of funny things imagined by Officer Dimples, but love in its simple purity of one being opening up to another, with no expectation beyond the gift of that love.

In the moments when I forgot how we came to live together, I believe that I came to love him. What had been a tentative flowering might have turned into a full blossoming. Then Zenzo entered our lives, and everything wilted.

2

I read in one of your columns that, on the night before their execution, death row prisoners in one of the Southern states, Texas or Georgia, I can't recall, will usually request, for their last meal, the foods that recall their childhood. And because a disproportionate number of death row inmates are black prisoners from the rural South, these last suppers tend to be the food of the poor, fried chicken and collard greens, grits and sweet potato pie.

I don't think I would want any food on the night before that morning. I imagine that it would taste like ash. And how would I ever eat that last mouthful, the last morsel, knowing that it *is* the last that I will ever eat? I would want just wine, I think. No – vodka, perhaps: strong, cheap vodka, and lots of it, enough to knock me out the night before and make every step the next morning shine with light.

When I asked Loveness on Sunday if we had the last supper tradition here, she clucked her tongue and said, 'You know we do not talk about that here.'

Any time that I approach the subject of my sentence, Loveness acts like a particularly judgemental hostess whose least important guest has been caught in a social faux pas. When I told her that, in America, people eat what they want on their last day, she said again that I should not think such things, and besides, I should hurry and leave my cell because I had a visitor.

I was surprised. As I told you before, I have never had a visitor in the two years that I have been here, apart from the Goodwill Fellowship people. You and Vernah Sithole do not count as visitors because you come at the special dispensation of the Chief Superintendent. As you saw last week, you can come in and out as long as you announce your planned visit and you don't visit more than twice in one week. So you are not visitors in the ordinary sense.

I thought it might be one of the Goodwill Fellowship women, though I was sure it would not be the one that they sent last time. 'Are you coping with prison conditions now?' the woman who came to see me had asked. 'Are you missing anything, anything at all?'

Her face was a symphony of manufactured sympathy. Something about her perfect assurance made me savage. Am I missing anything, anything at all? I mean, really. Not anything at all. Just everything. Books, books, books, books. Soap. A warm bed with clean sheets that smell of fabric softener. A hot shower. Sunscreen. The plopping sound produced by a Chablis straight from the fridge. Mosquito spray. The smell of old archives. The curling loops on old manuscripts. The cream-and-green ordinariness of my Tilley hat. Toothpaste. A comb. A comb with all its teeth attached. The Internet.

'You know what I really miss?' I said, and put on my most wistful look. I may even have managed a shimmer of tears.

She leaned forward, her face a rictus of concern, the Bic pen on her clipboard ready to note down desires she knew the Goodwill Fellowship could not possibly fulfil, her left hand on the verge of stretching out to clasp mine in solidarity.

'What I really long for, more than anything, what I miss above all other things,' I said, 'is a good, hard fuck.'

The outstretched hand was withdrawn. Her face collapsed into an O of shock. She fumbled for her clipboard and moved to record the longings of the next prisoner. I felt terrible until my irritation took over. What did she know, this little peach-faced do-gooder? It takes more than good wishes; it takes a spectacular failure of the imagination to ask if there are things we miss. Better to say nothing, to bring Bibles and leave than to open wounds that you cannot possibly heal.

But it was not the Goodwill Fellowship this time. Instead, my visitor was a student from one of the universities here. Synodia was not pleased to have another visit to supervise. Visiting days are on the first and third Sundays of every month. They are often deeply distressing, as so often the visitors bring bad news, and the guards have to threaten everyone and shout louder than usual to get everyone to settle. On those Sundays, the women who will have seen family during the day mostly spend the night in fits of weeping, which irritates the others and causes friction. That is when most of the fights in C cell happen.

My visitor had two letters from her university, one asking whomever it concerned to co-operate with her research, the other from the Prison Commissioner, approving her to see me, on condition that it was to be in the presence of a guard. Synodia was not pleased to hear her ask for a special room. As the guards were all occupied, she marshalled us into the canteen with all the others. We sat at one end of the room while Synodia stood over us with a sour face.

Synodia's manner had clearly unsettled my visitor. Without looking directly at me, she stammered something about the socio-pathology of the female murderer. She turned to open her lap-top bag.

'Eh, what are you handing her over there? I have to see what is in that bag,' Synodia said.

'But I have already been searched,' the student responded.

'And you will be searched again.'

At Synodia's command, the girl took out everything she had and put in on the table. As Synodia looked through her things, she kept a running commentary on how important it was for the student to know that there was nothing special about murderers like me, how it was important to make sure that murderers like me knew their place, and that the place for murderers like me was not in any fancy books written by students at a university, no matter how clever and educated they thought they were, but here in Chikurubi, where murderers like me belonged.

The student put everything back into her bag but her notepad and pens. Synodia was clearly getting to her. When she dropped a pen, she jumped as though to escape her own skin. She licked her lips and looked at her notebook. I waited for questions that did not come.

Eventually I said, 'So, Clarice.'

She looked at me blankly and said, 'My name is not Clarice.'

'Hannibal Lecter?' I said.

'Sorry, I don't get you.'

'"I'm having an old friend for dinner"?'

'Sorry?' she said again.

'*The Silence of the Lambs*?'

She looked about the room as though the silence that I spoke of was all around us.

'Sorry?'

The rhyme from the school playground in Mufakose came to my mind: 'Es-oh-ara-another-ara-no-more-ara-and-then-wayi!'

She looked as if she might know that rhyme. She is one of those students Zimbabwe produces, like my old friend Mercy at the Convent; she probably studied by the light of candles, her English coming to her, as mine did in the first three years, from teachers who had learned it third-hand, the accent undiluted, the ambition strong. She would have gone to a mission school, very likely as a scholarship girl.

And perhaps, like Mercy, she would meet some Pentecostal Christian man, if she hadn't already, who would have no interest in the sociopathology of the female murderer.

By the time she had recovered enough to stammer through a list of questions that assumed my conviction and guilt were one and the same thing, I had lost interest in Clarice. I gave short, bland answers to her questions, staying only so that I could spend more time looking around the room at all the visitors.

As Clarice talked and I looked about me, I wondered, for the first time, what my life might have been like if I had never met Lloyd.

3

It was Lloyd who first took me to the National Archives in Borrowdale. In our history classes, the walls of the classroom disappeared and I found myself fully immersed in the lesson of the day. The past came alive vividly before me. Chuma and Susi carrying the body of Livingstone, Gonçalo da Silveira's lonely death in the Mutapa Empire, Chiang Kai-shek crossing from the mainland, the Mensheviks and the Bolsheviks fighting the October Revolution, Queen Philippa pardoning the men of Calais.

If you ever go to the Archives, you must make your way through the main doors and up the stairs past the main desk. You will find yourself in an atrium that leads to the Beit Gallery. In this space are the symbols of the extraordinary juxtapositions that birthed this country.

There is a strikingly real facsimile copy of the Domesday Book, the result of William the Conqueror's comprehensive act of administrative control after crossing the English Channel to conquer an England that would eventually sprawl into the empire on which the sun finally set with the independence of this country.

There are large paintings by Thomas Baines, the artist who brought Africa to London as a lush rainforest inhabited by noble natives in neatly folded loincloths. There are two life-size bronzes of the rebels Charwe and Gumboreshumba, better known as the spirit mediums of Nehanda and Kaguvi, the spirits who gave the fight for black independence its moral force. And there are pictures of the ruins in Masvingo, the seat of the ancient empire that gave the country its name.

It was only in the months that I worked at the Archives, after my return to Zimbabwe, that I came to realise this arrangement was purely random.

If you go past this room and into the narrow corridor, you will find yourself in the treasure vault of the Beit Gallery. In here is the mace presented to the Federation of Rhodesia and Nyasaland by the British Parliament. In a glass cabinet, you will find the independence documents, a letter from the Queen of England handing over the country as one would hand over a gift to a friend. There are books and documents and portraits dating back to the seventeenth century, documents that quickened my blood as I studied the Mutapa Empire.

Right at the end of the gallery, in a wooden cabinet with a glass lid, is a worn piece of blue, red and white cloth that was stitched in South Africa by hands that have been lifeless for more than a hundred years. This is the Pioneer flag, the Union Jack that Cecil John Rhodes and his Pioneer Column, Lloyd's grandfather among them, raised at Fort Salisbury on 13 September 1890.

Sometimes, when I found myself in the Archives, or when Lloyd talked about his family, I thought of my own, undocumented past. The parents that I left behind in Mufakose seemed, like Melchizedek the Priest-King who came leaping in dance to Abraham, to have had no father and mother. We seemed like the Spartoi, the earth-grown men that sprang up, fully formed, from the teeth sown by Cadmus, to be completely unconnected to anyone but ourselves, to have emerged complete into the present, without a history.

There were no old letters, no mementos, no links to any kind of past. Even when we asked them, my parents answered no questions about their past, or any past. It was more than a lack of openness – it seemed an almost active secrecy. I had once asked my mother where my dead brother Gift was buried and she answered by shouting that I should not ask about things I did not understand. 'Why,' she continued, 'are the plates in the sink still unwashed after I told you again and again to wash them?'

She had, in fact, told me no such thing, but I hastily moved over to the kitchen to do as she said.

We had always lived in town, as far as I knew, until my father explained about Joyi's scar. I did not know that we had ever lived in a rural village until the day Joy looked at her small burned foot and said she wished it looked like the other one. 'That is a symbol of great love,' my father said. 'You should not wish it away.'

We pressed him to tell us what he meant and he laughed and said, 'She got it because of too much love. It happened when we lived *kumusha*. You had a little doll.'

'Did it open and shut its eyes like Promise's doll?' asked Joyi.

'This was when we lived *kumusha*, at your grandmother's village. It was not a real doll; it was a cornhusk that you had taken and made a doll of. When your grandmother burned it by mistake, you wailed and ran into the ash to rescue it. We got to you just in time.'

He told us about the white plaster that Joyi had; they had to crack it open at the hospital when it came off.

This was the only time that he had ever mentioned a rural home or a grandmother. Joyi was more interested in her plaster, but I pressed him on the grandmother. 'Where is she? Where is this rural home?'

Who was the grandmother, was she old, where was she now, was she dead, when would she come to see us, would she bring us peanuts and matohwe and watermelons, like Whizi's grandmother that time, or just horrible stinky old mufushwa, like Princess's granny?

He only laughed, and said, 'Why don't we go for our walk?'

In the excitement of anticipating sweets and treats, I stopped asking questions.

As I have said, it was only when I heard the neighbours talking at the wake when Mobhi died that I thought at all about what it meant that we had no relatives. MaiWhizi asked what had happened to all our relatives, why we were burying Mobhi alone, like we were 'born locations', meaning people born in the townships, people without roots; it was only then that I began to wonder why no one ever came to see us.

There was that scar, though, Joyi's burn scar. It was a hard fact that I could hold on to. It connected us to another life, to a grandmother, to a rural home, at least. Joyi, rarely aggressive, lashed out at me when she heard me tell the plaster story to Lavinia at breaktime. Only, in my retelling, the plaster had been on me and not on Joyi. She came charging at me and I found myself flat on my back as she pummelled me. And though I hit back, I knew she was justified in punishing me because I had claimed as my own something that was hers.

Perhaps more knowledge would have come in time and I would have found out more about the grandmother and the rural home and how my parents met and about the children they were, about their parents and where they had lived. All this may have been told to me one day, passed down like oral tradition.

It was the opposite at Summer Madness. Lloyd's past was an

active part of his present. It was in the Distinguished Flying Cross that Lloyd's father had obtained with the 44 Rhodesia Squadron, in the Victoria Cross awarded to his grandfather, and in the sepia-toned photographs from long-ago wars that hung on the walls of the library.

Lloyd could not have gone off on a more different trajectory from his grandfather, Assistant Commissioner Lloyd Douglas Hendricks, commander of the King's Native Regiment in Tanganyika and one of Rhodesia's only six recipients of the Victoria Cross. He was one of Rhodes's Pioneers, just the sort of man you wanted in a battle, especially if the battle happened to be against warriors in loincloths with nothing to shield them from the arsenal of a Maxim gun and other firearms than a goatskin shield, an assegai and the fleetness of their bare feet.

He appears on page 245 of the second volume of the *African Heritage* history book, a man with colourless eyes and a bushy moustache, looking out at Zimbabwe's schoolchildren with the glassy stare of the subjects of early photography.

My father was right to say that I was to live with a doctor, but Lloyd was not a doctor in the sense that my parents would have understood doctors. He had obtained his doctorate in classics at Oxford, where he had first gone as an eighteen-year-old to avoid the call-up, the conscription that required all young white men with complete limbs to fight for Rhodesia. At Oxford, he campaigned for the guerrillas, raising money for refugees and for scholarships.

Where he had really gone off on a tangent was in his role in the war. Instead of answering the call-up, or staying as long as he could in England, Lloyd had actually returned to join the comrades – or, as the whites called them, the terrorists. He worked in the refugee camp at Nyadzonia as a teacher of English and civic studies, and he wrote the pamphlets that were scattered from helicopters across the eastern regions. He was there when Nyadzonia was bombed.

Lloyd's refusal to join the war – I should say, his joining it on the wrong side – put him in direct conflict with his family. And after independence, he cemented his eccentricity by joining the university, but it was not to teach what he had studied. The new curriculum stated that students were better off learning how to make propane-gas-powered stoves and Blair toilets than learning Greek and Latin. Lloyd reinvented himself as a professor of classical literature, specialising in filtering Greek tragedies through the African experience.

Lloyd became another of that special class of Rhodesian eccentrics who were considered to have gone native in preposterous ways; men like Peter Garlake, whose insistence that the ruins in Masvingo were the work of black people alienated him from his fellow whites; or Michael Gelfand and Herbert Aschwanden, who collected Karanga mythology; Frank McEwen, who set up a village for sculptors; and George Fortune, who collected in one place all the totem names and poems of all the totem groups in the country.

It was during the war that Lloyd did just about the only thing of which Alexandra approved: he got engaged to a girl called Tracey Collins. Like Lloyd, she had been a teacher at a school in the Eastern Highlands; she had gone to Chimoio to volunteer as a teacher. She was killed in the attack on Chimoio by the Rhodesians.

Her face was in a frame on Lloyd's mantelpiece, a small plain woman with hair like Farrah Fawcett's, in a bow-tied blouse, her eyes earnest behind thick, round glasses, frozen for ever in the unflattering fashions of the late seventies.

4

From my new room at the back of the house, I heard the hum of the swimming pool. I was woken each morning by the sound of birds in the garden. In the first week, I slept on the floor, terrified of making the clean white sheets dirty. And I could not get used to not having Mobhi's warm smallness next to me, no Joyi to breathe in my ear.

In time, the room became truly mine as I filled it with the strewn evidence of the passions that I picked up and discarded over the years: shoeboxes in which I bred silkworms and fed them mulberry leaves, model horses and framed pictures of jockeys, portraits of Markova and Fonteyn and my mountains of *Archie* comics and *Misty* and *Jackie* annuals.

On my first night, I broke Alexandra's doll. It was an old one that had been passed down from Eleanor-Jean. It sat on the window ledge opposite my bed. It looked exactly the same as the doll with the porcelain face in Bester Kanyama's photo studio in Highfield. I vividly saw my sisters and me sitting and posing next to it for a photograph.

It made me shiver to think that this doll with its blank, empty stare had sat there all these years looking first at Eleanor-Jean, then Alexandra, and now me. During that first day, its eyes seemed to follow me. And later, when I woke up in the night, I found its face shining at me in the moonlight. Unable to withstand that steady, unblinking stare, I decided to move it to the back of my cupboard. But I had woken up from a terrifying dream, and my hands were unsteady as I lifted it down. It fell to the floor with a crack, and when I lifted it up it was to see that I had smashed its porcelain face.

I hid it at the back of the cupboard, afraid that Alexandra would one day ask for it. As I lay in my new room in Lloyd's house in Umwinsidale, I knew only that this room, with the new bed I did not sleep in until much later, was not big enough to contain the pain and fear that were within me. Fear of the doll, of Lloyd, of the unknown world in which I found myself.

The dream I had in Mufakose after Mobhi died came to me again later that night. I was pulled into the embrace of a horrible creature that spoke with my mother's voice and said I needed to bathe while my father screamed a protest. I woke up frightened, unsure where I was, and only remembered when I realised that I was alone. I clutched the troll doll to my chest. In the company of the ugly doll with pink hair, and a hidden one in the cupboard, I passed my first night in the room that was to be mine for the next nine years, and that remained mine long after I left Lloyd.

For two weeks, nothing happened, and I was safe. Then one afternoon, Lloyd's sister Alexandra walked over to where Lloyd and I sat outside on the veranda. As soon as I saw the doll in her hand, I waited for the kind of explosion that my mother would have produced in similar circumstances.

But she didn't look at me, or ask me what had happened.

Instead, she looked at Lloyd and said, 'If you are to make a success of this, you must teach her to respect other people's property. And you really ought to teach her better manners, too.'

She put the doll down next to me.

My heart was loud in my chest as I looked at it. Its cracked face and sunken eye seemed to reproach me.

Lloyd said, 'Memory can't have meant to do it. In any event, you have not cared about that hideous thing for years now. It should have been at your house if it means so much to you.'

'Memory, indeed,' said Alexandra and pursed her lips.

After the doll, my next moment of discomfort came from MaiJethro, who, with Namatai, was one of the maids who took care of the house and of Lloyd's grandmother, Poppy. They lived in the servants' quarters, which were at the back of the house, hidden by a large hedge, but I naturally saw them every day as they worked in the different rooms.

MaiJethro, as far as I knew, never had a child, Jethro or no Jethro. And there was no Ba'Jethro, though he lived every day in MaiJethro's conversation, serving, it appeared, no further purpose beyond agreeing with whatever view she wished to put forward. She told long stories about their conversations. His views served only to support hers, and she offered him to us as an authority on any subject, from the war in Mozambique to anything else she wanted to pronounce on.

I used often to see a small skinny man with gnarled hands, who smoked roll-up cigarettes outside the servants' quarters while reading Lloyd's newspaper from the previous day. I assumed that this was Ba'Jethro until Namatai told me that he wasn't, but did not explain any more.

The first time she saw me, MaiJethro made me stand before her in the kitchen while she assailed me with a thousand questions. Where was I from? What did my father do? Did I have many brothers? How had he died, this brother that was dead? Where was he buried? What did my mother look like? Where was she from? What about my sisters? What were they called? How old were they? Did all my family look like me? Why did I look the way I did? Had I been bewitched? How did Lloyd know my family? Did he give me any money? Where did I keep the money that he gave me? What was my totem? Where was our *kumusha*? When was I going back?

I tried to answer, but the questions kept coming.

I burst into tears.

'Otilda,' said a voice from the kitchen.

MaiJethro and I looked at the door and found Lloyd, looking stern. He put an arm around me and told me to go to my room. I left them in the kitchen. When I saw MaiJethro again, she looked at me for a long time. I looked back at her without blinking. She never again asked me any questions about my family or how I had come to live with Lloyd, but she looked at me warily, as though I were a dog of whose temper she was not entirely certain.

Namatai was one of the handful of people that I had met who did not do that visible double take on first seeing me. She reminded me of MaiWhizi, back on Mharapara, who talked constantly of other women's complexions, only Namatai was obsessed with hair — with who had nice hair and who did not. She gave me greasy green ointment that she said was hair food, and she plaited my hair. Unlike my mother's, Namatai's hands were not harsh against my scalp.

Both Namatai and MaiJethro had rooms in the servants' quarters. But more often than not Namatai spent the night in the cottage with Poppy.

Lloyd and Alexandra's grandmother, Poppy, was the oldest person I had ever seen. She lived in a small cottage on the estate, some way away from the main house. She spent most of her days lying in bed or sitting in her wheelchair on the veranda, looking out at the flowers, trapped in the dementia that had come upon her after her first stroke. In the rare intervals when she was lucid, she asked Namatai to play her jazz records.

When she was young, Poppy had come to the colony as a flapper, with suitcases full of daringly cut drop-waist dresses and strings of beads. Transplanted from the world of London nightclubs to the heat and dust of Rhodesia, and shut out from the currents and fashions of London, Poppy flapped determinedly right to the end, stuck in the jazz age. When I came to live at Summer Madness, I found her still playing the records she must have listened to when she first got off the boat from England.

Her one moment of glory was just a few years after her first grandchild was born, when Louis Armstrong came to play in Salisbury, and the 'colour bar', as they called the segregation that separated the races, was for that one evening put aside: both blacks and whites gathered to hear him perform.

With Namatai, MaiJethro and Poppy, I was happy enough, but I never recovered my relationship with Alexandra. I want to believe that she might have been kinder to me if she had known how. She only knew how to command black people or give them her charity. And I was a black child who was only black on the inside.

More than anything, I was relieved that Alexandra and Ian did not live in the valley, but on their farm in Chipinge. They came to town once a month. Alexandra's marriage to Ian Fleming gave her the improbable name of Alexandra Fleming, which, given her manic dislike of germs, seemed apposite.

Large, florid and moving always in the comingled smells of tobacco and brandy, Ian was a man of many prejudices and little humour. He hated Jews and Greeks and Italians. He hated the

Portuguese. He was not too wild about the Irish, either, or the Scots and Welsh, so you can only imagine how he felt about non-whites. His language was coloured by racial otherness. 'He was drunk as a mine munt on payday' was one of his favourite expressions, munt being short for *muntu*, a word that means person in its original, but truncated to munt was as dismissive as his other favourite words for black people: zots and Afs and kafs.

Above all, he hated the new leadership; he had gloomy predictions about what would happen to the country now that the zots had taken over.

His Rhodesia was one of excellence and possibility and he was given to enumerating its successes. He said all of this in my presence, but I was probably invisible to him, and he did not think that I understood anything he said – or if I did, that it did not matter. I was not sophisticated enough to take him on, to point out to him that this Rhodesia had worked only for a few thousand white people.

He also hated people he called 'poofters', an all-encompassing category that took in anyone who was not a zot or Jewish or Greek, Portuguese or Italian, Welsh or Scottish, who behaved in any manner that Ian saw as disagreeably different.

It was a category elastic enough to take in Lloyd's friend Sandy Knight-Bruce, Alan Milhouse, who was a psychiatrist and taught at the university, and anyone else who had the effrontery to act in contravention of how Ian prescribed men should act.

He talked mainly about his macadamia nut estate in Chimanimani, and about the wars that the Flemings and Hendricks had fought in. Between them, the Flemings and the Hendricks had been in every war from the Matabeleland suppression to the First and Second World Wars and the Civil War.

What tied him and Alexandra together was drinking. During their visits, bottles piled up. Looking back, there was something essentially joyless in their drinking, a determination that had nothing to do with conviviality.

Liz Warrender and Sandy Knight-Bruce, the most malicious gossips in Umwinsidale, told me later that Ian had another excitement in his past – a tragedy, even. He had had an affair once, but Alexandra had made him leave the woman and the baby. 'And I promise you,' said Liz Warrender, who told me this story, 'she's had him by the short-and-curlies ever since.'

Alexandra did not forgive easily. That smashed doll formed the strained basis of my relationship with her. I can connect a straight line from the crack in that doll's face to her testimony in the witness box at my trial.

She told the judge that I had killed Lloyd for the Hendricks money and for Summer Madness and everything in it. She knew about the will because Lloyd had told her that he would be leaving everything to me. She had not liked it, of course, and had tried in vain to plead with him, and she saw me only as one who sought to take the things the family had fought for and make them my own.

I could never forget that I had ruined her doll, and always I felt that I would say the wrong thing to her. I felt incomplete and inadequate before her cool scrutiny, and so I said as little as I could; for a long time afterwards she thought, as I heard her say to Ian one day, that I seemed 'slow, somehow retarded'.

This, then, was my new life at Summer Madness, with Lloyd who brought me there, Poppy, MaiJethro and Namatai, and Sandy and Liz and the dogs, and, happily on the periphery, Alexandra and Ian.

5

When I look back, those early years with Lloyd come to me as a jumble of books, horses and dogs, and a long series of journeys, both actual and imagined, but all real to me. In Mufakose, I moved between my rigidly defined worlds of home and school, my mother's churches, healers and hospitals.

In my tree house at Summer Madness, mercifully far from the swimming pool, I spent long days reading Lloyd and Alexandra's old books. I captured the castle. I went deep in the sea of adventure. I danced with Markova at Sadler's Wells, with Drina in Switzerland, and with Posy and Petrova and Pauline. With the Lone Pine Five, I hunted German spies on the Yorkshire Moors.

To Middle-earth and the Secret Garden I went, to the great grey-green, greasy Limpopo River, all set about with fever-trees. I brought Beth March back from the dead, and instead killed off Amy and married Laurie to Jo.

When it was too wet or cold to go outside, I stayed in the library, a dark, cool room at the back of the house, from which I could hear the burr of the swimming pool engine. In the library, and up in the tree house, I found the happiest and most peaceful moments of my life at that difficult time.

Crippled by fear and longing for home, I was saved by books. The worlds I travelled to allowed me to escape the pain of being uprooted from Mufakose. I had never seen so many books gathered in a single space as I saw in that room. I felt less afraid when I thought of all the other people who seemed to have had harder lives than mine. I disappeared completely to occupy the world of whatever book I was reading.

As I read more and my English improved, I often spent days in Lloyd's library. I spent hours before the television, watching *Flambards*, and *Flipper*, fascinated by adverts for Sunlight and Colgate.

I sometimes cried myself to sleep in the first months with Lloyd. When I did sleep, it was to wake from the terrible dreams in which the Chimera spoke in my mother's voice. It strikes me now that I was scared of many things in that first year: going to bed, the swimming pool, Alexandra, MaiJethro even, but I was never afraid of Lloyd.

I had thought him very old when I first met him, but I was seeing him through the eyes of a child, to whom all grown people are ancient. In reality, he was just over thirty-five when I came to live with him. If you want a physical description beyond the black-and-white blurs you have seen in the papers, then I would say he was tallish and thin, with ash-blond hair that he wore to his shoulders, and an amused face, as though he had just that minute remembered a joke someone had once told him.

The early years also come to me with the sounds of the eighties. Lloyd and I listened to cassette tapes by Fleetwood Mac and Depeche Mode. I hear 'Take On Me', 'Personal Jesus', as we drive under the umbrella trees on our approach to Nyanga, to Mutare to stay at La Rochelle, to Matopos to stand on top of the world, and to Mana Pools to track elephants – or at least, for Lloyd and Alan to track the elephants while I read in the tent, or listen to Salt-N-Pepa on my Walkman.

Alan Milhouse often accompanied us on our trips outside the city. He was Lloyd's best friend. On these trips, he and Lloyd shared a room, while I had my own. Alan was a man of quick enthusiasm; he spoke of the boiler at Lloyd's cottage in Nyanga with such passion that he might have invented it.

Though Lloyd was far from being a recluse, in the gregarious Umwinsidale set, with its endless round of cocktail parties, braais and sundowners, cricket and tennis and polo parties, he was considered something of a hermit.

Alexandra always tried to introduce him to women. She pulled together an impressive list of divorcees, who all seemed, curiously, to be real estate agents, and single women who were usually farmers' daughters called Debbie or Shirl, Sheila or Tracey, or jolly-hockey-sticks-type teachers with firm handshakes and *Fatal Attraction* hair.

Every woman she introduced to Lloyd was perfect, just the one for him; every one of them was clever: Alexandra was never able to distinguish between reading a scholarly work and reading *Look and Listen*, the TV and radio guide. When Lloyd stopped announcing our monthly visits to the farm, different women appeared, sent by Alexandra on errands that sounded spurious, even to me.

I particularly remember a woman called Avril, who sat too close to Lloyd on the couch, waving thin hands with rings on each finger in his face. She may well have had bells on her toes, too, like the fine lady upon the fine horse at Banbury Cross, but she did not stay long enough to get that comfortable.

All of Alexandra's efforts were in vain. Lloyd remained Lloyd, aloof and slightly amused, marrying none of the women she thrust upon him. The only adult person in whose company he seemed able to spend great lengths of time was Alan Milhouse. Alan was always friendly to me, but he sometimes disconcerted me by giving me hugs when I least expected them, and by questioning me closely, his eyes searching mine, about how I was, and whether everything was well with me.

I know that I impressed Jimmy when I told her that Summer Madness was a mansion, like the large houses that are the fashion today. You see them in places like Borrowdale Brooke, which is really just a township on steroids, with houses like promontories bloated on brick and concrete.

I did not know until Summer Madness became my home that it was possible to fall in love with a house. It did not happen at once.

What was meant to be a simple farmhouse became a little temple to grace and beauty; all Doric pillars and columns. Along its length runs a veranda. I loved to sit there during a raging storm, as one with the elements but protected from them.

I had no jobs to do, no cleaning, no washing, no Mobhi to tend to and care for. When I was not reading, and when I became used to them, I played with the dogs, first Chocolate, the little dachsie that took to following me everywhere I went and slept on my bed, then, when she died, Mrs Harris, the golden Labrador. In the garden, I dug up toy soldiers that had been forgotten through the decades.

There were no raised voices at Summer Madness, no sudden squalls, no explosions. It did not matter that Lloyd spoke to his sister or her husband, to his gardener and jack-of-all-trades, Biggie, to Liz Warrender or to me: he spoke always in a tone of supreme politeness and wry detachment. Not even in those awful moments after I found him with Zenzo did he ever raise his voice, not even after he came back from those two weeks in

[169]

the police cell did he shout or yell or look at me with anything like reproach.

He enrolled me at the Convent School in town, where, with four hundred other girls in blue skirts and beige blouses, we made prayers of supplication to the Blessed Mary, Ever Virgin, to pray for us sinners, now, and at the hour of our deaths. Catholic sisters with heavy shoes and equally heavy names taught me: Sisters Mary Gabriel and Ethelburga, Sisters Hedwig and Hildegarde.

At my new school, my life soon developed its own rhythm. The Dominican Convent was like the world outside, only in miniature. Money got me what a top girls' school gives: slight arrogance, self-belief. The blue skirt and beige blouse declared me a Convent girl, belonging by right to the upper levels of the school system. The straw boater linked me to the girls who had come before and those who would come after. I assumed a new identity.

It helped that money also bought me good skin, courtesy of a dermatologist. At school, I eventually became just another girl in a blue dress, and when I entered the secondary, another girl in a blue skirt and white blouse. In time I gained the confidence that comes with any expensive private education.

More than anything else, I felt an incredible sense of freedom: not from want but from scrutiny. I had not yet found home, but I found a place where I could belong.

6

It was a strange time to be living in a white family. Independence had come five years before. The news was filled with reburials of mangled corpses whose names would never be known, the Tomb of the Unknown Soldier at the new shrine at the Heroes Acre, and roll calls of the names of the fallen in Mozambique. A government minister had suggested a ritual ceremony to propitiate the spirits of the dead, lest they return as vengeful *ngozi* spirits. A tomb was erected to the Unknown Soldier. Kingsway became Julius Nyerere Avenue. North Avenue became Josiah Tongogara Avenue, and Railway Avenue became Kenneth Kaunda.

The 'Year of the People's Struggle' was followed by the 'Year of Consolidating the People's Struggle', the 'Year of Transformation', the 'Year of the People's Socialism' and the 'Year of the Child'.

It was a time of building a new nation, but there was conflict and upheaval. There were weekly explosions of landmines that had been planted in the forests during the war then forgotten about. The Mozambican rebels were waging war on the eastern borders. Our soldiers were sent to protect the Beira Corridor that gave the country access to sea routes. The apartheid government in South Africa was bombing targets all over Southern Africa. There were rumours of massacres in the south.

But at Summer Madness, I had long wet weekends in the

library or sunny days in the tree house. On our trips out of Harare, I watched the countryside sweep by in a rush of green. The wars and troubles were, at the closest distance, only reports on the news bulletins, and at the furthest, distant murmurs, far-off rumours that did not penetrate the ordered tranquillity of my new life.

The war closest to me was the one that had passed, and it came to me through Ian's stories as he talked about the hot extractions he had been part of, and the Afs he had shot. He terrified me by telling me that he had shot a boy my size, who had been a spy for the terrorists. 'He was as small as you are,' he said as he winked at me. 'Just two tickeys and a brick high.'

When I saw him again after my return home, it was hard to see the old Ian in this broken man in his wheelchair, his mouth permanently gaping, all liver spots and dribble. The once-upon-a-time hater of Afs and zots and kafs was clinging to the woman who cared for him, a woman from Chipinge who cleaned him and fed him and sang him Shona songs. He barely noticed when Alexandra left the room, but wept openly when his carer left.

My life found its total absorption in Umwinsidale. I made only one friend at school, a girl called Mercy, who came to the Convent in form two. She was a scholarship girl with milk-bottle spectacles. Her greatest value to me was that she did not ask questions that I did not want to answer. It also helped to have a friend because it meant that people did not think me stranger than I already was.

I did not want anyone to know that my parents had sold me: that was between Lloyd and me, and any time I got close to any of the girls I liked, I backed away, fearing the inevitable questions that further intimacy would have obliged me to answer.

I enjoyed my lessons and the library, but for the most part, school to me was a sort of temporary exile from Summer Madness. Umwinsidale had Liz Warrender and Sandy Knight-Bruce. They were Lloyd's friends, but I soon came to see them as part of my life. Liz must have been in her fifties then, a weathered woman with leathery skin who wore jodhpurs every day I saw her, except on the day of Poppy's funeral.

She smelled of a combination of gin, Charlie perfume and manure, with a dash of wet dog thrown in. She was the source of almost everything I knew about Lloyd's family: Lloyd had inherited her from Poppy. 'If the dog does not bite you', the sign on Liz's gate said, 'the owner will shoot you. If you survive you will be prosecuted.' Her cocker spaniel, Russet, was a mass of nerves and allergies. There was no dog more terrified of anything that moved.

Liz needed more protection from her maid, Rebecca, than from outside trespassers. Liz no longer knew how many times she had sacked Rebecca, but each time, Rebecca refused to go. Even when she did not pay her, Rebecca still stayed, helping herself to anything Liz left lying around. When Liz confronted her about the thefts, Rebecca insisted that the things were hers.

'That's my bag,' said Liz.

'No, medem,' Rebecca said. 'It is mine.'

'I know perfectly well what is mine, Rebecca.'

'You are mistaken, medem,' Rebecca said.

From Rebecca's mouth, the word medem fell with a particular contempt that was more pointed than if Rebecca had called Liz by her first name.

Liz often snuck into Rebecca's quarters to steal back her things, and Rebecca would take them again. This is how things were with them; Rebecca would steal something, and Liz would take it back.

Liz's house was often filled with Rebecca's relatives. They walked along Umwinsidale Drive in little knots, with little bundles on their heads. It was not unusual for Liz to walk into her kitchen and find Rebecca laughing with two women she had never seen as they drank her tea. 'This is my sister, medem. This is my aunt. They are staying a few days only, just a few days.'

The few days would turn into months, and Liz would retreat in fear, feeling like an interloper in her own home.

She could easily have sold her house to move into a smaller place, but she could not bear to leave her horse, Copperplate. She could not afford to keep him, so she housed him at the Compton-Jones's stud farm on Hazlemere Lane. In exchange for Copperplate's keep, she trained and exercised their horses. No one understood horses like Liz; she had remedies for colic that were better than any vet's.

She had been a jockey once, one of Rhodesia's only female jockeys, she said, but that lot couldn't put up with her. She was paid far less than she was worth; like her servants, the Compton-Joneses thought they were doing her a favour.

Whenever Liz came over, Lloyd would say, 'Quick, hide the gin. Here comes Liz, on the cadge again.' But the gin bottle would come out all the same.

In Mharapara Street, MaiWhizi peered through the curtains and polished her veranda. Liz was more direct; she simply went from house to house, picking up as much as she left behind. I soon discovered that she came to know as much as she did because she and Lloyd were the only whites in Umwinsidale who spoke fluent Shona. Liz picked up her gossip from the maids and gardeners.

She liked to tell the story of how she had gone one night to the compound that had sprouted behind her house, and was offered a drink of *masese*, a traditional beer drunk from a shared container, by Rebecca's son. Never one to turn down a free drink, she had taken up the proffered calabash, drunk deeply and passed it on to the next drinker. From that night had come the nickname her domestics gave her, Mukanya, not only for her monkey-like face, but also as a sign that she was one of them, and accordingly deserved a totem name.

The other neighbour that I saw often was Sandy Knight-Bruce, who lived in a cottage on Hazlemere Lane. He could have been any age from thirty-five to sixty. Like the waiter in the Shaw play we did for O level, he seemed to be a man whom age could not wither, because he had never bloomed. He played three musical instruments, and had wanted to be a concert violinist, but he thought his face too ugly. 'No one wants to see a violin below *this*, my dear,' he used to say. I had seen uglier faces in Mufakose, faces disfigured by scars, and thought he was not as hideous as all that.

Sandy's great vanity was that he was descended from Edward Plantagenet. He had spent most of his life working on a family tree that proved one of his ancestors was born on the wrong side of the Plantagenet sheets. As further confirmation of his royal lineage, he had a huge portrait of his presumed ancestral monarch in his living room, and always made sure to sit in a chair beneath it, the better to draw the eye of the viewer to the resemblance. But as the resemblance was really confined to the hairstyle, I often reflected that I, too, would have resembled Edward Plantagenet if I had worn my hair as he did.

For every day that I knew him, Sandy wore a cricket jersey and cream flannel trousers with white canvas shoes. He was going bald but that did not prevent him from wearing what little remained of his hair long, reaching his shoulders, while at the same time affecting one of those sweep-overs that are supposed to give the illusion of hair. He looked like a cross between the incarnation of Doctor Who played by Peter Davison and a male version of Miss Havisham.

I had no facility at all for music and never got beyond the basics. I preferred to be riding or reading instead of doing endless scales. It was just as well, because Sandy was not a particularly good teacher.

A typical lesson would see me sitting at the piano, hitting the wrong notes while Sandy winced in mock pain. He would then show me how to play it right, then he would play another piece to illustrate the mechanics of the first, and then another piece, and yet another, until he ended up playing his favourite songs to me, before ending the lesson with, 'There, dear child, you see how really simple it is.'

After the lesson, I ate Sandy's biscuits and drank Mazoe while he talked about the play he had seen that week. 'You should have seen it, dear one – oh, the spectacle, the impact!'

We soon abandoned all pretence of lessons, and instead I sat while he showed me his albums of press cuttings. When he was feeling less cheerful, he talked at length about Eastern mysticism, about chakras and auras and transcendental meditation. He had also met Lord Lucan and dined with him on a tea estate in Kenya. 'Sat there, he did, quiet as anything,' Sandy said. 'Not a peep from him. Not one blasted word to anyone the whole evening. Smoked a hundred cigarettes if he smoked one.'

With Liz I passed my time much more profitably, riding on the Umwinsidale downs or in her dog-smelling house, looking through her jockeys' autographs. Pride of place went to Lester

Piggott, Fernando Toro and Johnny Sellers, who had all been racing at one time or the other at Borrowdale Park.

I loved the story of the peppered moth. I did not see it then as science, but as a story, simplified in my mind so that I saw always the same moth fluttering through time, *Biston betularia*, the predominantly white-coloured moth with its dark speckles perching on the clean trees of pre-industrial England, more common and surviving longer than its predominantly black-coloured cousins.

Then, as mankind progressed and machines spewed the triumph of their industrial ingenuity into the countryside, soot collected on the trees and the black-coloured moths with white speckles prevailed over their white cousins, survived hidden from predatory birds, camouflaged by the soot of ages. And as England cleaned itself up again, the predominantly white-coloured moth reappeared.

I loved the story of the peppered moth because it seemed to me that it was the only creature that understood what it was to be black and white. Like the peppered moth, I adapted to my changing environments. Then Poppy had that last fateful stroke and died, and Lloyd and I met Zenzo and everything changed between us.

7

More than fifty women came in two trucks last Thursday, an unusually large number to arrive all at once. They chanted, danced and ululated as they entered the prison. The guards were forced to dispense with the usual routine.

Synodia's voice was drowned out by the chanting and singing. They were simply herded into the cells as they were. There were not enough uniforms for all the women, so they were spared the humiliation of casting off their clothes while Mathilda and Patience examined their naked bodies.

They sang all night and stamped their feet. In the canteen in the morning, they shook their bottoms at the guards as they performed vulgar dances to popular church songs, replacing the Satan of the original lyrics with the government.

Their arrival was our first real imitation of the upheavals outside Chikurubi. For the last year, the election has been just another thing happening outside, an external event that has little to do with our reality here. With these new prisoners, the election finally came to the prison. They were all supporters of the opposition party and had been rounded up by the police after a riot in one of the townships. Their frenzied denunciations of the government, their fearless confidence, were our first intimation that there might be change on the horizon.

The new prisoners had not learned that the only response is

deference – instant and absolute deference – eyes down, humility in every movement, submission in the tone of voice. At the prayer meeting the next morning, the women interrupted Synodia with long and loud prayers interlaced with political slogans. When Synodia tried to lead them in a song, they openly defied her. Instead, they sang their own party songs. Two of the women stood with their backs to Synodia, shaking their bottoms in rhythm to the music.

At breakfast, they refused to eat the food and instead sang and jumped on the tables. Truncheons and whistles failed to quell the riot, and it was only after Synodia called for guards from the men's section that any order was restored at all.

We spent the weekend in lockdown, leaving only when the guards from the male section came to shepherd us to meals. On Monday morning, the guards came back and pushed the new women roughly out of the cells and into the truck. I thought they were going to court, but Loveness told me that they were simply being moved to another place. 'It's how they deal with these opposition people,' she said.

~ ~ ~ ~ ~ ~ ~ ~ ~ ~

He is very successful now, Zenzo. If you know any of our artists, you will know him, because he is the most famous of them all. Perhaps you know him by that other, longer name, the new name that he gave himself to show the world that he is authentically authentic, genuinely genuine in the genuine fullness of his authentic Africanness.

He has had exhibitions round the world. Once, in a small gallery in Melbourne, I walked in and found myself face to face with his work. Another time, in London, I picked up the *Review*, the magazine that came with the *Observer*, and found him smouldering at me from the cover. 'His single-mindedness is impressive,' said his interviewer. Indeed it is.

When I think of him, I sometimes think of his girlfriend. Poor Sigrid. He mocked her often, imitating her accent, making sounds that he claimed she made when they were having sex. I did not see this as the cruelty that it was. I did not question at all that this was a violation of the worst kind. I thought she deserved it because she had what she had no right to: him. Sigrid was important to him, of course, because she was his ticket out of the country.

Lloyd and I were mere conveniences, but Sigrid was a necessity. When I look back to how things were between us, I have to face the reality that the only reason he was ever with me was because I pretty much threw myself at him and said, here I am, take me. The only reason that he ever looked at me at all was because I presented myself to him. I made myself available to him.

As I said, he is a famous artist now. He has been commissioned to paint huge, expensive murals in cities like Berlin and Tokyo and Geneva. People who know these things, the in-people, know that distinctive slashed-Z signature.

'I fled with nothing but the paint-splattered clothes that I had on,' he said in one interview.

His career has risen with our country's collapse. His paintings are different from the realist paintings that he said he wanted to paint. It is all tortured faces and screaming mouths now, slashed genitals and dismembered breasts. 'Evocative images of his tortured homeland,' as the reviewers will have you believe.

His painting speaks truths that the government wants to hide, it is said. He is the artist exiled from his homeland because his work shows a reality before which the government flinches.

None of it is true, but who cares for truth when there is a troubled homeland and tortured artists to flee from it? The more prosaic truth is that he did not flee, but rather left on the arm of his German girlfriend, on a ticket bought with her Deutschmarks, and that, having gone to Germany, he got himself a nice new passport before he traded her in for someone richer. I can't even say that he fled from my malevolence, because that was only ever directed at Lloyd.

This new Zenzo came into being much later, many years after Lloyd and I first met him. I had not thought that I would ever see him again, but I did. It was not my doing but Simon's. He thought it would be a treat for me to see someone from my own country. Nothing delighted Simon more than thrusting some countryman or other upon me. I sometimes think that I disappointed him because I was not African enough. I had no national dress, no foods of tantalising exoticism.

When Simon heard about Zenzo's panel at the Fitzwilliam, he insisted that we had to go. It was then that I learned that Zenzo now lived in Berlin.

Zenzo had lost the dreadlocks. He was still very good-looking – better-looking, in fact, than he had ever been. Money and success became him. I had already learned from the *Observer* interview that he had reinvented his past when he renamed himself.

He had wiped out Sigrid from his biography. He had not fucked his way to Europe, no, not Zenzo – he had left because he was persecuted for his art. He would only go back when his country was free. And the distinctive scar on his right hand, the hand that had once stroked mine, the scar he had told me was the legacy of sneaking across the barbed wire to steal tobacco leaves from the farm next door: that had come from a knife fight during ethnic battles in the township where he grew up.

At the reception afterwards, Simon wanted me to meet him. It seemed easier to go along, and besides, a part of me was curious to see if he would recognise me.

'I know you,' he said. 'Memory.'

He gave me a hug that I did not return. I found myself wrapped in his scent. This was certainly a new Zenzo, a more expensive one. His eyes darted about, looking at everyone but the person who was actually before him at the time.

As I watched him work the room, I wondered for the first time what it was that Lloyd had felt for Zenzo. And I hoped – I longed to know – that it had not been love.

~ ~ ~ ~ ~ ~ ~ ~ ~

Poppy died in the September just after I turned seventeen. By then, I had been living with Lloyd for almost eight years. My life in Mufakose seemed like a parallel episode in someone else's life.

I could, at times, persuade myself that this life, the life that took in the Convent and Summer Madness, my horse, my books and the dogs, had always been my life.

My dreams no longer troubled me as much as they had when I first arrived. In those moments when I forgot how I came to live with Lloyd, I found myself warming to him.

Unlike Ian, who would later spend the last pain-wracked months of his life at Island Hospice, Poppy spent her last days in her own bed. Namatai came to the house the morning after the evening of her death to tell us that she had gone. I went with

Lloyd to see her. She looked fragile in death. Lloyd kissed the papery skin of her forehead.

She had wanted to have her ashes scattered at the same place her husband's ashes had been, in Matopos National Park. It had been her favourite place when the Commissioner was alive. They had spent every anniversary of their marriage there.

We drove in a convoy of three cars to the Matopos hills. It was a family tradition. 'We don't do it for Rhodes,' said Lloyd. 'We do it for the Matopos. You will see what I mean, Memory. I hope you remember that when I go, I want my ashes there too.'

I am sure you have been to the Matopos by now; it is the 'must-see' place in every tourist guide. Rhodes's grave is there, as is Allan Wilson's of the Shangani Patrol, and Leander Starr Jameson too. But before they were buried there, it was a holy shrine, to Umgulumgulu, the god of the sky. The people who lived in the surrounding areas regarded it as a sacred place that was full of magic and power.

I saw immediately why Poppy would want her final rest there. As I stood next to Lloyd, at the top of the world, the graves of Rhodes and Jameson and Allan Wilson before us, I could not help but be affected by the splendour of the stillness.

The air seemed alive with the spirits of the nameless dead. I was struck by the hushed glory of this beautiful place, and I understood why the Ndebele had held it to be sacred, and why its eerie, peculiar beauty had so attracted Rhodes, and why the Commissioner and Poppy and Lloyd would want their ashes scattered here.

As Lloyd scattered Poppy's ashes up into the whispering trees, my mind went to the only other funeral that I had attended, Mobhi's funeral, my mother almost jumping into the ground with her, and where the frenetic dancers raised dust around the grave as the drumbeat thundered.

But there were no wailing voices in Matopos, no mother to jump into the grave. Only Lloyd and Ian, Liz and Sandy, Namatai and me.

Lloyd made a short speech about how much Poppy had loved this place. He wanted to come here when he too died, he said. Every time he came here he felt he was in a place where nature had begun, and it felt like the last place that would be here when it all ended. Alexandra read from a poem that she had chosen. 'I am not there, I do not sleep,' she said.

A small gust of wind took up the ashes, danced with them a little before blowing them over us. 'I am not there,' muttered Sandy as he wiped his face, 'but I am in your hair.'

I was afraid to laugh because I feared that if I opened my mouth, bits of Poppy would find themselves down my throat. Poppy's ashes fell on the flowers; the wind carried them into the trees and into the air around the top of the world and far into the distance.

8

Lloyd saw Zenzo before I did. We were at a garden party thrown by the Compton-Joneses. They threw a summer party in June, which, of course, is winter here, but they were not people to let an inconvenient thing like being in the wrong hemisphere get in the way of what they considered unassailable English traditions.

Tim and Val Compton-Jones spoke in the kind of accents that made them sound like they had been taken from one of those Thames Television productions that were screened on ZBC all the time in the eighties. An hour in their house made you feel like you were an extra in a Bizarro version of *To the Manor Born* or some other drama about distressed gentlefolk in the English countryside.

Tim Compton-Jones aimed to look like a jovial country squire, if, that is, a country squire wore khaki shorts and shirts and Farmer shoes all the time. His laugh was a loud braying sound, and he began his sentences with 'I say', and, in imitation, Lloyd and I took to beginning sentences like he did.

'I say, old chap, it is raining rather hard, what?'

'I say, old bean, the fire needs another log.'

'I say, old chap, I need money for the school bus.'

'I say, my foot,' said Liz. 'He grew up in Karoi. I know his family. None of them sound like that – his brother Dennis wouldn't know a Pimm's if you poured it down his arse.'

Lloyd replied that Tim had got his accent when he married Val. She had one of those frozen faces with precisely matching eyebrows, like she was Botoxed to the eyeballs even before the invention of Botox. Her hair was sprayed into such stiffness that it seemed as though nothing could move it, not even the blistering high wind of an August day.

Lloyd used to say that her voice was exactly like Sybil Fawlty's. 'She sounds,' he said, 'like a seal being machine-gunned.' But I was reading Stephen King by the bucketful, and privately thought that she spoke like the wife in *Pet Sematary* after she had been brought back to life, or like her voice was being filtered through a cement mixer.

Theirs was a highly stylised simulacrum of England. Their garden boys sweated as they trimmed their bushes into topiary animal shapes. Val Compton-Jones had yet to meet an indigenous tree that she did not want uprooted and replaced with a foreign import. Liz made sour observations about all the water that the trees absorbed, how their wretched gums and firs lowered the water table, how they had long roots, and took more water than they should.

They held carols by candlelight at which children lisped about chestnuts and sang about the holly and ivy, and St George's Day celebrations in which they chewed overdone roasts. At their parties, the children played croquet, and the adults tennis, the players in blinding white, as if they were just minutes away from stepping onto Centre Court. They would have fled in horror from the real England, with its Indians, Pakistanis and Jamaicans.

Lloyd would not normally have gone to the Compton-Joneses' summer party, but he had been talking for some time about how I had no friends in the valley. Bridget Compton-Jones was at the Convent with me, but I had never seen her outside school. When

I told him that I would rather stay at home, he said, 'Just think of all the other children who will be there.'

It seemed to have escaped him that I met any number of other children during the week. And that I never actually enjoyed the youth dances he drove me to at the Anglican Cathedral, where I stood drinking Fanta while people danced badly to Dire Straits and David Scobie. And I was seventeen, after all; in another year I would be at university. I knew about existentialism and solipsism. I had read Sartre and was reading Camus.

The only attraction of the party was the drinks. I was much more interested in tasting the Pimm's than anything else.

I was working out how I could get a drink without Lloyd noticing. I headed for Liz. She had elbowed a waiter, delaying him so that she could finish the drink she held and take another before he moved on. 'Tally-ho,' she said in an exaggerated accent. 'You are here, then, are you?'

I offered to hold her drink for her. She picked two from the tray and handed them both to me. 'In the language of the old country,' she said, 'chin-chin.'

She knocked back her glass and handed it me, taking one of the two full glasses that I held. I could not resist drinking from the remaining glass. It was just as delicious as it looked. I drank it in quick gulps. A heady feeling began to sweep over me. Everything was lovely and green; the hedge animals looked as though they were about to stretch and prance across the lawn. The laughter seemed louder than any laughter I had ever heard. The grass was dazzling green. The powder blue of Val Compton-Jones's eye-shadow was as one with the sky. She dazzled, they all dazzled, I dazzled.

It was in this state that I saw Zenzo. He was the only other guest there who was not white. The only other black people there were the staff: the maids in colourful uniforms, the men in white shirts and black trousers, carrying glasses and food.

He stood in jeans and a black tee-shirt with Bob Marley on it. He wore his hair in dreadlocks. I stared at him as though my eyes were on stalks. He had white eyes and a smile as white as the tennis clothes around him. I could not take my eyes away from his hair.

Dreadlocks are much more ubiquitous now than they were then, so you may not understand how shocking it was to see a man in dreadlocks at a party in Umwinsidale. Dreadlocks were what the Bob Marley on his shirt wore: they belonged to another world, of Rastafarianism, which nobody understood, but everyone frowned on.

I had only ever seen two people with dreadlocks: the homeless man who slept at the Post Office in town and the son of one of MaiWhizi's brothers, who had once visited her. That nephew had dreadlocks, and everyone had crowded around him because MaiWhizi had said he did not eat meat. No one in the township actually believed that there was a person alive who could refuse to eat meat; Nhau got Whizi and her sisters to watch him to see if he ate meat.

And here before my eyes was this beautiful young man with dreadlocks. I believe that I would have noticed him even without the dreadlocks because he was the most beautiful person I had ever seen. It seemed to me that he was standing a little apart, watching the party and taking it in. The people around him did not seem to know what to make of him.

I looked around to see whom he could be linked to.

When Val Compton-Jones introduced him to Lloyd, I made

sure to get closer. I walked up to them and put my hand in Lloyd's. I was not normally this demonstrative, and Lloyd looked at me. He squeezed my hand as he said, 'Have you exhibited much?'

'Have you exhibited much?' I said.

Lloyd shot me a probing look.

Before the man could talk, a woman came up to him. She put her arm through his. Young as I was, I recognised it for what it was, an act of claiming. And she was so old, I thought, so old you could see wrinkles around her face.

They introduced themselves as Sigrid and Zenzo. They had just moved into Hazlemere Cottage, the small house on the Compton-Joneses' estate. She was a German economist. She worked for a German foundation in town, she said.

He was an artist from Bulawayo.

I knew then, of course, about sex. Sister Gilberta in biology had told us all about it in clinical, dry-as-dust terms, the spermatozoa, and fallopian tubes, complete with line drawings. Jackie Collins, Harold Robbins and Jacqueline Susann had filled in the rest. That this beautiful young man, Zenzo, should be with old Sigrid, that he should be making her melt and tremble while thrusting his manhood at her and filling her uterus with spermatozoa, which was expelled if there was no conception to form a zygote, seemed unutterably grotesque. He was young, as I would find out, only twenty-four, and she was thirty-seven.

He was beautiful; she was not.

They moved on to join another group and my eyes followed them, or at least him. While Lloyd was distracted, I downed his Pimm's, too.

The next thing I remember is waking up in my room. Lloyd had carried me to the car, as I had passed out.

~ ~ ~ ~ ~ ~ ~ ~ ~

I saw him again when I was riding. I had been riding for more than three years now, and Liz trusted me out on my own. He was walking down Umwinsidale Drive. I recognised him at once. As I nudged Pugsley into Hazlemere, preparing to go home, I saw him.

'The light here is good,' he said. 'This is how it must have been for Vermeer in Delft.'

I had no idea what he was talking about, but I memorised the names. I went to Lloyd's *Encyclopaedia Britannica*. The next time that I saw him, I said, very quickly, 'Vermeer was born in Delft.'

I need not have bothered with Vermeer. He had been looking for me, he said, he had walked this way hoping that I would ride past. 'I want to paint you,' he said.

'Will I have to take my clothes off?' I said.

He laughed and said, 'It is not necessary.'

I saw at once that this was the only way I would ever see him on my own. Surprised by my own boldness, I said, 'Do you want to start now?'

At his laugh, my heart plummeted down into my stomach, where it turned to water. He was busy at that moment, he said. We agreed to meet the following day. It was the holidays, so I had the whole day free.

The next day, I walked down the valley and up to Hazlemere Manor. He was waiting in the cottage. He smoked. Then he said, come here, and he held and then kissed me playfully, and then not so playfully. I was caught up in the smell of him, a mixture of cigarette smoke and sweat, and something else, a smell that seized all my senses.

I found out all about him. Like me, he was the third child in his family, but they were seven. He had gone to schools in Bulawayo and had transferred to Harare to attend the Birch School of Art. He talked to me as he worked, about the work he wanted to do and the work he had to do. No one, he said, was interested in visual art from here – it was all sculpture in serpentine and soapstone.

He wanted to be a Vermeer, a Brueghel, a Lucian Freud. He did not care for abstract art at all; he wanted to be a realist painter in the old school, he said. Until he could get to be what he wanted, he had to be what the world wanted him to be: a sculptor of headless women with jutting breasts and bulging bottoms.

He drew me on my horse, a delicate pencil sketch. I sometimes wish I had kept it – it would have been worth a lot of money now. Instead, I tore it up in the passion of my rage.

So this was love. I felt like I was riding at breakneck speed, the exhilaration tempered only by the fear that my horse would stop suddenly and I would find myself hurtling over and onto the ground. I lurched between fear and longing, between triumphant certainty and aching insecurity.

Everything was much more vivid. How lovely was the sky! And yet everything was so much more terrible. Why did time move so slowly? Why did Sister Hedwig talk so much? What mattered the French Revolution, what mattered the organic formula for lithium, what mattered the peppered moth, when there was something bigger than this classroom, than all classrooms?

He liked Queen, he liked Black Umfolosi, he liked Lovemore Majaivana. I loved Queen. I worshipped Black Umfolosi. I adored Lovemore Majaivana. He peppered the language with his own. A simple word like *wena* came to mean more than just you. 'You' was ordinary, prosaic. *Wena* invited me in; it said I existed to him.

On his lips, the word *faka*, simply meaning to put, was imbued with thrilling meanings.

He laughed at my accent; until he mimicked me back to myself, I had not realised how my voice had taken on the voices of those around me. I had not realised how much of the Convent was in me, how much of Liz, of Lloyd and Sandy. I wanted to stamp out my voice. I liked the sound of his voice, the way he said bottley instead of bottle, cattley instead of cattle and wiggley when he meant wiggle. He did not take it well: we fought when he thought I was making fun of him. Imitation, in this case, was no flattery.

I shut out thoughts of Sigrid.

He was mine, not hers; rightfully mine. That is how I thought of him, in the possessive mode. There was a claim of ownership, a sense that we belonged. My claim, my stake in him, was nothing more than my love for him, but it was enough. It was everything. Sigrid's existence simply fortified my love for him. To me, she did not exist in her own right: she existed only to test our love.

I look back now at my time with Zenzo, and then I look at my brief life with Simon, and I wonder that I should have given myself so completely to someone who so obviously did not love me. Simon wanted me; he loved me; he wanted to heal me. He gave me the very best of himself, his devotion; he plied his troth to me. All I had to do was to take what he offered.

I want to believe that I know a little more now about people than I did then. Then I thought that Zenzo was just moody. I thought that he was pouring his soul into his work. I see now that he used his art, and would always use his art, as a cover to get what he wanted, and as an excuse to be less than he knew he should be.

As I lay in his arms in that cottage on Hazlemere, I fantasised about our life together. Europe was our focus: it was where we aimed the trajectory of our dreams. He would look at paintings, and I the buildings that contained them. It was a beautiful fantasy, a dream, which came crashing down the day I found him with Lloyd.

9

When Loveness brought me the newspaper today after lock-up, she was in a voluble mood. She talked about her daughter. Her daughter's condition was better, her daughter's teachers were still bad, her daughter's uniforms needed taking in. I wanted to say that I knew about the damn uniforms because I ironed them every week, but I said nothing and instead tried to read the headlines from the newspaper she was waving in her hand. My mind was on the election, and it was only with effort that I heard her say that her daughter's father left her when the child was a baby. 'He could not cope with what, with her condition.'

My mind wandered until she said, 'Memory, did you hear me? You are eating *matemba* today.'

The big smile on her face suggested that I should be giddy with excitement. The Goodwill Fellowship had donated sacks and sacks of the stuff, she explained, and we were to have some for our supper. I was clearly supposed to be excited about this, which I suppose I should be, as the Goodwill Fellowship usually just donates Bibles along with lashings of sympathy. My immediate thought was that the Goodwill Fellowship must have donated more *matemba* fish than the prison guards could steal.

I am certain that Synodia, Loveness, Patience and the rest of the guards have not had to buy toilet rolls or sanitary pads in months. Or toothpaste. Or soap. Or washing powder. Or anything else that can be carried off to use at home. So when she said that we were to have *matemba* for about a month I could only imagine that they must have driven entire lorries of the stuff to the prison. We get only what the prison guards choose not to take.

It is strange how associations can come just from a fractured image, a phrase, a word, a smell. It was while she was talking of how lucky we were to have this bounty that I remembered the only time that I met Simon's mother and father, Domenica and Hugo. I could see as soon as I met them that Simon had only told his parents where I was from, but not what I looked like.

I had developed by then the affectation of braiding my hair into long plaits that matched the colour of my skin to produce a somewhat otherworldly effect. Simon, in the first giddy moments when we could not stop touching each other, said I looked like something that lived in the water, like the Ondine.

When we sat down to dinner, Domenica startled me by asking, 'Are you Matemba?'

'Am I what?' I said.

'Matemba. That's it, isn't it, darling, that thing I read you the other night? It was the Matemba, wasn't it?'

Without waiting for an answer from her husband, she continued, 'Or was it Malemba? No, it was definitely Matemba. The Matemba people. They have a forgiveness ceremony, don't they, darling?' To the rest of us, she added, 'In the middle of the night. The whole village comes out and sings. Then the person who did whatever it is stands in the middle and everyone sings, we forgive you, we forgive you.'

'*Matemba*,' I said, 'are very small fish.'

'Small fish?'

'Yes, also called *kapenta*. From Zambia.'

Her husband, who had turned to speak to Simon, now broke away to hear the tail end of the conversation. 'The Matemba people are Zambians? I thought you said they were from Zimbabwe.'

'Well, yes, but they are fish, apparently,' said Domenica.

She gave me a look that was almost accusatory. 'Are you sure?' she asked. 'When were you last there?'

'I have eaten the fish myself,' I said. 'But maybe these Matemba people have sprung to life since I left two years ago. Like the earth-grown men.'

'Well, it must be some other Africans, then,' she said.

Domenica began to talk about something else. I focused on the wine. I had never lived in a village or even been to one, but I could not imagine any villagers, between the harvesting and the tilling, between the water-fetching and the shifting cultivation, having time to stand and murmur forgiveness chants in circles in the middle of the night. I know I did not convince Domenica because I heard her tell that story again at another, bigger dinner party.

Since that night, this mysterious forgiveness ceremony has popped up many times in other places, always attributed to different tribes. It even appeared in your magazine, in an excerpt from the memoir of an American writer who always looks as though she is weighed down by both the thickness of her dreadlocks and the ponderousness of her prose.

I can see, I suppose, the attractiveness of it.

It speaks to the human need for validation, for acceptance, for belonging. It affirms the power of words. It says that words can be even more powerful than deeds; that dreadful acts can be wiped out by the simple sincerity of the right combination of words; it speaks to the power of contrition. If you say you are sorry enough, often enough, you can wipe out pain.

'I stole maize that did not belong to me.'

'We forgive you.'

'My cow wandered into the wrong pasture.'

'We forgive you.'

Even as I pour scorn on this forbearing tribe, I wonder what would it be like to have my own little village of all the people I have known, standing and saying they forgive me. Mostly it is Lloyd. He died before I could tell him how sorry I was, before I asked him if he forgave me. I long for him to speak to me, to say to me, 'I forgive you, I forgive you, I forgive you.'

~ ~ ~ ~ ~ ~ ~ ~ ~ ~

It was all because of a cancelled hockey game. Played in the winter months, when the sun burned less, hockey was one of the games that I could play and I made a competent right wing for the second team. On that afternoon, we were supposed to play Arundel School, but when we got there we found there had been a mix-up about the dates. The school allowed us to go home early. When I got home, I saw Lloyd's car. I looked for him but he was not in any of the places that he usually was if he was home. The first thing that told me I was not alone was the murmur of voices.

I followed the sounds to Lloyd's room. The door was slightly open. The laugh came again, Lloyd's laugh rich with happiness. And then the murmur became Zenzo's voice. Without thinking, now only reacting, I pushed the door ajar. Zenzo was sitting up, smoking, laughing down at Lloyd, who lay looking up at him from his pillow. They did not see me at once. Lloyd looked up and Zenzo laughed. On Lloyd's face I saw something that might have appeared in my own face. And in Zenzo's face, I saw something that I recognised as reciprocity, acceptance.

Lloyd turned and saw me. This was the tableau: Lloyd's face of horror, Zenzo's disappearing smile, the bed, the smoke wafting up to the ceiling, the men.

My blood froze to form sharp pins of ice that stabbed me with their heat. I must have made a sound. Zenzo said something. With his left hand, Lloyd grabbed a shirt from the floor and ran towards me, his right arm outstretched.

'Don't touch me,' I said. 'Don't come near me.'

He stopped, as though recoiling from my hatred.

I turned to leave the room before I could cry.

In the many years that followed that day, after I had moved away and could look back with a calmer mind, I finally began to think about Lloyd's life, about Tracey Collins, the woman in the photograph with the Farrah Fawcett hair and thick glasses, the woman who served as a protection to blind the world to what he was. I thought about what it meant to live in a country where you could never share such an essential part of yourself.

Many things made sense all at once: Alan Milhouse, the women he refused to be involved with, the strange voices that I heard at night. I did not think all of this at the time. I hated Lloyd. He repulsed me. I felt contaminated by him. I could not make the imaginative leap that would have made me see how trapped he was, that could have made me see the lie he was constantly forced to live.

I judged him with all the prudish and priggish self-righteousness of a Catholic schoolgirl with narrow, dogma-driven certainties.

In the years since the shock of that moment, I have come to

understand Lloyd. Even as I write this, I see how presumptuous it is for me to say that. If I had been mature enough I could have seen how lonely he was, how terrifying it was to live in a country that did not accept you. Not even Lloyd's whiteness could have saved him from the stigma of homosexuality because it is a stigma that cuts across race and tribe and religion and class and sex and political beliefs and all the artificial divisions this country has erected to keep people apart.

If I had been mature enough or had sufficient imagination, or generosity of spirit, I might have seen that Lloyd was as different to those around him as I was, that the fact of our difference bound us. But I felt only repugnance.

Would I have seen things differently if the object of his affection were not also the object of mine? Because I also hated him with all the passion of scorned love. But if I am honest I will admit my prejudice. I was as much a victim of my society as anyone else.

But the sin, for such I considered it, was nothing compared to this ghastly situation in which he was now my rival for Zenzo.

I saw him as someone who had taken away everyone that I had loved. I forgot the privations of my earlier life; I disregarded everything he had ever given me. I saw only the wrong that he had done me. He had taken the one person who made me happy.

In the hot fever of my pain, I saw him as existing only to block my happiness. I remembered every disagreement, every small thing he had ever denied me. My family – he had bought me from my family and now he had taken Zenzo. It was grotesque to be love rivals with someone who stood in place of my father. I did not stop to consider that Zenzo might have had his own agency. It was all Lloyd. Alone in my room, I slapped my face hard enough to leave angry red welts.

The next day, he tried to talk to me. I hurled at him my disgust and abhorrence. 'Is this why you bought me? To make me see what you do? Is this why you brought me here?'

His face went white as he said, 'What on earth do you mean, I bought you?'

'You know very well what I mean,' I flung at him. 'I saw it all, at Barbours, remember? I was there. I may have been a child but I know what I saw.'

He walked away without talking and I was left to enjoy the savage satisfaction of my victory.

The next day I saw that he had put a letter for me under my door. It would be full of justification, I thought, and burned it in the fireplace without reading it. For the rest of the week, I stayed away from him. I took myself to school, and shut myself in my room as soon as I heard him come into the house.

Without knowing it, Zenzo gave me the idea for my revenge. The morning after I found him with Lloyd, he came to the house. I was sitting at the kitchen table, trying to eat toast and marmalade as I read.

I looked up from my toast to find him staring at me. I stood up quickly and went to the door. 'You can't tell anyone what you saw,' he said. 'You can't.'

I tried to push past him but he held my hands. 'Please,' he said, intending a caress. 'I get that you hate me right now.'

He put his hand on my waist, as though to draw me to him. I was filled with anger and outrage. I fought myself free.

'If anyone finds out, if for any reason the police get involved, I mean, do you really want me to be in trouble?'

Even then he was thinking of himself; he had no thought at all for Lloyd. I pushed myself from him violently, and tried to pass the door. Lloyd stepped into the kitchen. Immediately to my mind's eye came the two of them, naked on Lloyd's bed.

I managed to reach the door. As I left, I heard Lloyd say to him, 'You have to go.'

'She could tell someone – you have to stop her.' Zenzo's voice was now a whiney panic.

I moved out of earshot, but not before I had seen Lloyd stretch out his hand and pull Zenzo into an embrace.

That is what decided me.

I wrote to the police. 'There is a man who is committing sodomy with other men. His name is Lloyd Hendricks and he teaches at University of Zimbabwe.'

I dropped the note in the police box at Highlands. I do not know what I wanted, what I expected to happen. Almost as soon as I dropped that note in the police box, I regretted it. But I could not unpost it, so I let it be. Things continued as they had before. Then Lloyd didn't come home one night.

He didn't come home the next day.

Alan Milhouse came over, worried and anxious. Ian and Alexandra drove down from Chipinge. Liz and Sandy came to ask every day. They held a conference, Alan and Alexandra and Ian. Alan said Lloyd had missed their usual lunch in the Senior Common Room. He had gone to Lloyd's department and found his rooms empty. Someone in the department said the police had come for him, but that could not be true, could it?

Only Alan thought to ask me if I knew anything about where Lloyd might have gone. But it never occurred to him that I might have anything to do with it.

Alan then suggested calling all the hospitals, and the police stations. They drove to all the hospitals and inquired at every station.

They finally found him at Highlands police station, two weeks after he had disappeared, and three times after they had been to ask. He had refused to sign an admission of guilt. They had no knowledge of the other party, as the police described Zenzo. All they had was an anonymous accusation. It was impossible for them to prosecute.

On the night that he came back, I stood behind the door in the next room and listened to their conversation.

'I had hoped all that was over when you met Sue,' Alexandra said.

She put her arms around him and he put his head on her shoulder. As I moved away from the door, our eyes met across Alexandra's shoulder. I knew without needing to hear it from him that he knew that it was I. Later, as I lay in my room, reading in bed, I heard his footsteps at my door. I thought he might come in, but after a pause I heard him move back to his own room.

10

From the laundry room where Monalisa, Evernice and I were ironing yesterday, I heard running feet, muffled voices and then shouted voices. The sounds seemed to come from the admissions office at the end of the corridor. Evernice ran out into the corridor. Monalisa and I continued with the ironing.

She returned ten minutes later, her eyes shining.

'That *n'anga* woman is here,' she said.

Evernice ran back into the corridor without explaining what she meant. I continued alone. It was only when Synodia and Patience arrived to collect the ironed clothes that I understood what she had meant.

They were talking at the same time. I had never seen Synodia that animated outside one of her church services.

Evernice said, 'Have you heard that the diesel *n'anga* is here? They finally caught her, she was about to cross into Mozambique . . .'

'Pwozambique, Pwozambique,' said Synodia. 'Who said anything about Mozambique? It was Zambia, that's where she went to buy the diesel in the first place.' Then she became almost confiding. 'In all my time here,' she said, 'I have never seen anyone so difficult. It took two whole hours just to process her. She collapsed to the floor and went into a trance. We tried to lift her, but we had to call two more guards. She was heavy, stiff, like a dead body. Like she had rigor – what is it called?'

'Do you mean rigor motion?' said Patience.

'That's right,' Synodia said, 'rigor motion.'

Synodia continued, 'She was stiff as anything, I tell you. We could hardly move her, only when she came out of it did she finally move.'

I found out then that the excitement is about the woman called Rotina Mavhunga or Nomatter Taruza. Her story was one of the things that Lloyd and I laughed about, uniting our mirth in disbelief.

You must know about her. She is that woman from Chinhoyi who convinced the Cabinet that she could make diesel come out of a rock. In exchange for this miracle, she is supposed to have received a farm and seventy billion dollars. Chinhoyi is a mystical place, of course, with its deep caves that are said to contain all sorts of *njuzu*. I am sure that on that basis alone the government believed her. She was the medium of the spirit of Changamire Dombo, she said; she was the medium of the great emperor of the Rozvi people.

Almost half the Cabinet went to her. They took off their shoes and socks. They exclaimed and clapped when the fuel came out. The women ministers ululated. All the while, behind the rock, she and her boyfriend had a tanker of diesel from Zambia.

I saw her later that day at lunch, a small, light-skinned woman with eyes like she was recovering from a hangover. She sat apart from the others. Around her women ate their *sadza* and boiled cabbage.

She belched and said, '*Mudzimu wangu unoti ndinoda nyama.*'

Synodia said, 'You can tell your spirit that it is in the wrong place. There is no meat for it here.'

She belched again and broke into song, 'Black September, *wairamba kubire* Charter *mukoma, wakatozobira watombodzu-ngudza musoro mukoma.'*

As suddenly as she had broken into song, she stopped and seemed to go into a trance. The women around her moved away.

She belched again and said again, '*Mudzimu wangu unoti ndi-noda nyama.*' She spent the rest of the lunch period belching and shaking her shoulders.

There was a commotion later when she began to sing very loudly, '*Gandanga haridye derere mukoma. Chukucha mwana weropa! Chukucha rega kudaro!*'

The guards rushed to keep her quiet. At supper that afternoon, she again insisted that her spirit demanded only meat. Again, she ate nothing. At lunch the next day I saw her wolfing down boiled cabbage like her spirit depended on it.

~ ~ ~ ~ ~ ~ ~ ~ ~

After he returned from the police cells, Lloyd and I spoke little to each other. When we spoke at all, we were stilted and formal. The air between us was heavy with what was not said. The previous Christmas, Lloyd had given me a battered Beetle. I no longer needed him to drive me to school, and took care to leave the house before he did. He left after I did, and arrived when I had long gone to bed. At weekends, he drove on his own to the cottage in Nyanga. He accepted every conference invitation that he received. I frequently found that I was alone in the house.

The tension became so unbearable that all I could think of was escape. But where could I have gone? I could not go back to Mufakose. I had no relatives who could have taken me in. And the only friends I trusted, Liz and Sandy, were more Lloyd's friends than mine.

I was desperate to escape. I knew that my only escape was a scholarship to study abroad. I threw myself into my studies. Against Sister Mary Gabriel's wishes, I opted to write my A level exams in the June of the next year, and not wait for November. And I applied to every university I could think of that was out of the country.

My efforts paid off. I did well enough to get the scholarship, and I was admitted to read history at Sidney Sussex in Cambridge.

In the first days I wrote to him long, discursive letters about my lectures and tutorials. Alexandra would say, as she said at the trial, that I wrote to him only to ask for money. She produced letters in which money was a constant complaint.

When I left, I did not come back. The only time that I returned home was for a month in the first year of my postgraduate degree. In that year, Lloyd had been on sabbatical leave in America.

I met Simon, I studied, I travelled, I was happy. I won't tell you much about Simon; he mattered to me then but does not matter to this story. The distance blunted the painful memories. The distance also allowed me to give more space to the circumstances that had brought us together. I wanted to ask why he had bought me.

But I kept it to myself. Even when I met Simon I could not tell anyone. That, like all my attempts to connect, soon fizzled away, and I was free from all the explanation and analysis that talking would have required. I had eventually come to forget it; I did not care about forgiving because forgiving meant actively remembering. I did not want to forgive because I did not want to remember.

After university, I was barely in the same place for more than six months at a time. A few months before my studies ended, one of the fellows at my college had recommended that I continue on to doctoral work. He also recommended that I spend a year at an East Coast university in the United States. I had the idea to convert my thesis on the Mutapa into something bigger. I planned to go to Portugal. I would even register for language classes at the University of Lisbon.

And then I was seized with a lassitude that made the smallest task seem like endless labour. To get to the United States required me to apply for a visa. I collected the forms; I put everything together. Then I did nothing. The thought of taking the train to London, following up on papers, submitting my passport for a visa, exhausted me. I was tired, too tired to do anything; all of it seemed too difficult; everything seemed too difficult. And so I stayed where I was, taking any job that came my way until I decided that it was finally time to go home.

~ ~ ~ ~ ~ ~ ~ ~ ~ ~

I came back to a country whose outlines I recognised, but which was different in the details. I had not been home in more than ten years. So I was not there to see for myself how quickly everything had gone wrong. All that had happened in my absence – the political paralysis, the economic collapse – had been nothing more to me than news headlines. Now it revealed itself everywhere. You arrived after everything had calmed, after the political settlement, but Vernah, who was here throughout everything that happened, can tell you all about it. It is different for Vernah and people like her, for people who were here all the time.

I had not prepared Lloyd for my arrival. I wanted to believe that he had forgiven me, but the possibility of another rejection kept me quiet.

I called him from the airport in Johannesburg, and told him simply that I would be on the flight that landed in three hours. He was waiting for me at the airport when I landed. As I saw him again after all that time, it was as though I was seeing him for the first time, really seeing him. Had he always looked so weathered? It seemed as though someone had taken out his spine and he was collapsing in on himself. And what had happened to his hair?

He waved down at me from the transparent platform overlooking the arrivals hall at the airport. I did not know what I would say to him, how I would tell him about the revolution in my ideas and feelings. Would I ever be able to talk about Zenzo? How would I overcome the constraint that had arisen between us, how would I cross the distance of all those years? I did not know how to begin to tell him all the things that I wanted to say; how to tell him that I was sorry for my betrayal.

My bags were searched and I was allowed through. I blinked in the bright light as I walked through the glass doors.

'Mnemosyne,' said Lloyd as he put his arms around me and lifted me off my feet.

And as I hugged him tightly, I realised that he knew already all that I wanted to say, and that it was unnecessary ever to say anything because he knew all that I wanted to say even without my saying it.

II

Since Loveness overheard Jimmy and Benhilda telling Monalisa that the Commissioner forced the guards to vote for the ruling party, or else they would lose their jobs, she has not brought me any more newspapers. She came to my cell during lock-up and yelled at me through the bars. I have been telling the others things they should not know, she shouted, and she had trusted me, and look what I was doing, did I want things to go back to what they had been, before the papers and the favours?

There was no point in arguing, especially as she was right that the information came from me. Since the opposition women left, the election is the talk of the prison. From the snatches we overhear from the guards, from the information filtered through visiting Sundays, it is clear that something big is happening outside, perhaps something big enough to affect us here.

Verity came back from the hospital with more news. She collapsed at the prison farm three days ago. Patience and Mathilda half-dragged, half-carried her to the sanatorium, where she lay groaning on the bed until Synodia grudgingly signed release papers for her to be taken to hospital. It was appendicitis: she returned with her appendix removed and news of the victory, her dimples straining against her face.

It was hard to resist Verity's infectious excitement as she described the spontaneous celebrations she glimpsed through the grille of the prison truck.

Things would change, she predicted. Now she would really get out. Her connections would pay off.

'But I thought that your connections were all on the side that has lost. Isn't this bad news for you?' said Jimmy.

'I have friends where it matters' was Verity's cryptic answer, and she went back to telling us all the things that she would buy in Dubai the minute she landed there. Next to her, Benhilda and Beulah spoke happily about the food that would come, and the blankets too. They only seemed uncertain about whether the new government's magnanimity would extend to fizzy drinks.

We stopped talking when Synodia and Loveness came to inspect the shirts we had ironed. Synodia looked more sour than usual, and Loveness was shorter than usual in her commands. Jimmy could not resist and said, 'Congratulations, Mbuya Guard, on the new government.'

Synodia sneered and said, 'Pwongratulations, pwongratulations. Don't talk as if it is your father's government.'

Patience added that there was nothing to celebrate because the new president would be leading a government of people who barely spoke English. 'They are all alphabets,' she said. 'Literate alphabets.'

Jimmy said, 'Well, it is still better because the last president led a government of thieves.'

Patience gave her two weeks of sanitary duty.

The excitement is less to do with a new government than with the certainty of an amnesty. 'There will be an amnesty international after the election,' said Verity. 'There is always one after an election.'

'What Amnesty International now?' said Monalisa. 'What do you mean, Amnesty International?'

'You know what I mean. Prisoners are allowed to go after an election,' said Verity.

'Then why are you calling it Amnesty International?'

'That is what it is called.'

'Amnesty International is an organisation,' said Monalisa.

'Yes, it is an organisation that makes sure prisoners get out of prisons after elections. What, you think you know everything just because you said yes baas, no baas to white people?'

'What do white people have to do with anything? I already told you that Amnesty International is an organisation.'

'Pwamnesty, pwamnesty,' said Synodia. 'Pwoganisation, pwoganisation.' She had snuck up unnoticed. Monalisa and Jimmy were too busy arguing to see her appear, or to see our frantic attempts to warn them. 'What do you know about amnesties? Will you stop talking and get on with your food? As for you,' she said to Monalisa, 'let's see just how hard you worked for your white people. Pwite people, pwite people.'

Whatever revolution is raging outside has – in here, at least – clearly been postponed.

~ ~ ~ ~ ~ ~ ~ ~ ~

This time, coming to Summer Madness felt like returning home. Lloyd's gentle kindness to me was just as it had ever been. We settled back into our old rhythms, as though I had never been away, as though those two weeks had never been, and as though I had never betrayed him.

We had long conversations about the elections that had been delayed yet again. He feared that the country was on a precipice. I watched the news, stunned at the mix of bare-faced lies and superstition presented as fact. A convicted murderer who had been pardoned was declared a national hero. A house was blown up by witchcraft in Chitungwiza. A goblin was stealing women's underwear in Gokwe. The adverts were all in celebration of the ruling party: I gazed in amused disbelief at the most unlikely figures ever to grace a football field, three big-bottomed women from the city's oldest and most chaotic township, dancing on a football field in ruling party 'team colours'. They shook their thighs of thunder as they sang in praise of the ruling party. They danced to the beat of their own oppression.

In the first two weeks of my visit, I took to driving around and walking about town. Outside Bay's department store, two little boys spoke threateningly to the naked breasts of the semi-clad statues of Artemis and Aphrodite. 'We will drink all your milk. We will drink every last drop.'

I began rereading the books that I had read as a child, capturing the feelings of wonder I had known then. I had no definite plans; I did not know how long I wanted to stay. I had no job anywhere. There was really nothing for me to stay for, but there did not seem anything to go back to, either. I would find my way, I thought, I would find something.

Lloyd suggested that I consider teaching at the university. I chose to volunteer at the Archives instead, while I decided what to do. The place had its old pull on me still, and comfortable as I now was in my skin, I did not think I could bear to stand before the unblinking gaze of staring students.

I had few people to visit. I saw my old friend Mercy, who told me how infinitely she had been blessed, how the Lord had moved in her life and made everything that she touched prosper.

Sandy had moved to Cape Town to live with a sister. And Liz Warrender was dead.

Lloyd had emailed me about Liz's death the year before. I passed her old house many times, now bursting with Rebecca's relatives and other squatters.

I even went back to the Convent to see Sister Mary Gabriel, but found that she had been moved to a school in Masvingo. It was then that I realised that, without Liz, and Sandy, I really had no one left.

In my wild moments of loneliness, I thought of driving to Mufakose. But that wound, though partially healed, still throbbed enough for me to want to leave it undisturbed. I stayed away.

Ian and Alexandra were no longer on their farm in Chipinge. It had been one of the first farms to be invaded. Ian was dying at Island Hospice. He did not know me at all when I saw him. He had had a stroke that left him paralysed on one side and oozing constant tears from one eye.

Alexandra seemed even older than Ian. She told me about the stand-off at the farm, what the leader of the invaders had said, what she had said to him, what he had said back to her, and how Lloyd had called 'a connection of his', one of the ministers he had been with in the camps at Chimoio, who had said, if they packed their clothes and things, he would make sure that they were not harmed.

She told me about what had happened to the farms of people I did not know, or who, if I had ever known them, I had completely forgotten, like Keith and Suzy Granger, who had left with nothing at all, just what they had on; not even proper shoes. 'I promise you,' she said. 'they are now in Nig*ee*ria.'

The Grahams had fled the farms, shots ringing in their wake; their dogs were killed as they tried to defend them. The

Chisholms of Chimanimani had tried to defend themselves, but both father and son had been killed. It was their faces that had been splashed across the international news.

The invasions were the talk of Umwinsidale. My feelings were ambivalent. I had lived long enough among them to understand and feel pity for their losses, but I found it infuriating that they spoke as though there was no context to this, as though this is something that had just happened, with no history to it.

They spoke as if the Pioneer Column had never invaded a land that was not theirs, as if land had not been stolen, as if this had not been a crisis long in the making.

I don't want you to think that I am in any way defending the chaos of the way the farms were parcelled out, or the greed with which the top people took farms for themselves. From what Lloyd told me, Alexandra and Ian's farm had gone to the second wife of an army general, who had also taken a farm in addition to the one that went to his first wife and two children.

The whole thing had been reduced to the simple matter of blackness versus whiteness. White people stole the land. Black people took farms and ruined them. Black people took control and ran things down. White people stole.

Alexandra believed that it was not inexperience that made black people incapable of being farmers, but something intrinsic to their identity. For her, the ability to farm had nothing to do with access to loans and cheap labour, but had everything to do with the genetic accident of whether you were born white or black. 'Africans can only farm communally, you see; they can't do the big commercial farming. They are used to only little pieces of land. It is a miracle they grow anything at all.'

Lloyd said, 'What about all those historical advantages that the commercial farms enjoyed? The tilted and unjust land-tenure system, the bank loans and the guaranteed markets?'

Alexandra changed tack and said, 'It's the wrong people at the top.' She looked directly at me and said, 'You always choose the wrong leaders.'

'And Ian Smith,' I said. 'What was he, the white Mandela?'

Alexandra got up abruptly and left the room. Lloyd made a face at me, smiled, and when she came back, steered the conversation to other, safer waters.

There had been two robberies in the area, with the most serious being at the Collinses' on Hazlemere. Alexandra was convinced that the squatters from the camp that had sprawled out on Liz Warrender's property were behind it. In one of the robberies, the white couple that lived at the targeted house had been shot and their bodies thrown in the swimming pool. 'Inside jobs,' Alexandra said, nodding in the direction of the squatter camp. The police had taken some of the squatters away, had beaten them senseless, but no one had confessed, she said. 'Mind you don't pass that lot at night,' she added. 'And make sure you load the gun.'

I looked up, surprised. Lloyd had never been comfortable with guns.

He noticed my surprise and said, 'Alexandra gave me a gun, but I sometimes forget that it is there.' That conversation came back to me the night that Lloyd died.

I have replayed in my mind, over and over again, the events of that last Friday in November, my last day of freedom. I had woken up just after six to go for a run. I left the house through the kitchen. Mrs Harris lay in her basket next to the pantry. She raised her head and panted. I made a soothing sound and tickled her under her neck. Exhausted with the effort, she put her head down again and went back to sleep. I left the door open so that she could go out.

The rain had come down the night before. The ground was soft beneath my feet as I made my way down our lane and turned left into Umwinsidale Drive. I met no one in the first stage of my run. It was two hours before the road would be filled with the children of Umwinsidale's domestic servants, chattering as they walked to their school in the Chishawasha Valley on the other side of Enterprise Road, and leaping out of the way when the Range Rovers and Jeeps of their parents' masters zoomed past.

Only the birds kept me company. From the stud farm on Umwinsidale Drive, I heard the sound that I had missed the most in my absence, the sound of horses. At the intersection of the drive and Hazlemere Lane, I ran past three white women who were walking at a brisk pace. We said 'Good morning' as we passed each other.

On the first day that I had seen them, I saw in their faces the look of confusion that I often see on strangers. From a distance, I looked like I could be one of them, but seen closer, the difference became visible. They were used to me now – we had passed each other on the same spot every day since I had started running. It was customary for us now to exchange nods or greetings.

'I promise you,' said the woman in the middle, 'I am absolutely the only one in Africa who does this.'

I smiled to myself as I ran on and my mind idled over her words. She was the only one in Africa who did what? Was she the only person in Africa who gave French pedicures to African poodles? The only person in Africa who made small scarves for bats? Who knitted mittens for kittens? Who made velvet gloves for monkeys' paws? The only person in Africa who eats her peas with honey, who has done it all her life; it makes the peas taste funny but it keeps them on the knife?

The morning was right for running. The air was crisp and cool. I ran up Hazlemere Lane and rested there for a minute as I looked at the valley stretched below me. In the distance, a small herd of zebras from the private game park grazed in the morning mist.

I ran past the new houses that had come up in my absence, hideous promontories jutting out against the sky. I ran on, up the hill to the Compton-Joneses' place, then down again. By the time I ran back to Summer Madness forty minutes later, I was breathing hard. I did some stretches on the veranda. In my bathroom, I showered, careful to keep my face away from the rushing water, washing my hair with my eyes open.

Lloyd was up by the time I returned. From the kitchen came the smell of the coffee. As I walked to the kitchen, I sang along to the music that he was playing that morning, about becoming lovers, and marrying fortunes together.

He was sitting at the table, eating toast and marmalade with his coffee while he caught up with the news on his laptop. He said something about Obama and the election in America. I turned down the music, poured myself some coffee, and sat in the chair opposite him. I took a naartjie from the fruit bowl on the table, peeled it, and ate it with my coffee. Mrs Harris moved from where she sat at Lloyd's feet and came panting up to be patted. I ruffled her head and neck. She thumped her tail and nuzzled my hand.

'You should eat more than that,' Lloyd said after his morning greeting. 'You are all skinny *mabhonzo*.'

It was the same discussion that we had had since my return.

He finished his toast and got up to go. 'We may need another voucher for the Internet,' he said.

'I will pass through Sam Levy's on my way back from the Archives,' I said.

'See you when you see me,' he said.

He closed his laptop, shoved it into a bag that he slung over his shoulder, and left. Mrs Harris lifted her head and dropped it again. In the old days, she would have scampered after him, but it was all she could do to lift up her head and watch him out. Her head between her paws, she went back to sleep. In the background, I heard his car making its way down the lane to join Umwinsidale Drive.

As I got up to make toast, I saw that he had left his phone behind. Lloyd was so absent-minded that I had sometimes thought that his household, such as it was, existed for no other purpose but to find the things that he lost.

I hummed with the music as I chuckled at the headline stories on Gawker, read the news story that Lloyd had talked about on the American election, brushed my teeth and drove for the Archives.

I would take him his phone around lunchtime, I decided, because the university was just a few minutes from the Archives.

I stopped for a newspaper at the intersection of Enterprise and Glenara. A vendor in an Arsenal shirt ran into oncoming traffic, shouting a triumph as a speeding van almost hit him. The lights changed as he reached my window. He threw the paper into my car, and then, like a runner stretching for a baton from the team member ahead of him, ran alongside the car, his hand outstretched for the wad of notes that I handed him. I drove up the Enterprise bypass, round the roundabout, into Churchill and turned into the Archives.

I spent the rest of the morning going through photographs in the picture archives. I was curating an exhibition of photographs for display at the National Gallery. I selected my pictures: the first young woman to get a medical degree in Rhodesia, market women in Mbare in the fifties, colonial wagons pulled by a team of zebras, naked warriors from the 1896 rebellion hanging from trees, southern fruit in the Rhodesian bush.

At lunchtime, I drove to Sam Levy's. At the intersection of Churchill and Borrowdale, nimble-footed young men thrust their wares towards me: flotation devices shaped like the Teletubbies, chargers, adapters, Springbok and All Blacks flags – South Africa and New Zealand had a rugby match that weekend. A man with dreadlocked hair and beard ran up to my car; the three national flags billowing behind him made him look like a demented Rastafarian.

When I first came back, Alexandra had encouraged me to buy a flag to hang in the car. It was the only way to get past the police roadblocks, she explained. 'You'll get less hassle that way, I promise you,' she said. Like many whites under siege, she thought flying the flag from her car was a badge of patriotism, a visible sign that she was not a 'detractor'.

Lloyd had mocked the talismanic effect of the flag. He used to joke that he would fly a Union Jack instead. If he could be sure that the police would know it, he would fly the old tricolor, he said. Alexandra had obviously not seen the funny side of this.

Lloyd was right; I had been amused to see that the focus of hatred on the nightly news was not the Rhodesians, but the British. According to this new history, the war had been fought not against a white minority regime that had opposed black rule to the extent of unilaterally declaring independence from British control, but against the British themselves.

I was even more amused to see that Alexandra and Lloyd had exchanged places. Lloyd, who had fought in the liberation struggle on the side of the black forces in favour of majority rule, could joke about the flag of Rhodesia, while Alexandra, whose husband and favourite brother had defended it, was anxious to show loyalty to the flag of Zimbabwe.

At Sam Levy's, I was thrust into the middle of the usual lunchtime crowd, skinny white girls in denim shorts that skimmed their butts, aggressively coiffured black women tottering in vertiginous heels, walking like they had something uncomfortable between their legs as they tried to sneak up on a particularly skittish rabbit, and workers in blue overalls queuing to buy a cheap lunch from TM. I bought my lunch at Antonio's, shopped for a bagful of groceries at TM, and bought an Internet voucher at the Apple store.

In the TM parking lot, a man with an armful of flowers ran up to me. 'Some flowers, madam,' he said in a wheedling voice. 'I have some very nice flowers – nice, nice flowers.'

Our eyes met. There it was again, that familiar double take, the recalibration that played out on his face as his mind adjusted to the reality of what I was. He immediately changed to Shona, his voice stronger, cockier. 'Some flowers, sister. *Zvakadhakwa nhasi*, sister. Come on, sister, you are my first customer today.'

I smiled at the switch from formality to familiarity, from 'madam' to 'sister'. He pushed his flowers at me, flame lilies and calla lilies, strelitzias and proteas. I bought two bunches of strelitzias. They were Lloyd's favourite flowers. I liked their other name better – birds of paradise. I put them in the back seat with my other parcels and drove back to the Archives.

I ate my lunch in the garden, finished selecting my pictures and drove to the university. Lloyd was still in a lecture, his department secretary told me. As I followed her directions to the lecture room, it occurred to me that I had never been to one of Lloyd's classes. I threaded past little knots of students. I wrinkled my nose against the pungent smell from the toilet in the corridor.

Lloyd was in a large lecture hall but had only a few dozen students in front of him. I took a seat and listened. He was in the middle of the lecture, and he spoke without notes. In the vastness of the lecture room, with a few students before him, his voice echoed a little as he spoke.

'Nothing operates by chance. If we hold a fatalistic worldview or believe in fate, we give that fate a name or series of names. Giving fate a name is a necessary imaginative act that permits us to establish a relationship with the controlling forces of our existence. We can convince ourselves that such fatal presences do listen to us, that prayer can persuade them, as can sacrifice, blood or penitence.

'Take our local concept of *ngozi*, which appears in various forms in African and other ancient cultures. How does it differ from the Erinyes, the Furies who followed murderers and drove them mad? The idea that *mhosva haiori*, that a crime as serious as murder is felt until it is appeased is a common belief across humanity.

'In Shona mythology, you can propitiate a *ngozi* spirit in the same way that the Greeks poured libations before the Oracle at Delphi. A *ngozi* can be appeased with live animals and with a young girl to carry the children the murdered victim was unable to have.'

As Lloyd spoke, I looked at his students. A girl in front of me scratched her head and played with her phone. A boy two rows beneath her was taking notes with such ferocious speed that his pen almost tore into his paper. Two were entering notes on laptops, and one, I saw, was open to Facebook. I turned my attention back to Lloyd.

'Oedipus was pursued by *ngozi*. And it was Antigone's desire to avoid the *ngozi* that drove her to defy Creon and bury the corpse of Polynices. When we talk of fate, when we talk of a fatalistic vision of human experience, what we mean is that the most important forces that shape human lives are out of human control.

'It is to say that there is something, an external force that controls the rules of our lives, that determines the things of particular importance to us, our good and bad fortune, our happiness and sorrow, and, above all, our death. To have a fatalistic sense of life is to hold that our destiny is out of the control of any human being and that non-human actors will always determine the outcomes.

'This is both comforting and terrifying. On one hand, we have no control and can give ourselves over to the forces that control us. On the other, we have no control, and are carried along on a tide we cannot control.'

I realised then something that I could not have not known as a child in his house. Lloyd was a fine teacher. He finished the lecture, and I waited while the avid note-taker spoke to him. When he left, I gave Lloyd his phone. He had a department meeting to go to; he would see me at home. I am glad that I saw this side of Lloyd because when I went back home that Friday, I found him dead in his room, a dry-cleaner's plastic bag over his purple face.

13

I have had more than two years to think and reflect on everything that happened to me from the moment that I found Lloyd in his room to the moment the judge pronounced my sentence. And I have concluded that the judge had no choice but to reach the conclusion that he did. What else was there to believe? They had a confession. They had a witness who had seen me moving Lloyd's body. They had the gun.

The police came for me on the day that Lloyd died, the second last Friday in November. By Christmas, I had been tried, convicted and sentenced.

The speed and swiftness of my trial also had something to do with other events that took place around the time of Lloyd's death. Vernah Sithole will tell you that the trial was quick, much quicker than any murder trial has ever been. Within two weeks of the start of the trial, the judge had reached his verdict.

I have become convinced that the death of three white farmers in the month before Lloyd's death had something to do with the swiftness of my trial. There had been an outcry around the world about these deaths, but no one had been arrested; no one had been tried.

So when Lloyd died, another white man over whom the world would make a hue and cry, something had to be done. And there I was, a readily available suspect, caught with the body, ready to make this a simple domestic murder, nothing at all to do with the vexed and anxious questions of land and its ownership.

I did not go back to Summer Madness after they arrested me. I was deemed a flight risk. I had no apparent ties to anyone in the country, and so I spent my time on remand in Chikurubi.

On the first day of the trial, I was brought to the High Court. I was led up to Courtroom A through a series of quadrangles, passing groups of lawyers in gowns and jabots, crow-like figures bursting with mirth and legal glee.

In the wood-panelled courtroom, the judge and his two assessors sat on green leather chairs with backs as high as gravestones. The judge spent much of the trial looking into the middle distance. The assessor to his right was asleep. The assessor next to him, a woman of Indian origin, had a face that was twisted into a rictus of concern.

The door behind the judges' dais opened every few seconds and from the corridor behind would come snatches of conversation that floated disconnected into the courtroom.

'*Ende makafitwa nekaweave ikako vasikana.*'

'*Ndakafitwa?* I wanted to take it off.'

'He was abusing me in the vilest terms, with the utmost contempt and contumelia.'

'*Kafish aka kari right manje.*'

'Yah, he always brings good fish.'

The dock I sat in was in the middle of the courtroom, facing the judges and assessors; the prosecutor and my lawyer had their back to me. The prosecutor wore a lace jabot that did not connect at the back of his neck, the ends stuck out of his gown as he talked.

Behind me was Alexandra. I could not see her, but I could feel her gaze on me, burning me with the heat of her hatred. After giving her evidence, she sat on her own, on a bench behind the journalists. She was the only witness. Beyond her statement, there was no other evidence. There were no forensic reports, and no post-mortem: the last pathologist had long left the country. The signed confession that the prosecutor produced sealed my fate.

The judge concluded that I was guilty of the crime that I was charged with, a cold and calculated murder: an unnatural act for a woman. The motive didn't matter. The law, the judge said, is concerned only with action and intention, with the necessary combination of the *actus reus* and the *mens rea*. Was the mental element present, was there an intention to kill, and did the intention to kill translate into the action of killing a human being who was alive at that time? Both elements were present in this case.

The deceased's own sister, a competent and credible witness, had seen the accused with her own eyes, dumping the body of the deceased into the pool. The demeanour of the accused told against her, the judge said; she had been particularly remorseless and cruel.

The relationship between the accused and the deceased was unclear, but it was not necessary to go into the exact nature of that relationship. What was beyond question was that the deceased had left the accused his house in his will, and his money. So the accused had also acted out of greed; she had killed for money that she would have inherited anyway had she been happy to wait for the natural course of events.

The accused had committed murder, and he had not been able to find any extenuating circumstances. He could not discount that the accused had confessed, thus saving the state from wasting valuable resources to prove what was essentially an open-and-shut case. In any other circumstances, that confession would have gone some way to mitigating the sentence. But it was important to send a message to the world that this country did not condone violence. The only competent sentence he could impose under the law, and in view of all the circumstances, was the death penalty.

~ ~ ~ ~ ~ ~ ~ ~ ~

Lloyd was dead when I found him. I had spent the day at the Archives. I reached home around seven in the evening. His car was in the garage, but he was not in his study, or the library or the living room. I called out his name, but I met only silence. I thought he might have gone to bed early. When I found him, I did not understand immediately what I was looking at. The naked body, dressed only in yellow socks, the plastic bag around his face – but it made no sense to me then.

It is ridiculous, the tangentially connected, orphaned thoughts that come to you in a moment like that. 'He died with his socks on' was the first thought that came to my mind. Hysteria and shock then took over. I burst into tears. They were immediately followed by hysterical laughter. I reached for the phone. There was nothing but a dead sound. My mobile was not charged, and nor was Lloyd's.

My first instinct was to remove the bag on his face. Beneath it, his face was purple with strain. His eyes were wide open. As I moved towards him, I tripped on his laptop computer cable but managed to regain my balance. I touched the open laptop and it came to life. As soon as I saw what was on his screen, what he must have been watching, I understood at once.

I thought at first that I could save him. I tried to give him mouth-to-mouth, but even as I put my mouth towards his face, I knew it was too late. Still, I tried. I sobbed out the numbers as I counted to myself.

Even as I tried to revive him I knew that my efforts were in vain. After minutes that seemed like hours, I stopped. Even as I had tried to revive him, the governing thought in my mind had been that I could not let anyone find him thus. With comprehension had come the conviction that I could not let him be found like this.

When I think of those moments now, more than two years after it all happened, it is hard for me to explain just what I thought I would achieve. All I know is that I did not want them to find him, without articulating to myself who exactly it was that I meant by 'them'.

I did not want anyone, even strangers, to see him like that, or for his death to be a lurid headline in a newspaper, or the subject of titillating speculation on the news websites.

It was this governing thought that led me to my wild plan: I would make it look as though he had died accidentally. He had indeed died accidentally, but I would transform this accident into another type, to make it seem as though he had died in another way.

In that moment, I remembered what Alexandra had told us about how the Collinses on Hazlemere had died, how their bodies were found floating in their swimming pool, how their attackers had still not been caught. I remembered the squatters on Liz Warrender's property. And I remembered that Alexandra had insisted that Lloyd keep a gun.

It was then that my plan came to me in its completeness. In the turmoil of my wild panic, I decided to make his death look like he had been shot during a robbery. I would shoot him with his gun, and then I would drop his body in the pool.

You will understand from this that I was clearly not thinking straight: in the extremity of my panic, I was even prepared to go to the swimming pool, the one place that I had always kept away from. Nor did I think about ballistics and forensics and post-mortems. I imagined that the police would simply see his floating body in the pool, connect it to the Collinses, and conclude that things were just as they seemed.

The first thing to do was dress him. But as I looked down at him, my courage almost failed me. His discarded clothes lay on the floor of the bed. His body was floppy beneath my ministra-tions. I pulled his briefs and trousers on. I could not manage a shirt – my hands were trembling too much for me to even con-sider putting all those buttons into the button holes – so I pulled out a tee-shirt from his wardrobe.

I was sobbing as his arms resisted my efforts at manipulating them into his sleeves. I ran to the safe and took out his gun. If this were to work, I would need to make it look as though he had been surprised.

I stood some way away and shot him in the back. The report rang in my ears. The recoil of the gun made me drop it to the ground.

I picked it up from where it had fallen and tucked it into the front of my jeans. There were forests and trees in Umwinsidale where I could get rid of it; I could even drive out of the area alto-gether and dump it in a river – the Hunyani, perhaps, in far-off Chitungwiza.

My tears were hot on my cheeks. I needed to get him to the pool. I dragged him through the living room. We stopped. His foot had hooked a lamp and I could not move him. I sobbed in frustration, and pulled harder. The lamp fell over and smashed to the floor. I managed to get him out of the room and onto the veranda. It was just a few metres away now. I dragged him across the veranda, and towards the pool.

I approached the pool from the shallow end. Without looking, I pushed him to the side of it. There was a splash. It was the gun. By the time I realised what had happened, the gun rested on the final step of the shallow end.

I cried out my frustration.

I willed myself to walk in. The old fear held me back. I could have gone in; it was just one step, two steps, three steps to where the gun lay. But the thought of stepping into that water paralysed me into inaction. The *njuzu* would get me; the Chimera would drown me. I thought wildly that I would get the long-armed net that Biggie used to remove leaves from the surface of the pool, but even that seemed beyond me.

By now, I was overwhelmed by exhaustion. Tomorrow, I thought; tomorrow. I will do it tomorrow.

I turned back to Lloyd's face. With my eyes closed, so that I did not see the water, I pushed him. There was a heavy splash. It was immediately followed by a scream. It seemed as though the sound came from the body in the pool. There was another scream, and I realised that it came from behind me. In confusion, I whirled to face the veranda.

Alexandra looked at me, her eyes wide above the hand clasped over her mouth. The phone in her left hand fell to the ground with a clatter. As though in slow motion, I saw the battery go one way, the phone and SIM card another. Alexandra made a strangled sound.

Babbling and weeping, I made to move towards her, my hands turned to hers in supplication, pleading with her, willing her to understand. Now that she was here, I could let go of my preposterous plan, what I had planned to do. Now that she was here, I would tell her everything. She would help me, I thought; we would decide what to do, the two of us.

As I moved towards her, she backed away. I understood in that moment that she thought I had done this.

'You have to believe me,' I said. 'I found him dead.'

But the words remained in my mind. I could not speak them.

'Alexandra,' I finally managed to say.

She backed away and went round to the side of the house where she normally parked her car. Overcome by the wild emotion and exhaustion, I sat down on a chair and closed my eyes. When I opened them a few seconds later, I heard the sound of heavy breathing and running feet followed by the sound of her engine starting and her car driving away from Summer Madness. From the veranda I saw the twinkling lights of her car winding down Umwinsidale Drive, headed towards Enterprise Road, towards my fate.

~ ~ ~ ~ ~ ~ ~ ~ ~ ~

You will hear many stories about the inefficiency and corruption of the police, about impunity for sale. But, as I found out, in cases that have nothing to do with the poisoned politics of this country, the police are much more thorough. Perhaps they would have been more inclined to believe me if I had not moved his body. But I *had* moved his body – there was Alexandra's statement of what she had seen.

There was the will. He left me the house.

They asked me how I came to live with him. I told them. They did not believe me. 'We don't sell children in this country,' they said.

When they failed to believe that truth and cast it as a lie, it naturally followed that everything else I said was a lie. Even when I told them the truth, *chokwadi chaicho*, the real truth, as Officer Dimples called it, they exploded with laughter at the mere thought.

'Whoever heard of such things?' Officer Rollers said. 'We know they are strange creatures, these whites, but really.'

'Whoever heard of such a thing?' echoed Officer Dimples.

As soon as Alexandra arrived back at Summer Madness with the police, they took me to Highlands police station. They left me alone in a room for more than an hour. Officer Dimples, the man who said my crime was no laughing matter as he laughed jovially, then came in to ask me what had happened.

I said nothing.

Then Officer Rollers came in and asked if I would like a drink: water, maybe, she suggested, or maybe Mazoe. The kindness in her voice disarmed me, but it was a short-lived relief. I was left alone for another hour.

Then Officer Dimples came back with the same questions. Officer Rollers followed him with offers of food and drink. This was not so much good cop, bad cop as it was bad cop, worse cop.

In my first week there, I did not talk. I had no lawyer. No one came to see me; no one knew where I was. I thought then about what it must have been like for Lloyd, alone in the cell for two weeks, with no one knowing where he was.

They finally charged me with murder two weeks after they

arrested me. I have read different accounts of what they do in police cells here – the beatings on the soles of the feet, the twisted arms. Nothing like that happened to me.

They played a much subtler game that was, in the end, more terrifying than actual pain would have been. They removed me from the first cell, in which I had found myself with women arrested for prostitution, and moved me to an empty cell, a small windowless space filled with the smell of many bodies. When they first put me there, there had been a power cut, and all I got from my new surroundings was the smell, overpowering and fetid, of urine, sweat and faeces.

When the power came back, I wished the darkness had remained. There were stains that looked like blood had dried on the walls and floors. On the wall immediately opposite me were marks that looked like they might have been made by a bloody hand moving along the width of the wall. On other parts of the wall were traces of dried faeces, vomit and blood.

I felt then the terror that Lloyd must have felt. More than the discomfort of my surroundings, I felt an unshakeable guilt. I could not disconnect the act that had led to Lloyd's death from my own actions all those years ago. That is wildly exaggerated – I see that now, of course – but I am telling where my frenzied reactions at the time sprang from, and not the reasoned conclusions that I have meditated over for the last two years.

So this is what was in my mind then. He had been in this very police station all those years ago when Alexandra found him. I had not killed him, but I had been cold and cruel to him. I had rejected him. I thought then about Lloyd, about why he had died the way he had. Was it because of me that he had rejected all human touch? Was it the fear of discovery? Or had it always been like this for him? What did I know about Lloyd beyond what I saw? What had I ever known? What did I know about the things he dreamt about, fantasised about?

After three days in that place, Officer Rollers made the threat that finally broke me. When she said it, it was not even a threat. She said it casually, as if it was the most reasonable solution to their administrative problem.

'Now look here,' she said. 'Do you see all the women in the cell?'

They had committed minor crimes, these women, a bit of theft here, a bit of soliciting for prostitution there. They were not hardcore criminals but minor offenders – an admission of guilt and a fine in most cases would cover their offences. They had not committed serious crimes like I had. They had not killed anyone. My crime was far too serious for me to be with these other women.

But there was one problem now, she said. The only other serious criminals they had arrested were four men who were members of an armed gang that stole from the cars of female drivers after raping them. One of those victims had died, she said. They needed to put them somewhere, these men. And the only other place possible was the cell that I occupied. At the same time, they could not put me in the women's cell, because my crime was too serious.

'You see how it is,' she said, and scratched her nose.

I signed the statement that Vernah Sithole may have shown you, the statement that sealed my guilt. The words were dictated to me. The statement was then read back to me and I signed it. I did not think it meant anything beyond an escape from my present hell. I would explain it all to the judge.

It occurred to me then that, even if Alexandra had not come to Summer Madness that night, my plan would never have succeeded. Now I pinned my hopes on the very things that I had hoped against. I became certain that there would be a post-mortem. There would be forensic evidence. It would become clear that Lloyd could not have been shot. The judge would see that he had been shot after his death. There would be technical and detailed reports about lividity and rigor mortis, gunshot wounds and the state of his blood. It would all come right at the trial.

By the time my trial began, the Law Society had appointed a pro bono lawyer for me. That is how I ended up with my first lawyer. Vernah has explained to me much that puzzled me about him, why he would barely look at me, why he spent more time laughing with the prosecutor than going over my case with me, and why he was so obsequiously anxious to please the judge.

I know now that the Law Society obliges all law firms in the country to take on pro bono cases. And the High Court requires that everyone accused of capital crimes be represented by lawyers. But there are no large fees that the law firms can make from this kind of case. On the other hand, there is money to be made from conveyancing and selling houses and commercial contracts. So the senior lawyers, the most experienced lawyers who know the law best, do the undemanding work that brings in the money, while the lawyers who charge the least because they are the least experienced, the lawyers who are barely out of school, get the murder cases in which they fight for people's lives.

I was brought before the court for a bail hearing. My lawyer said very little beyond trying to be as agreeable as possible. 'Accused has been out of the country and has a passport. Accused is likely to abscond or interfere with witnesses. And as accused has already pleaded guilty, accused may as well stay in prison,' said the prosecutor.

The judge denied my bail. There was the trial, then Chikurubi. The cracking of my skin was the first indication that my nightmare was beginning. It was as though I was going back to the child that I had once been. And when I slept, the dreams came to me and I was drowning and Lloyd was speaking in my mother's voice and the *njuzu* that was like the Chimera was telling me that I was dirty, I was dirty, and I needed to bathe.

PART THREE

CHIKURUBI

I

I have finally understood Loveness's unexpected overtures to me. I know now what it all meant, the newspapers, the lotions, the extra pens and notebooks, the dropped confidences. Yesterday afternoon she came to fetch me from the laundry, where I was ironing with the others. As we worked, we helped Beulah to prepare for her trial. She had finally been given a date.

'Make sure you don't look directly at the magistrate,' Jimmy was saying. 'Look down on the ground, like you do with the guards. If you look directly at them they think you are challenging them.'

'Unless the magistrate is white,' said Monalisa. 'I have worked with whites all my life. It is different with them. If you don't look straight at them, they think you are lying.'

Evernice turned to her. 'White people, white people, *chii cha-cho*? Why are you always going on about white people? Where is she going to see a white magistrate? Where is she going to see one, tell me that. Where have you seen a white magistrate?'

Sinfree said, 'There is a white magistrate in Bulawayo. He was the one who sentenced me.'

Evernice rounded on Sinfree. 'What has Bulawayo to do with anything? Is she going to Bulawayo? Are we in Bulawayo? Does she look to you like she is going to Bulawayo?' She let out an explosive sound of disgust and accompanied it with a matching moue. Then she calmed down as quickly as she had flared up and, her voice less strident, said to Beulah, 'If they ask you if you are sorry for your crime, just tell them that you are the only breadwinner in your family.'

'*Ehunde*,' Jimmy added. 'You can also say that your sister or brother passed and left you their children to look after, or you can also say the whole thing is based on heresy.'

'Do you mean hearsay?' asked Verity.

Jimmy nodded. 'That's right, heresy. But honestly, I won't lie to you,' she continued, 'the best thing you can do for yourself is to just say that you have really come to know Jesus.'

Loveness came in at that point. We stopped talking at once. After ordering us to work in silence, she turned to me. 'I want you to come with me,' she said.

The others looked at each other. I could not think of anything that I had done that would warrant my separation from the others during the day. In silence, I followed her out of the laundry room, down the corridor and out of the courtyard and into the compound.

The ground was muddy. I blinked in the sun. It had rained almost every day of the week before. We had not been out in more than a week. Synodia and Patience were in the yard, talking while they watched their charges sweeping the rainwater that had collected in the courtyard. Patience waved to Loveness as we passed. I kept my eyes to the ground, keen to avoid drawing any further attention to myself. I did not dare to glance back but I knew that the others must have looked up from their work to follow us with their eyes, because as we passed them I heard Synodia say, 'What are you staring? Get back to work at once.'

Loveness led me past the garden and the fields, where small

clusters of A and B prisoners were resting after planting the new beans. As we passed the administration block, my right flip-flop remained stuck in the mud. I stopped to rescue it. Loveness stopped with me. 'Don't worry,' she said. 'As soon as the next donation comes from the Fellowship month-end, I will make sure to get you some nice shoes.'

Curiouser and curiouser.

On we walked, past the perimeter fence, until we had left the prison compound altogether and were approaching the staff houses. The homes of the guards are set back from the prison; you do not see them when you drive in. Before I could ask Loveness where she was taking me, we had stopped at a little house with a green hedge around it.

A group of children played a game in the open space before the houses. The girl whose turn it was to be in the middle had tucked her dress into her panties. Her thin legs kicked up with practised agility.

'Sweetie, sweetie, day by day,' the children sang. 'Upside down. *Tula madhebhula, tula madhebhula*. Oh fish!'

'And fish!' cried the girl in the middle.

'And upside down!' echoed the others.

A toddler sat in the mud, splashing dirty water over herself in happy disregard.

As soon as the children saw Loveness, they ran to her, shouting, 'Aunty, aunty.'

Was this Loveness, this aunty, aunty that the children clamoured around with laughing faces?

'Where is Yeukai?' Loveness asked.

'She is at Tadiwa's house,' a little girl answered.

'Tell her to come home,' Loveness said.

Two small girls broke from the rest and ran as with one motion towards the end of the row of houses.

Loveness opened the door to her house. 'Come in, come in. This is where I am,' she said. There was an unmistakable note of proprietary pride in her voice as she ushered me in to the pin-neat, overstuffed room.

The room felt suffocatingly familiar. The lace curtains at the window, the lounge suite with cloth covers, the display cabinet with miniature figures on doilies, and in the corner, a dining room table, which did not appear, from its resolute position squashed into the corner, ever to be used. I was in a more expensive version of the living room in Mharapara Street from which I had watched the children play.

And just as it had been then, the voices of the children came through the open windows, continuing the game that they were playing as we walked past them. 'Oh fish,' they cried. 'And fish, and upside down.'

'I have just the one bedroom and a spare,' Loveness said. 'I should have moved into the one at the corner after my promotion, the one that is occupied by Patience now, even though she has not been promoted like me, but, well, you know, there is this thing between the Assistant Commissioner and Patience . . .'

She indicated that I should sit. I took the armchair nearest the television and turned towards it. It had a sleek, flat screen, with the store display labels saying 'high-definition', '40-inch LCD' and 'Phillips' with two Ls stuck in the bottom corners.

'Patience brought this from Dubai,' she said as she switched it on. 'Just three hundred she charged me, can you imagine, what a bargain, and she paid no duty, no nothing. That is the good thing about being connected.'

She surfed though the channels until she found a Nigerian film. 'Oh, my daughter,' said the television. 'What have you done with my daughter? I want my daughter, *wo-o*.'

'Your daughter will not come back. She has married a creature of the waters.'

'She has married a marine husband!' screamed a voice.

'A marine husband,' echoed the first.

Mesmerised by the television, I did not realise that Loveness was not only talking to me; she was also handing me a glass of Coke that she had poured out for me. As I drank greedily, I tried to focus my attention away from the television.

Loveness was uncharacteristically nervous – bashful, even. She talked in a circumlocutory way about how much she liked Nigerian films, the problems with teachers these days, the things that Patience brought back on each trip to Dubai and why it was good to have Patience on her side. It was obvious that all of this was a lead-up to something. But I could not think of anything that would warrant such hospitality. I concentrated on my drink and the television, until finally she came out with it.

Her daughter was having problems at school and she wanted me to help. I had gone to university, she said, so I knew all about it. She was writing Cambridge exams in two years. She had saved and saved for her daughter because she wanted her to write the very best exams.

'You have been where, you have been to Cambridge, there where they set the papers,' she said. 'Can you help me?'

'Ajana says the girl must remain under the sea.'

'Will you help me?' said Loveness again.

'Yes,' I said, and turned my attention from the television. 'Yes, of course I will help.'

The door opened and in came a little girl with that robust thinness that only very young girls have. The sound of the television receded, and even Loveness seemed to be speaking from a long way off. She was a small girl, maybe twelve or thirteen, a small albino girl with freckles on her face and arms and thick glasses on her nose. In that moment, I understood everything that had baffled me about Loveness. The little girl blinked and scratched at the alabaster skin of her right arm. In that gesture, I saw myself again.

~ ~ ~ ~ ~ ~ ~ ~ ~ ~

Every afternoon, after Yeukai returns from school, Loveness takes me to her house. Yeukai is not at the prison school, but at a government school in Highlands. Funnily enough, it is Alexandra's old school. It was once a government school only for whites, but it now takes mainly the children of the domestic staff who work in the affluent areas surrounding it.

The uniform is still the same, the children are obliged to wear hats, but there are fifty children in each class. Yeukai is behind in every subject. For this term, I am teaching her history, geography, English language and literature. In February, we start on biology and chemistry. They are not my strongest subjects, and I have to stop at physics and maths, but Loveness said not to worry: they had been Synodia's favourite subjects at school.

With the reawakened memories of the children at my first school in Mufakose in mind, I asked Yeukai if the other children gave her problems at school. She was not the only albino child in her school, she said; there were three others, so everyone was used to her. The school absences are Yeukai's only problems. I have said that in her I saw myself again, but we differ in one respect. She wears glasses, but is otherwise healthy and well cared for. Loveness told me that there is now an Albino Society that gives out free sunscreen and advice.

I would rather that you not tell Vernah Sithole about this arrangement. I know that she will not approve of this – she has, after all, been appointed to the new Anti-Corruption Commission. She will get into a tizzy about corruption and get Loveness into trouble for abusing her position. It is corruption, but it is a form of corruption that happens to benefit me.

In Loveness's house, I get to shower in hot water, the first hot water I have had in two years. I get lotion for my skin. I watch the television when there is electricity. It is limited fare: Loveness sticks resolutely to Nigerian and Korean melodramas and channels with Pentecostal preachers, but I have managed, on one or two occasions when she was not here, to catch reruns of sitcoms like *Seinfeld* and *Friends*.

In the effusion of her happiness, Loveness even offered me some of her old clothes until she recalled that I could not wear them in prison. If Yeukai passes this term's tests, I intend to ask Loveness to buy me a bottle of wine. I can almost taste it in my mouth.

Above all, I get books.

I suggested to Loveness that she should go to the flea market at Avondale and buy any books she could find. She brought back the *I, Claudius* books by Robert Graves, and some Frederick Forsyths and Jeffrey Archers. She apologised because the only books she manages to find are old. I have told her that this is what I prefer.

The world has changed, but the curriculum has not. I am teaching Yeukai all the things that I learned myself. I find myself looking forward to the lessons, planning them, impatient for the next one, and missing them when they are cancelled. I teach her about the Mensheviks and Bolsheviks, I teach her about igneous rocks and sedimentary rocks, I try to smooth her way as she stumbles through the iambic pentameter.

We had started on the Russian Revolution when Loveness came to see me last week; it was on the day that I normally go to teach Yeukai. I was thinking already of ways to make the revolution come alive for her. Maybe I would tell her about Rasputin. I would teach her the standard story in the text, about the rightness of the revolution, but I would try to make her see the pain of the children shot one by one, the pitiful waste of it. My mind was on the little Tsarevich and I did not immediately understand what she said.

'Your sister is here to see you,' she said.

I thought I had misheard her as soon as I saw my visitor. Sitting in the visitor's room was a small, light-skinned woman in a plain grey skirt, a white blouse, and a short veil covering her hair. I had misheard Loveness. There is *a* sister to see me, she meant, a Catholic sister, perhaps a volunteer from the Goodwill Fellowship. As I hardened myself to meet her platitudes, she looked up from the book she was reading and smiled.

Then my heart contracted because my mother faced me across the years. 'Memory,' she said, and burst into tears.

Immediately, I saw my mistake. My mother's face had never been this gentle, or her voice ever this soft.

2

———————

How do you begin your life again after you find out that everything you thought was true about yourself is wrong?

How do you begin to understand your life all over again? My mind is in the Mukuvisi with my parents, in the murderous waters of the river in which the Baptist almost drowned me until my father put his strong arms around me. Had those same arms pulled my mother to her death? Who had killed whom? Had they died at the same time, weighing each other down?

I do not even know if there was a funeral. But who was there to bury them, when they had died together? How long had it been before they were found? Did our house on Mharapara find new tenants? Or did it become another place of horror, like the haunted house that we were afraid of when we were children? MaiWhizi, how did she take it? Did she go from house to house, spreading the news to those who had not heard about this bioscope in which her neighbours died?

All these questions, but they are all really one. How do you begin again? How do *I* begin again?

3

Mavis Munongwa died last night.

From my cell I heard her crying out, but I was too filled with my own pain to think that the sounds meant she was in any particular distress. When the siren went in the morning and Synodia unlocked the cells, she did not come out to wash in the ablution block with all of us.

No one noticed her absence until breakfast.

When Synodia came back, she held a whispered consultation with the others. They all left together, and it was then that we knew that something must be wrong.

After a few minutes, Synodia said, 'Let us now say prayers for our sister Mavis, who has gone to sleep with the Lord. She has gone home, to a better world.'

Loveness ordered Jimmy, Evernice, Benhilda, one of the baby dumpers and me to fetch Mavis's body and put it in the sanatorium. She weighed so little, her eyes had been closed, and she was light to carry. We carried her out feet first and laid her on the bed nearest the door.

Loveness said Mavis had no family, and she would be buried in the grounds of the prison. We buried her the next day. The December heat meant that she could not be kept in the clinic for long. From the window of the Condemn later that morning, I saw in the far distance some khaki-clad figures from the men's prison digging a grave for Mavis, in the shared cemetery at the corner where the men's and women's prisons touch. Separated in life, together in death.

Only the old graves have gravestones. The new mounds of earth have no gravestones above them. It was to a new grave that we carried her the next day, wrapped in a prison blanket, and threw her body into the ground. She landed with a soft thud. Jimmy must have seen something in my face, because she squeezed my hand and whispered, '*Iza*, Memory, *iza.*'

Synodia led us in singing. The women's voices were beautiful in the hot afternoon. They induced in me a terror, not just for Mavis, but also for myself. This could be me one day. Even if I escape the hangman, I might still end my life here, in a prison blanket, buried by Synodia. Maybe I would even watch the men from the prison digging my grave.

After the funeral, I went back to my cell. I was unwell, I said; could I lie down. Loveness let me go. I had been looking forward to reading the old edition of *I, Claudius* she had given me before the meeting with my sister; I tried to read it now, but the words of Robert Graves blurred and mixed with the horror of what my sister had told me.

I, Tiberius Claudius Drusus Nero Germanicus, am now about to tell you that your entire life has been a lie. I, Tiberius Claudius Drusus Nero Germanicus, am now about to write this strange history of how your mother killed her children.

4

When my sister was eighteen years old, and I was seventeen and falling in love with Zenzo, a policeman called Constable Mapfumo came to her school in Chishawasha to tell her that our parents were dead. They had both drowned in the Mukuvisi River. Perhaps it was a murder-suicide, or a mutual suicide pact, who knows.

What matters only is that they both died.

Joy says that when people rage against the police and talk of corruption and inefficiency, she remembers that man, Takawira Mapfumo, who drove his own car to see her because he wanted himself to put in her hand the letter that my father had written. He sat beside her in the headmaster's office as she read it, and afterwards held her hand while she cried.

This is what our father told her.

My father was not my mother's first husband. He was not even her husband, because she was not his wife but rather belonged to another man. She had been just thirteen years old when she was married, or, I should say, when her parents married her off to a man four times her age.

She was married off to this man because a very long time ago, before 13 September 1890, before Lloyd's Pioneer Column ancestor dreamt of Zambesia, of England's El Dorado in Africa, long before there was a war of liberation, before the Internet and electricity, an ancestor of my mother had killed an ancestor of her first husband.

The story of this murder was passed by one generation down to the next. The spirit of the dead man came back as an angry *ngozi* spirit and wreaked havoc on my mother's family. Fields failed to prosper, children rotted in their mothers' wombs. My mother's father was told that something had to be done, the debt repaid. A life for a life.

That life was to be my mother's.

Her family decreed that that long-ago death had to be honoured through the gift of a girl to the family of the murdered. My mother was to be the currency that paid the debt.

Pledging girls is illegal now, of course. As Vernah will tell you, the government outlawed it almost at independence, but this was in the late 1960s, deep in rural Rhodesia, where the chiefs decided what was law and appeasing the sins of the past mattered more than securing one girl's future.

So there was no one to protest, no one to dispute the authority under which a girl, a child, my mother, should be given over in marriage to a man to appease a murder committed long before she was even thought of. There was no one to stand up for my mother.

At the age of thirteen, my mother found herself married into a family that was poor, polygamous and plentiful. She became the third wife. The other wives lived in acrimony and conflict, and their children carried on their mothers' quarrels. Into all this violence and ugliness came my mother. She could not escape because continuing in this marriage was necessary to appease an angry spirit.

She was unhappy and she was lonely. She ran away and escaped to her father's house. Her father beat her and brought her back to her husband, who also beat her for her insubordination. With little education, and a family that had approved this enforced slavery and desired her marriage in the first place, where could she go? She tried to hang herself but was caught and tied down for three days. She was locked in her hut to prevent it. They would not let her go but they feared that, if she killed herself, her own *ngozi* spirit would come back and haunt them, and begin another cycle of endless death and despair.

In the end, my father was her escape route.

She met him four years after her forced marriage, when she took one of her stepchildren to the clinic near the new school in her village. He had a job there as a carpenter, making shelves and cupboards. He saw her when she came to the school and fell in love with her at once. That she was married did not deter him. But by this time she had a young child, a boy of three years. She was afraid that her husband would hunt her down if she took him. So she left him behind, that little boy whose name I will now never know. She left him to be raised in that family, and with my father she began a new life.

The loss of the child caused her great unhappiness. After a year together, she and my father could not bear it. They were expecting a child. They returned to her home to make an offer: my father would repay the family of her husband; they would take her son and my father would marry my mother.

My mother then learned the horrible truth: her little boy had been drowned in the river while bathing. She and my father saw it as the *ngozi* striking back in terrible vengeance. I can see her weeping at the news, weeping like she did at Mobhi's funeral, tears running into her mouth, hands clasped together behind her head, body moving from side to side.

My mother's father refused to accept the money that my father offered as a penance. 'You cannot marry another man's wife,' he said. And in addition to the original *ngozi* of her family, which remained unpaid since my mother had run away, there was now the *ngozi* of her dead child. There was only one thing to be done: my mother had to return to her husband. My father would pay compensation for having run away with her. But my mother could not bear that thought.

They went to my father's village. Gift was born there, and soon after, Joy. A cow drowned in the river and the family blamed my father. 'She will bring nothing but tears to you. You shall suffer every day of your life.'

They left to live in another village. And then I was born, with no darkness in my skin, with no pigment, an albino, *murungu-dunhu*, with my ghastly whiteness. My mother believed that I had been cursed inside her womb. Joyi says my father told her that my mother was unable to feed me, and that I spent my first year at a mission hospital.

They were asked to leave their new village as soon as the headman heard about my condition. My parents moved to town. Unmarried, they remained together, my mother sinking deeper and deeper into despair.

My mother killed Gift when he was three, Joyi was eighteen months and I was just a baby. She drowned him in his bath and told my father that her dead son had appeared before her and commanded it. 'It was the only thing that could save them,' he said she said.

They were not detected. He said the child had been playing. This was in the townships, before independence. The war was on; there was a state of emergency. There were so many African children – what did it matter if one died? It was just one less person to demand inconvenient things like majority rule and electricity and education and jobs. If I sound bitter, it is because I am. There was only the most cursory of investigations.

Then came Moreblessings.

My father could not unmake us, or wish us gone. He might also, though Joy did not say this, have believed that this was the curse that was playing out, that he could not prevent it but could delay its dreadful effect.

After I was born, they had seen a traditional healer who had told them that the only thing to do was to make sure my mother returned to her husband. My father was fatalist in his belief that they could not escape.

I now understand my mother's persistence in seeking out a cure for me. She believed that there was someone out in the world, in Manicaland, perhaps, and maybe even Mozambique, who had a different answer, the right answer. She and my father travelled up and down the country.

Only the war on the eastern border, flowing in from Mozambique, stopped my mother, and defeated they turned to Harare, where they could get lost. My mother remained convinced that there was an answer out there, if only she could find the right diviner to give it to her.

They had spent more than half of their earnings consulting diviners. My father saw, I think, that they might eventually give all they had to finding this mysterious answer. He refused to allow any further trips. When my mother insisted, he fought her like he did the day she took me to the healer. He could not stop fate but he could be vigilant and make sure that it did not act through his wife. He could not send us to our mother's relatives because they would not have accepted us.

His own mother had taken us in for a few months, when my father had to go to Salisbury for work and could not bring his family. But when the accident occurred that produced Joyi's scar, the local chief said my parents had to leave.

But something more serious had happened that the chief was never told about: it was at my grandmother's that my mother tried to kill me for the first time. She tried to drown me in a zinc bucket, and only my grandmother's sudden arrival stopped her.

My father decided that he would work from home; he decided that he would spend every waking moment protecting us from our mother.

Then she killed Mobhi.

Her son had made her do it, my mother said. My father saw that we could never be safe as long as we were in that house. He did not let us out of his sight. But he did not blame her. He continued to believe that it was not she who did it, but a force external to her, a supernatural force that possessed her and drove her to kill. The best protection he could think of was constant vigilance.

At night, he tied her to the bed. But she broke free. The final straw came two weeks after Mobhi had died, when he found her standing by our bed in the middle of the night, trying to lift my sleeping form from the bed. 'She needs a bath,' she said. 'She is dirty.'

The following day, after he took us to school, he walked along Crowborough without knowing or caring about the direction that his feet took him. He found himself in town and walked to the Harare Gardens. He and my mother had sometimes come here when they first came to Salisbury. He had brought us to those gardens often, passing through on our way to the Show Grounds every August for the Agricultural Show.

He had thought then of his grandfather, whom he had never known because he had died in the forests of Burma in the Second World War. That thought took him to the monument in the park commemorating the fallen from the two world wars. As he looked at the words on the plaque, 'We fought and died for our King', the intensity of his emotion moved him from his bench. Perhaps it was the simple beauty of those words, but something in him broke. He put his hands in his arms and wept long and hard. He was not aware of the passing people, or of the man who came to sit beside him. It was Lloyd.

5

I was supposed to be in court yesterday. This is the second appointment that I have missed this month. From what Loveness told me when she came to give me the message from Vernah Sithole that I would not be leaving, it may be another month before anything happens.

From what Vernah Sithole said the last time, the new Minister of Justice has appointed a commission to re-examine all sentences before they announce an amnesty. It is primarily meant for the new government's supporters who were locked up on spurious charges, but the review will extend to all prisoners serving sentences of more than two years. They have delayed the opening of the judicial year to allow the new Commission on Sentencing to complete its work.

The Minister is also appointing new court officers, magistrates and prosecutors, and the Judiciary Services Commission is reviewing the appointments of all judges. In cases not covered by amnesty, Vernah explained, they may even order new trials.

A flicker of hope leapt up in me when she said this. I found myself making plans, tempting fate. But it soon died. Mine is not a political case, and perhaps I will never leave. That is what Loveness would want. 'With all my heart,' she said, 'I hope it goes well for you. I want them to give you life, or at the very least eight years, so that Yeukai is finished by the time you leave.'

I had not realised before then how pink her gums are or how yellow the teeth that frame the missing ones on her upper jaw. I thought suddenly of Mr Todd in *A Handful of Dust*, trapping Tony into a nightmare of reading all of Dickens, over and over and over for the rest of his life, buoyed only by the thought that the Amazon jungle termites had disposed of one hated volume.

The new Minister of Justice arrived in person to inspect the prison. In the weeks before she came, detergents and mops appeared as if by magic, along with tubes of toothpaste, soap and sanitary pads and toothbrushes. When we stood before her in our clean uniforms and with our newly cleaned teeth and feet with shoes on them, singing a song that we had been practising while we worked, it was with stomachs full of porridge made with the right amounts of sugar and margarine.

And from the kitchen wafted the smell of fried beef.

The Minister walked among us. When she got to the Ds, she asked, in the cheeriest voice possible, how things were in prison. Just as I was thinking how best to answer such a question, how to address in one succinct sentence the bad food, the poor plumbing, Synodia, how the guards treated us, Evernice said, 'Everything is very well, very nice.'

'Everything is just wonderful,' Beulah added.

'Just wonderful,' simpered Benhilda.

Behind the Minister, Synodia, Loveness and the guards smiled their approval. The Chief Superintendent stood next to them, the buttons on her epaulettes reflecting the glow of self-congratulation that came from Synodia and Loveness. After this hearty endorsement, the Minister seemed to lose her assurance and her speech fell a little flat.

She spoke of the standards that the United Nations has set for the treatment of prisoners. Prisons should be places of human rights and human dignity, we were all on the same page, everyone in this room was on the very same page. We all wanted the same things, and those same things were, primarily, human rights and human dignity.

She spoke as though these were tangible gifts that we had only to reach out and take. Indeed, if we had had a piece of meat for every time she said those words, we would have gone to bed fuller than we had been in all of the time we had been in prison.

I cannot say I have seen any human rights since her visit – or much human dignity, for that matter – but Synodia's voice is certainly less loud. Her blood-and-thunder seems straggly and ineffectual.

Loveness is even more subdued. No doubt she fears that the Stygian effects of the new Minister's reforming zeal will flow all the way to Chikurubi. In this, she and I are of the same mind. If I am to stay here any longer, I would rather that my pact with Loveness continues. I can only cling to what I know, which is that my life since I started to teach Yeukai has some even tenor. If I am to be honest, I do not want to think of changes here.

6

Somewhere in the Archives, where I once worked, is a newspaper that has the report of my parents' death. It will not be very long; maybe just ten lines headed 'Man, Woman Drown in Mukuvisi'. This is the only time that my parents' lives will be recorded. Had they not ended their lives, there would have been no reason at all for even this, but a double suicide will have been news.

How did they keep it from the township, their terrible secret? But the township encourages familiarity, not intimacy.

Joy says that Lloyd talked to my father for a long time. He asked to see him again in town the next day. He said to him that my mother was not cursed, that she was ill, dangerously ill, and that their children were in great danger. Could he not send us all to school? Lloyd asked. Then he could help my mother to get treatment.

When my father said he didn't have enough money, Lloyd offered to pay the school fees for Joy and me. But my father said Joy could go to a school, but what about Memory, his daughter who was always unwell?

'Could she not go to a special school?' Lloyd had asked.

When my father had explained my condition, Lloyd had said that he would take me in, that he would look after me until my mother was well. When we met that first day at Barbours, it had been so that he could look at me, so that he could see if my mother agreed. He had told my father that my mother needed help – a doctor's help, he had said. He had even made arrangements for them to see a friend of his who taught at the medical school at the university. And once they had seen this friend, he would make sure that he would support my father to look after me.

Lloyd had thought that my mother would be locked away for treatment. Perhaps my father thought so, too, because they did not go to see Lloyd's friend, and they did not go back to see Lloyd.

So I was never meant to live with Lloyd. They had been right, after all, when they told me that I was to go there for a short time.

But then they died.

It was a simple act of kindness.

Our father finally allowed my mother to go to the Annexe. He had woken up to find her standing over him with a knife. He had tied her hands behind her back that night, and the next morning he had dressed her and taken her to Parirenyatwa, to the Annexe, where she remained for six months.

When I told Joyi everything that had happened to me, she wept with her veil over her face. She had been teaching at a school in India when Lloyd died and had not known about the trial until she came back. Through the Goodwill Fellowship, she heard about the albino woman called Memory, a woman who was in prison for killing a white man.

7

It has been two months since Joyi told me the truth about my family. My dreams have gone. The Chimera no longer pulls me down to the water; it speaks no more with my mother's voice. I understand now that the dreams were not dreams, but faint imprints of buried trauma fighting memories of my mother.

In the first days after Joyi told me the truth, it was hard for us to talk without breaking down. But now, together, we have been sharing the many moments of snatched joy: my father's music, my mother's records, and the birthday cakes that were really just rock-hard candy cakes with a candle on them.

The ablution and the Condemn and the corridors are silent without the others. The Commission on Sentencing gave up – there were too many prisoners needing review. So they went for a straightforward amnesty. They released all the A and B and C prisoners. In D, they let go everyone who had served more than half their sentences. The only prisoners excluded from the amnesty were those convicted of murder and aggravated rape.

Vernah is still campaigning hard to have my sentence commuted to life, but that has not happened yet. Mavis Munongwa has found her own amnesty, which means that I am the only person left in the whole prison.

The prison is open to me now; I go where I please, when I please. There is no lock-up. I eat at Loveness's house, and spend most of my time there. Synodia and Mathilda have asked me to teach their children, too, and that is how I spend most of my time. Teaching the children, thinking about my parents and all the things that I will do if they ever let me leave. I spend most of the time in a small room that used to be the library, and which I have persuaded Loveness to let me rebuild as one.

I am also rereading these notebooks that you sent back before you left for New York. I did not thank you enough for what you have done for me. Even if nothing comes of the magazine feature you were planning to write, I am grateful to you for setting me on the path to the truth.

I asked you to bring them all back because I wanted to go back, to see where it was I made that fatal mistake. My mind keeps going back to that memory of seeing Lloyd hand over the bills, a false memory on which I have built the foundation of my life, or, to put it more accurately, a true memory from which I have made false assumptions. My utter conviction that my parents sold me rested only on that exchange of money.

I understand now why Lloyd adopted me. He was as different as I was and knew what it was to be different. I did not see that he lived in pain and fear. He had paid my father for Joy's school-ing, as promised, and the money took her right up to her O levels. She lived at school during the holidays. When she decided that she wanted to take the veil, the nuns took over her education, and only when our parents died and my father wrote her that letter did she understand how she had come to be there.

There are things that I understand, or that I have grasped. My parents thought that it was a fate from ancient days that controlled their lives, but it was actually random chance. It was chance that led Lloyd to that park bench. He had left his car to be fixed up near Herbert Chitepo. It was not ready when they said it would be, and he had decided on impulse that he would walk to the park and look at the memorial. It was chance that brought Lloyd to that bench; it was chance, too, that my father found himself in the company of one of the few white men in Zimbabwe who understood what a black person meant when he talked about *ngozi*.

There are still many things that I do not understand. Some I can guess at, but I have no certainty. Above all, I am wondering if Lloyd knew where Joyi was, and if so why he kept us apart. Chishawasha and Umwinsidale are in opposite valleys. I am seeing the times we drove past Chishawasha, the time we drove to St Ignatius to see an old priest who had taught him at his old school at St George's. In all that time Joyi was in the valley below. Did he never try to find out what had happened to my parents? And if he did, why did he not tell me about Joyi, why did he keep me with him still, without once telling me that my sister was at school in the neighbouring valley?

In one of her prayer meetings before the prison emptied, Synodia spoke about a baptism of fire. I feel as though I have walked through fields of fire to emerge into shining coolness. I tell myself to fight the hope that rises like a flare when I imagine that I might actually leave. I look forward to leaving because finally, my life makes sense. My discomfort has not just been feeling ill at ease in my skin, but a discomfort in myself.

One of the hardest things about prison is the lack of choice. There are choices, even here, and the most important one is the life within. I will not think about tomorrow. All I want to do is to live in the moment. It will not be possible for me to escape the past. But if I go back there, it will only be to find ways to make rich my present. To accept that there are no villains in my life, just broken people, trying to heal, stumbling in darkness and breaking each other, to find a way to forgive my father and mother, to forgive Lloyd, to find a path to my own forgiveness.

To stop living what has been, until now, this pale imitation of life.

I thought today about the peppered moth. Like that insect, I have had to change my shape and shade to blend into my surroundings. And like the peppered moth, I was fluttering, blindly, changing colour, struggling to adapt, to survive. Maybe that is enough – for me to resolve that I will survive. And to start my life all over again, whether in here or out there, but to start it over with the full truth before me. Maybe that is enough to begin with.

8

Verity, Jimmy and Beulah came to see me yesterday. As part of their amnesty conditions, they are not supposed to visit the prison. But there they were, in the canteen, with things for me: food, drink, toiletries, soap, a new toothbrush, a towel and sunscreen lotion.

As if they had set out to look as different as possible from how they were when they were here, Jimmy wore tight red trousers and a lurid yellow blouse while Beulah's hair was covered in a long ginger weave that came down to her waist. The sweat shone through Verity's thick foundation. Her red-and-blue heels were so high that her knees buckled. They had come in her new car, Verity said, as she jingled the keys casually, but not so casually that Synodia missed them.

'*Hesi kani*, Mbuya Guard,' Jimmy said, and slapped her hand against Synodia's, like they were best friends reunited. '*Nayo nayo tirongo.*'

'*Zvipi,*' said Synodia. 'You will be back here soon enough. With your temper, Beulah, and your permanently open legs, Jimmy, you will be back with us before you know it.'

Beulah and Jimmy shrieked with laughter and clapped each other's hands so hard that it was like a small thunderclap had been unleashed in the room.

Joyi arrived just after they did. They sat side by side on the bench. Jimmy was soon talking to Joy like she had known her all her life, drinking Cream Soda and Cherry Plum, the things Beulah said she missed most when she was here. 'There is something about this place that just makes me so hungry,' Beulah said as she tore into a drumstick.

Verity told us about her new car, which seems intricately connected to her new boyfriend, while Jimmy told us about the work she is now doing. There is a project funded by the European Union that is persuading women to give up prostitution in exchange for working together on a co-operative farm. The thought came to me that they should call it the 'Hoes for Whores' programme.

I could not keep a straight face as Jimmy explained that she was only doing this as long as she has to report to the parole office. 'As soon as they forget about me, I will stop. They are insane, those Europeans. Like I can't get more money in thirty minutes on my back than a month on my feet,' she said.

Monalisa has started her own business, consulting on aid projects. Evernice has reinvented herself as a victim of political repression.

Jimmy is going to move back to Manicaland, but not to her village. She plans to make her way to the diamond mines in Marange and on to Manica in Mozambique, where there are many white and Asian men with exotic tastes. 'Just a little licking here, a little sucking there, and I will make more than I make in Harare.'

I listened as they laughed and talked about their plans until Synodia came to tell us that it was time. We all got up. 'We will see you soon,' Jimmy said.

I wondered for how long they would come. Will they still come in one year, in three years, in five? Will they come in ten? Will they care if I die here, if I am given a pauper's funeral and buried in an unmarked grave, like Mavis Munongwa? They will forget this place. They should forget this place. They will forget me.

'Memory, don't cry,' Verity said, and reached for my hand.

'It is nothing,' I said. 'My eyes are hurting today.'

They all embraced me before they left, Jimmy so strongly that she lifted me off my feet, and as I walked back to my cell I carried with me the mingled smell of their perfumes.

9

I am reaching the end of this notebook. I will not write again. I will give this to you when I see you, together with the other notebooks that I asked you to give back to me so that I could read over them again. We will know next week whether or not I will get a new trial. There is enough in what I have told her to make my conviction unsafe, Vernah says. All the evidence pointing to my guilt is purely circumstantial.

Joyi has read them all. With all the treachery of my imperfect recall, the notebooks have helped us to construct our collective memory. Joy marvels at what I remember. 'What you have here is a book of memory,' she said.

'Isn't that in Shakespeare?' I said.

'It's in the Bible,' she said. 'The Book of Malachi. "Those who feared the Lord spoke to one another and he gave attention to them and a Book of Memory was written before Him."'

Joy told me something that I had forgotten, or perhaps had never known. 'Baba says she chose all our names. She never regretted us.'

'Just look at what she named us.' I smiled. 'Gift and Joy.'

'Memory and Moreblessings,' said Joy.

We talk about the past, but when the pain is too much to bear we reach for other subjects. Joy has told me about what it means to be in her order. She is a female Jesuit. She has told me about

Ignatius of Loyola, who says that to be spiritual means to listen to the deeper levels of our experiences, to the knowledge that there is something good and worthy to be found even in suffering. That God means for us to find meaning in things that happen to us, even the very worst.

She has chosen to respond to our past by choosing to see it as a mysterious way in which God operates. There is a neat and terrible logic to the idea that these were no random events at all, but a pattern drawn by an unseen hand. But no god can be that terrible, that vengeful. That God is not relentless or sardonic enough – but maybe something like the Moirae, the three Fates spinning for each man the thread of life, measuring it out and then snipping it with those abhorred shears at the appointed time.

It makes more sense to think that it is that *ngozi* reaching out from the past. Anything else is too horrible, the idea of a knowing hand directing all of this merely to put me in prison to learn a life-affirming lesson; that this all happened so that I could find a sense of purpose behind bars.

I have not said any of this to Joy, and perhaps I never shall, for the simple reason that I love her. But it makes more sense for me for all of this to have been a random series of things that happened, with no celestial hand to direct any of it.

I have been obsessing over the moments, small in themselves, that brought me here. I see in my mind's eye my father, wandering into the Harare Gardens and pausing to look at the statue of the dead soldiers. I see Lloyd, also stopping and looking at that same statue, those two thoughts occurring to both men at the same moment and leading them to that fateful union. The cancelled hockey match, and coming home to find Lloyd with Zenzo.

We also talk about Lloyd.

When I think about Lloyd now, it is not those difficult first days that I see. It is not even the tumult of our life after Zenzo. Instead I think of our drives to Nyanga, I think of going to bookshops. I think of the day that we buried Poppy in Matopos. That period of equilibrium that came after my return home. Because what I had with Lloyd was love. There was love and warmth and generosity of spirit. I was smiling when I recalled our trips to the Archives.

'You must have loved him very much,' Joy said.

In the bare simplicity of her words, I recognised a truth that I had long run from. I think that handing me to Lloyd was a leap of faith for my father. I don't think that it was such an extraordinary leap. He had seen what everyone saw as soon as they met Lloyd. He had seen his warmth, his generosity, and his shining goodness.

Was it Pericles who said that grief is felt not in the want of what we have never known, but rather in the loss of that to which we have been long accustomed? Lloyd would know. That is the way it is with me. I find I grieve for my parents as remembered persons. But it is for what I have been long accustomed to that I grieve the most. It is for Lloyd that I grieve the most. I think over the four phases of my relationship with Lloyd: the distance and uncertainty of the first years, then the gradual tranquillity, the turmoil of Zenzo and the bitter aftermath, and the new equilibrium after I returned. He gave me an understanding that took me outside of myself, that there was a life beyond things; there was an existence that went on long after the self had gone.

A line from my mother's favourite song came back when I was with Yeukai and the children today, about a summer's day, and placing flowers on old family graves.

If I ever leave, I will drive out to Matopos. Vernah managed to get Alexandra to tell her that Lloyd's ashes were scattered just where I thought they would be, and where he said he wanted to be when he died, at World's View in Matopos.

That is where I will go first, to Matopos, to throw flowers over the place that he loved the most. Not funeral flowers, not lilies, or carnations, or roses. I will give him strelitzias, birds of paradise with long, strong stems and orange and purple plumes, the flowers that I bought on the day that he died. I can see them now, blazing with colour in the air, purple and orange against the blue sky, falling from every direction that I throw them, falling to the ground of his resting place. If I ever get out, I will throw birds of paradise from the top of the world.

ACKNOWLEDGEMENTS

That I managed to reach this last page is due to the support of the ace professionals who nursed this book to life, and the love and support of my friends and family. I must acknowledge above all others the wonderful people at Faber, particularly my editors, Mary Morris and Silvia Crompton, who managed to combine their enthusiasm for this novel with forensic eviscera-tion of it; Walter Donohue, who wrote a brutal but kind assessment that lifted me out of a very tricky place; and Hannah Griffiths, who poured sunshine into the gloom. I also acknowledge with gratitude Sophie Portas, drumbeater of First Chimurenga pro-portions; Donna Payne for the breathtaking cover on the UK edition; Stephen Page, my infinitely patient and abiding pub-lisher; and Lee Brackstone, poor thing, who aged quite visibly with each draft that he read.

I also wish to thank my former agents, Claire Conrad and Rebecca Folland at Janklow and Nesbit, and also Kirsty Gordon, for shepherding me into the world and linking me to Mitzi Angel in New York, Sylvie Audoly in Paris, Catherine Bakke-Bolle in Oslo, Luigi Brioschi in Milan, Martjin David in Amsterdam, Päivi Koivisto-Alanko in Helsinki and Charlotte Weber in Stockholm, wonderful visionaries who saw a novel even before one existed, and who kept faith with me even as I struggled to keep mine with them.

I also thank my current agents, Cathryn Summerhayes and Raffaella de Angelis at WME, who truly make me feel like I am their only author. And if there is such a thing as a literary god-father, mine would be Eric Simonoff. Thank you, Eric, for being there at the crucial moments: for where you go, I will go and your people shall be my people.

In Geneva, I wish to thank my old boss, Frieder Roessler, and my current bosses, Niall Meagher and Leo Palma, who made it possible for me to move back to Zimbabwe for three years to write while guaranteeing my security. Thank you, truly, for the best of both worlds.

In Amsterdam, I want to thank Nederlands Letterenfonds, the Dutch Foundation for Literature, for the beautiful apartment on the Spui in which I wrote a crucial part of this book in the summer of 2011. In Den Haag, my profound thanks go to Ton van de Langkruis, director of Stichting Writers Unlimited, whose invitation to three memorable literary festivals in Aruba, Curaçao and Sint Maarten finally convinced me that I may have written a novel that other people might actually want to read.

In New York, I am grateful to the brilliant minds I met as an Open Society Fellow in 2012, particularly those belonging to Deprose Muchena, Tawanda Mutasah, Leonard Bernardo, Stephen Hubbell and Glen Mpani. That crucial year of travel and reflection on questions of spirituality and religion affirmed my commitment to writing the truth about my people in all their beauty and ugliness, in all their maddening complexity.

I did not manage to visit Chikurubi Prison. I had one opportunity, but it would have required me to sign the Official Secrets Act. As the point of the visit would have been a little frustrated if I could not write about the prison, I declined the opportunity.

The Chikurubi of this novel is thus from my imagination, and from archival research. I am particularly grateful to Simon Mann, who, in his memoir *Cry Havoc* (John Blake, 2011), brought humour to his vivid account of his time in Chikurubi; to Thelma Chikwanha, who, as the Community Affairs Editor of the *Daily News*, made a commitment to telling the stories of Zimbabwe's prisoners; and to Irene Staunton and Chiedza Musengezi, whose lovely collection of short prison memoirs, *A Tragedy of Lives: Women in Prison in Zimbabwe* (Weaver Press, 2003), moved me deeply. I am also grateful to Julie Stewart and the Women's Law Programme at the University of Zimbabwe, and to Tendai Biti, who not only made me big in Gokwe, but also, together with Farai Rwodzi, shared with me his own prison experiences.

In Harare, I want to thank all my friends, particularly these comrades-in-arms who were directly connected to the struggle for this book: Penny Stone, Richard Beattie and Magnus Carlqvist, best beloveds and library titans; Patrick Mavros, who gave me more Umwinsidale stories than I knew what to do with; Tatenda Mawere and Munyaka Makuyana for their unparalleled support and kindness; Dominic Muntanga and Naomi Mapfumo for that whooping cheer over Sunday pancakes; Lisa Orrenius, a Zimbabwean writer in disguise, and whose eagle eye gave me Loveness; Firle Davies, Raphael Chikukwa, Andrew Chadwick, Nick Marq and Jill Coates, friends and fellow travellers; Alf Torrents and Deborah Bronnert for that spectacular send-off and Jeane Wessels for the gift of the tea estate in Chipinge at which it all fell into place.

I also want to remember with love my beautiful friend Pilar Fuertes Ferragut, the Spanish envoy to Zimbabwe whom we lost in a tragic car accident in April 2012. She suffused everyone she met with her warmth, intelligence, elegance and radiance. Thanks to her relentless and generous encouragement, I accepted an invitation to read to the members of ZIMAS, the Zimbabwe Albino Association. Their kind reception, and the stories they shared with me, encouraged me to rescue this novel from the bin into which I had thrown it. I miss her very much.

Then there is a group of people who have meant everything to me wherever I have been in the world because they are part of my interior world. I was excited to find one morning that I had found the perfect name for a character, only to find to my horror that my perfect name belonged to one of the many friends on Facebook that I have never met. I am grateful to my beloved Gang of Lunatics. I cannot name you all, partly because there are so many of you, but mainly because I suspect that some of your names may not actually be your own. You stretch my thinking, sharpen my arguments and force me to re-examine my assumptions and prejudices. You fill my heart with laughter. I cherish you all dearly.

Finally, to my son, Kush Gappah, who could not read when I started writing this: I promise that the one after the next one is for you; to Silas Chekera, I thank you every day for helping me to this path; and to all the members of my family: the Gappah Gapas—Tererayi Mureri, Simbiso, Regina, Ratiel, Vimbayi, Vuchirai and Babamunin'Pheneas, the bookseller of Harare, who sold the last book like it was cooking oil on the black market: ndinotenda vana Mukanya, Makwiramiti, Bvudzijena, vaMbire nemi mhai, Musinake, Shinda, Zimbabwe. Kune zvese zvinoitika mumhuri medu, munogaroti dai Pet'na aivapo, zvokwadi ainyora mabhuku. Mukasafadzwa nerino, musavhunduka, nokuti ariko mamwe achatevera.

Hokoyo nenhamo!